MW01505855

Pr:
Better Dreams, Fc

"Ken Scholes is a force of nature, and his best stories read like they were written by a whirlwind."
Jack Skillingstead, author of
THE WHOLE MESS AND OTHER STORIES

"Scholes is a bard for all occasions. His new collection is enchanting, like the unholy lovechild of a mermaid and Bob Dylan. Get ready to meet your new friends: a spaceship-guitar, a sassy cactus, a gay space pirate, and more."
Emily C. Skaftun, author of
LIVING FOREVER AND OTHER TERRIBLE IDEAS

"Ken Scholes is intensely, unrelentingly inventive. His newest collection, *Better Dreams, Fallen Seeds, and other Handfuls of Hope*, includes stories from his treasured Psalms of Isaak series, tales that offer a slightly dark turn on our modern world, and a sprinkle or two of lighter modern fantasy. Always surprising and beautifully written, this collection is a great escape that will leave readers touched with hope."
Brenda Cooper, author of
WHEN MOTHERS DREAM: STORIES

"A truly original voice. Ken Scholes has the goods."
Josh Rountree, author of
THE LEGEND OF CHARLIE FISH

"Ken Scholes mixes wildly beautiful imagery with the sharply visceral; the profoundly mythic with the profanely human."
Tina Connolly, author of
ON THE EYEBALL FLOOR

BETTER DREAMS, FALLEN SEEDS AND OTHER HANDFULS OF HOPE

ALSO BY KEN SCHOLES

THE PSALMS OF ISAAK
Lamentation
Canticle
Antiphon
Requiem
Hymn

COLLECTIONS
Long Walks, Last Flights and Other Strange Journeys
Diving Mimes, Weeping Czars and Other Unusual Suspects
Blue Yonders, Grateful Pies and Other Fanciful Feasts

NOVELLAS
Last Flight of the Goddess

COLLABORATIONS
METATropolis: The Wings We Dare Aspire (with Jay Lake)

BETTER DREAMS, FALLEN SEEDS AND OTHER HANDFULS OF HOPE

BY

KEN SCHOLES

FAIRWOOD PRESS
Bonney Lake, WA

Fairwood Press
21528 104th Street Court East
Bonney Lake, WA 98391
www.fairwoodpress.com

Front cover art and design © Paul Swenson
Book design by Patrick Swenson

ISBN: 978-1-958880-32-6
First Fairwood Press Edition: August 2025

Printed in the United States of America

For Virginia and her sturdy feet

TABLE OF CONTENTS

INTRODUCTION
by Sarah Chorn

KEN SCHOLES TORE INTO MY LIFE LIKE A HURRICANE that not even the meteorologists could predict. *Unexpected* is the word I would use to describe him.

I started reviewing books in 2010 on a small website called Bookworm Blues. Ken released his epic fantasy series, *The Psalms of Isaak,* around the same time. This is how I became aware of him. I was a reviewer watching an author release one mega-hit after another and I was overcome with awe, inspired by his journey, and enchanted by his storytelling.

Even then, so many years ago, I knew he was a force to be reckoned with.

Over the years as I have moved from a book reviewer to an editor and author, and I have watched from the sidelines as Ken has continued to perfect his craft.

In 2022, *Grimdark Magazine* (which I edit), was looking for more authors to add to their publication pool, and I naturally thought of Ken Scholes first.

I believe people come into our lives for a reason, and Ken entered mine at a time when I was starting a slow spiral into one of the deepest, darkest depressions I have ever experienced. Through sheer tenacity and force of will, he chipped through the armor of isolation I built myself, helped me prune the trees in my jungle, and allowed the light shine through.

Ken's humanity is his greatest asset.

And it serves as the backbone for all of his writing.

Ken has a long and storied career. He's an award winning author and celebrated talent with plenty of accolades. His corresponding list of strengths is long. I could discuss his smooth, effortless prose and thought provoking plots, or the nuance with which he handles sensitive topics at length, but what I really want to talk about are journeys.

Knowing Ken has been like going on an adventure. I can never guess, from one day to the next, what ideas he'll have or what he'll start planning. Ken Scholes is never stationary for long, nor has he ever been. He is, ultimately, a seeker. His life has been a pilgrimage peppered with oceanic emotional depths, mountainous peaks of happiness, and jungles of struggle. With titanic strength, he has forged his way through all of it becoming more *himself* through every trial waged and victory celebrated.

Ever evolving, is Ken Scholes.

He allows you to see bits of his journey here, in these stories, from the man taking his first tentative steps toward discovering who he truly is, to the vital force I know as my friend today. There is an evolution in his style, his voice in this collection that I find compelling. Like the author, change is present in these pages, both large and small.

As I've said, Ken's humanity informs everything he writes, and I am convinced it is his greatest strength as an author. Ever attuned to the emotional journey, his stories work on numerous levels, but it is the humanity in them that shines like a light. He writes a myriad of people across landscapes both far-future and fantasy, and yet I somehow see bits of myself in all of them.

More, Ken has an uncanny ability to cut directly to the beating heart of each moment and that beating heart . . .

Is where his magic is most potent.

This an exploration of the journey of Ken Scholes.
And it's magnificent.

Sarah Chorn
2024

SOMEDAY, 25 YEARS LATER
ᴮʸ Patrick Swenson

KEN SCHOLES SUGGESTED I WRITE AN ADDED INTRO-duction, looking back on that first published story collection *Long Walks, Last Flights and Other Strange Journeys* and musing about how far he's come in the last twenty-five years. At the time I told him, "You know, I think it isn't necessary. Look at that intro by Sarah Chorn! Says it all succinctly, and what could I possibly add at this point?"

Well, he *thought* I was begging out of it. As I write this, he has no idea, but of course by the time *you* read it, you'll know he found out about it because, *here it is.* That first introduction was called "Someday," so let's take a quick look back at it:

First, there was my small press magazine *Talebones.* I published Ken's first short story, "The Taking Night." Later came the vastly popular "Edward Bear and the Very Long Walk." We became friends *before* that, however, following a fiction class Ken attended. I'd sent him a flyer along with a story rejection encouraging him to join up. He proudly calls me his "literary dad" and blames me for teaching him the ins and outs of publishing; I may have also hinted he pay closer attention to point of view, and . . . well, all that "starting out writer stuff."

So I bought some stories from him, and seven years later, my "literary son" turned in that first story collection. Along the way he wrote more stories, two more collections, a handful of novels.

Now, *seventeen* years after that *first* collection, here is the *fourth* collection from his Imagination Forest. And lo, I was also extremely lucky to have my brother Paul come on board to do a new cover. You *have* seen his wonderful covers on the other three collections, right?

Along the way, Ken also actively pursued one of his other loves: music. That man can strum a guitar and throw that golden voice around with the same ease he types a story and sells it for gold. I have his CD *Live at the Village Inn Lounge* that boasts music as unique as his fiction. Only Ken could woo us with "Love Song to My Future Self" and "Land of Bears and Honeybees."

For now, let me just say, regarding the stories in this collection (and his entire back list of titles), that I agree 110% with Sarah Chorn's praise for it all. He's a bit Bradbury and Ellison, a touch Houdini, a smidge Don McLean, and a pinch Bob Dylan.

Ken's back to writing regularly, including a new series of novels based on his original Psalms of Isaak series. He's gonna take us to the moon, baby.

Who knows where he'll go next? He never *really* leaves his Imagination Forest, just stops for some reflection and quiet strolls from time to time.

What it all means for us is that something wonderful is coming in the next round of Someday.

Patrick Swenson
2025

FIRST BAR *at* THE END *of* THE DAY

A MAN WALKS INTO A BAR. HOW'S THAT FOR A BEGINNING? Well, here *I* am and here *you* are. Me? No, I'm not gay. It's just the first bar I saw and let's just say that after *my* day at the office, I needed a drink or three. Any bar will do.

Talk? Sure, let's talk. But I have to tell you, straight up, that I don't have time in my life for a new relationship. Frankly, you don't either. What am I drinking? Bourbon. Thanks.

So, what do you do, Tom? Security guard? Nice.

Me? I'm in nonprofit. Well, at least that's what we call it. Called it, I mean. What kind? Oh . . . you mean like homeless shelters or saving seafaring mammals? No. More like . . . research. I'm not allowed to talk about it but you seem like a good guy so what the hell.

Ever hear of SETI? Bunch of geeks pointing radio receivers at the sky listening for voices. That's not us. We're a bit . . . unusual. We listen to the sky with our minds. I know. Far-fetched? Extremely. Ever hear of the Foundation for a Better World? That's us. We're in the bank tower down on Sixth.

How long? Well, I've been with them for about twenty years. They recruit us young. I was fifteen, doing card tricks at the county fair. Couple of suits watched me for two or three hours, asked me to take some tests. And here I am.

I quit today.

Then I came here to get shitty drunk.

Slow down? Why? How about another? No, let me get this one. I *insist*.

Well, there we were, working in shifts, hooked to machines they called boosters, stretched out in recliners in the basement.

Exactly. Going to work for the last twenty years basically meant
crawling into a recliner and spending the day *thinking*. Reach out
and touch someone, you know?

Say again? Well of *course* we found stuff. That's why we did it
in the first place. Not much. Glimpses of strange skies. Nonsensi-
cal mutterings. Snippets of alien song. Flashes of temples on crys-
talline sands. But nothing really solid. Officer of the Watch logged
it and we kept right on casting.

Then, three days ago, I got something no one else could hear
or see or sense or whatever the hell you want to call it. They always said I had more reach than the others. Made sense: I'd been
at it longer.

Do you believe in evil, Tom? Yeah, I didn't use to. But I
touched something . . . or maybe it touched me. And it was so
fucking dark it made my balls ache and my stomach lurch. I
started crying—not just a tear or two but full-on sobbing. I saw
it. Worse: It saw me. You ever see a woman so pretty, so . . . *perfect*
. . . that you just hurt from wanting her? Oh. Sorry. Okay . . . a guy
then. Ever see a guy tha—

Well, I'm flattered, Tom, but like I said: Bad timing.

Anyway, imagine that craving for her—for him—only flip it
so that what you want most is to smash that pretty face, crack
those slender bones, chew that tender meat until you've completely broken and devoured your love.

That's what I touched. Out there. And it touched me back. And
it *moved*. Like I was the guest star in its dreams and it suddenly
woke up, saw me there, and turned towards me with open eyes.

They unhooked me. They told me it was an anomaly, a problem in my booster. But they didn't look like they believed that.
My nose bled, my head throbbed, my hands shook. They sent me
home for the day; told me to get some rest.

I chicken-shitted instead. Excuse me? Chicken-shitted. I had
a bottle of sleeping pills. I don't know how many I took. Obviously not enough. Why? Because I knew what it meant, Tom. I'll
get to that.

Anyway, I took a bunch of pills. Went to sleep. Woke up two
days later in a pool of cold vomit. Yeah, sorry about that. Not a
pretty picture.

I knew it was closer now. I could feel it without the booster.

It moved with slow, hungry, intent. I cleaned myself up and went to the office. Thought maybe there was something we could do to stop what was coming.

All of the other casters were dead in their chairs, eyes and mouths open. The handlers were nowhere to be found.

I decided to call it a day. I came here and met you.

One more? Sure, you can pay for this one.

Tom, do you ever think about how the world will end? Do you ever think about what you'd do or where you'd go? Is there someone you'd call? Would you pray? Would you cry? Or would you just find the closest bar and get shitty drunk?

No, wait. Don't go. I know, I know. Poor taste and all that. Sit down. Please?

I'll tell you the truth. I make shit up all the time. I'm a science fiction writer. No casters. No boosters. No psychics in basement recliners. No strange hungry space monsters. I'm sorry; I'm a little drunk.

Let's just sit together for a while. Maybe later, we can go back to your place or back to my place and see what happens. Sound good?

My nose is bleeding? I know it is, Tom. Yours is bleeding, too.

Feel that? Me, too. Hurts like hell, doesn't it?

It won't be long now. It won't be long at all.

MAKING MY ENTRANCE AGAIN WITH MY USUAL FLAIR

NO ONE EVER ASKS A CLOWN AT THE END OF HIS LIFE WHAT he *really* wanted to be when he grew up. It's fairly obvious. No one gets hijacked into the circus. We race to it, the smell of hotdogs leading us in, our fingers aching for the sticky pull of taffy, the electric shock of pink cotton on our tongue. Ask a lawyer and he'll say that when he was a kid, he wanted to be an astronaut. Ask an accountant; he'll say he wanted to be fireman.

I am a clown. I have always wanted to be a clown. And I will die a clown if I have my way.

My name is Merton D. Kamal.

The Kamal comes from my father. I never met the man so I have no idea how he came by it. Mom got the Merton bit from some monk she used to read who wrote something like this: We learn humility by being humiliated often. Given how easily (and how frequently) Kamal is pronounced Camel, and given how the D just stands for D, you can see that she wanted her only child be filled to the brim with humility.

My mom is a deeply spiritual woman.

But enough about her. This is my story.

"Merton," the ringleader and owner Rufus P. Stowell said, "it's just not working out."

I was pushing forty. I'd lost some weight and everyone knows kids love a chubby clown. I'd also taken up drinking which didn't go over well right before a show. So suddenly, I found myself without prospects and I turned myself towards home, riding into Seattle by bus on a cold November night.

Mom met me at the bus stop. She had no business driving but she came out anyway. She was standing on the sidewalk next to the station wagon when she saw me. We hugged.

"I'm glad you're home," she said.

I lifted my bag into the back. "Thanks."

"Are you hungry?"

"Not really."

We went to Denny's anyway. Whenever my mom wanted to talk, we went to Denny's. It's where she took me to tell me about boys and girls, it's where she told me that my dog had been hit by a car.

"So what are you going to do now?" She cut and speared a chunk of meatloaf, then dipped it into her mashed potatoes and gravy before raising it to her mouth.

"I don't know," I said. "I guess I'll fatten up, quit drinking, get back into the business." I watched her left eyebrow twitch, a sure sign of disapproval. I hefted my double bacon cheeseburger, then paused. "Why? What do *you* think I should do?"

She leaned forward. She brought her wrinkled hand up and cupped my cheek with it. Then she smiled. "I think you've already tried the clown thing, Merton. Why don't you try something different?"

I grinned. "I always wanted to be a sword-swallower but you wouldn't let me."

"What about . . . insurance?"

"Well, it gets steep. The swords are real, Mom."

The eyebrow twitched again. "I'm being serious. Remember Nancy Keller?"

Of course I did. I'd lost my virginity to her back in eleventh grade. It was my second most defining moment that year. Three days later, Rufus P. Stowell's Traveling Big Top rolled into town and my first most defining moment occurred. They said I was a natural, I had the look and the girth. Would I be interested in an internship? I left a note for Nancy in her mailbox thanking her for everything in great detail, hugged my Mom goodbye and dropped out of high school to join the circus.

Mom was still waiting for me to answer. "Yes, I remember her."

"Well, she's some big mucky-muck now at CARECO."

"And?" I took a bite of the cheeseburger.

"And I told her you were coming home and asked her if she'd interview you."

I nearly choked. "You did *what*?"

"I asked her if she'd interview you. For a job."

I had no idea what to say.

So the next morning, Mom took me down to J.C. Penney's and bought me my first suit in thirty years. That afternoon, she dropped me downtown in front of the CARECO building, waved goodbye, and drove away.

The CARECO building was new. I'd visited a few times over the years, had watched buildings come and buildings go. But I had never seen anything like this. It looked like a glass Rubik's Cube tilted precariously in a martini glass full of green Jello. Inside, each floor took on the color coding of the various policies they offered. Life insurance was green. Auto, a deep blue. I can't remember what color Long-Term Disability was. Each color had been painfully worked out, according to a plaque near the door, by a team of eminent European corporate psychologists. Supposedly, it would enhance productivity by reducing the depression inherent within the insurance industry.

While I was reading the plaque, a man stepped up to me. He was as tan as a Californian, wearing sunglasses and a Hawaiian shirt despite impending rain. I went back to reading. "Excuse me," he said.

"Yes?"

"Have you seen a monkey around here?"

I shook my head, not really paying attention to the question. "Sorry."

He smiled. "Thanks anyway."

I went inside. I rode three escalators, two elevators, and talked to seven receptionists. I sat in a chair that looked like plastic but was really made of foam. I filled out long and complicated application forms.

An hour later, someone took me into an office at the top of the highest point of the inside of the glass Rubik's Cube.

Nancy Keller looked up. She smiled until my escort closed the door on her way out.

"Merton D. *Camel*," she said, stretching each syllable.

"Kamal. Hi Nancy." The view from her office was spectacular. The walls were glass framed in steel and I could see the city spread out around me in a wide view that pulled at my stomach. The office had a modern desk, a few chairs and some potted plants.

"I'm surprised to see you after so long. Back from clowning around?"

"I am." I smiled. "You look good." And she did. Her legs were still long but her hair was short and she'd traded her Van Halen tank top for a crisp blue suit.

She ignored my compliment and pointed to another of those foam chairs. "Let's get this over with."

I sat. She sat. I waited, trying to ignore the places where my wool suit created urgent itching.

She studied my application, then she studied me. I kept waiting. Finally, she spoke. "This interview," she said, "consists of two questions." She leaned forward and I realized the button on her suit coat had popped open to reveal more cleavage than I remembered her having. "First question. Do you remember the day you left for the circus, three days after our . . . *special* moment?" She made little quote marks in the air when she said special.

I nodded. "I do. I left you a note." I grinned. "I think I even said thank you. In some detail."

She nodded, too. "Second question. Did you ever stop to think that maybe . . . just maybe . . . my *father* would be the one getting the mail?" She stood and pushed a button on her desk. I stood, too. "Thank you for coming, Mr. Camel. Patrice will see you out." She extended her hand. I shook it and it was cold.

Later, I was working on my third bowl of ice cream and looking over the Twelve Steps when her assistant called with the offer.

"It's easy," Nancy Keller said again. I wasn't sure I'd heard her right. "I want you to drive a monkey to our branch office in New Mexico."

"That's my job?"

She nodded. "If you don't futz it up, there'll be another."

"Another monkey?"

"No," she said. "Another job. This monkey's one of a kind."

"And you're sure you don't want me to just take him to the airport and put him on a plane?"

"I'm sure."

I should've asked why but didn't. "Okay. When do I leave?"

"As soon as you get your mom's car." She noticed my open mouth. "This monkey," she said, "needs as much anonymity as possible."

"I'm traveling with an incognito monkey in a twenty year old station wagon?"

"Yes. You'd better get changed."

"Changed?" I knew I'd worn the suit two days in a row but I figured the first day didn't really count.

"You can't be seen like that. What would a guy in a suit need with a monkey? I need a clown for this one."

I was opening my mouth to question all of this when Patrice came in with a thick envelope. Nancy took it, opened it, and started ruffling through the hundred dollar bills.

"I'll get changed, get the car, be back in an hour," I said.

Nancy smiled. It was a sweet smile, one that reminded me of eighties music and her parents' ratty couch. "Thanks, Merton."

The monkey and I drove southeast, zig-zagging highways across Washington, crossing over the Cascades into dryer, colder parts of the state. There was little snow on the pass and the miles went by quickly.

The monkey was in an aluminum crate with little round holes in it. They'd loaded him into the back in their underground parking garage. Two men in suits stood by the door, watching.

"You shouldn't need anything else, Merton," Nancy said. "He's heavily sedated. He ought to sleep all the way through."

I looked at the map, tracing my finger along the route she'd marked in blue highlighter. "That's . . . around seventeen hundred miles, Nancy." I did some math in my head. "At least two days . . . and that's if I really push it."

"Just bring his crate into your hotel room. Discreetly, Merton." She smiled again. "You'll be fine. He'll be fine, too."

Naturally, I'd said okay, climbed into the car and set out for Roswell, New Mexico.

When we crossed into Oregon, the monkey woke up.

I knew this because he asked me for a cigarette.

I swerved onto the shoulder, mashing the brakes with one

clown-shoed foot while hyperventilating.

"Just one," he said. "Please?"

I couldn't get out of the car fast enough. After a few minutes of pacing by the side of the road, convincing myself that it was the result of quitting the booze cold turkey, I poked my head back into the car.

"Did you say something?" I asked, holding my breath.

Silence.

Releasing my breath, I climbed back into the car. "I didn't think so." I started the car back up, eased it onto the road. I laughed at myself. "Talking monkeys," I said, shaking my head.

"Monkeys can't talk," the monkey said. Then he yawned loudly.

I braked again.

He chuckled. "Look pal, I'm no monkey. I just play one on TV."

I glanced up into the rearview mirror. A single dark eye blinked through one of the holes. "Really?"

He snorted. "No. I don't. Where are we supposed to be going?"

"Roswell, New Mexico."

"And what does *that* tell you?"

I shrugged. "You got me."

"Let's just say I'm not from around here."

"Where *are* you from?" But it was sinking in. Of course, I didn't believe it. I had laid aside the cold turkey alcohol withdrawal theory at this point and was wondering now if maybe I was tilting more towards a psychotic break theory.

"Unimportant. But I'm not a monkey."

"Okay then. Why don't you go back to sleep?"

"I'm not tired. I just woke up. Why don't you let me out of this box and give me a cigarette?"

"I don't smoke."

"Let's stop somewhere, then. A gas station."

I looked back at him in the rearview mirror. "For someone that's not from around here, you sure know an awful lot." More suspicion followed. "And you speak English pretty good, too."

"Well," the monkey said. "I speak it *well*. And I may not be *from* here but I've certainly spent enough time on this rock you call home."

"Really?" Definitely a psychotic break. I needed medication.

Maybe cognitive therapy, too. "What brings you out this way?"

"I'm a spy."

"A monkey spy?"

"I thought we'd already established that I'm *not* a monkey."

"So you just look like one?" I gradually gave the car some gas and we slipped back onto the highway.

"Exactly."

"Why?"

"I have no idea. You'd have to ask my boss."

I pushed the station wagon back up to seventy-five, watching for road signs and wondering if any of the little towns out here would have a psychiatrist. "Where's your boss?"

"Don't know," the monkey said. "I gave him the slip when I defected."

"You defected?"

"Of course I defected."

"Why?"

"Got a better offer."

It went on like that. We made small talk and Oregon turned into Idaho. I never asked his name; he never offered. I found a Super Eight outside Boise and after paying, hauled his crate into the room.

"So are you going to let me out?"

"I don't think that'd be such a good idea," I told him.

"Well, can you at least get us a pizza? And some beer?"

"Pizza, yes," I said. "Beer, no." I called it in and channel-surfed until it arrived.

The holes presented a problem. And I couldn't just eat in front of him. I went to open the crate.

It was locked. One of those high powered combination jobs. "Odd, isn't it?"

"Yeah," I said. "A bit."

He sighed. "I'm sure it's for my own protection."

"Or mine," I said.

He chuckled. "Yeah, I'm quite the badass as you can see."

That's when I picked up the phone and called Nancy. She'd given me her home number. "Hey," I said.

"Merton. What's up?"

"Well, I'm in Boise."

"How's the package?"

"Fine. But. . . ." I wasn't sure what to say.

"But what?"

"Well, I went to check on the monkey and the crate's locked. What's the combination?"

"Is the monkey awake?" Her voice sounded alarmed.

I looked at the crate, at the eye peeking out. "Uh. No. I don't *think* so."

"Has anything"—she paused, choosing her word carefully—"*unusual* happened?"

I nearly said you mean like a talking space alien disguised as a monkey? Instead, I said, "No. Not at all. Not really." I knew I needed more or she wouldn't believe me. "Well, the guy at the front desk looked at me a bit funny."

"What did he look like?"

"Old. Bored. Like he didn't expect to see a clown in his lobby."

"I'm sure he's fine."

I nodded, even though she couldn't see me. "So, about that combination?"

"You don't need it, Merton. Call me when you get to Roswell." The phone clicked and she was gone.

In the morning, I loaded the monkey back into the car and we pointed ourselves towards Utah.

We picked up our earlier conversation.

"So you defected? To an insurance company?" But I knew what he was going to say.

"That's no insurance company."

"Government?"

"You'd know better than I would," he said. "I was asleep through most of that bit."

"But you're the one who defected."

He laughed. "I didn't defect to *them*."

"You *didn't*?"

"No. Of course not. Do you think I *want* to be locked in a metal box in the back of a station wagon on my way to Roswell, New Mexico, with an underweight clown who doesn't smoke?"

I shrugged. "Then what?"

"There was a guy. He was supposed to meet me in Seattle before your wacky friends got me with the old tag and bag routine. He represents certain *other* interested parties. He'd worked up a bit of an incognito gig for me in exchange for some information on my previous employers."

I felt my eyebrows furrow. "*Other* interested parties?"

"Let's just say your little rock is pretty popular these days. Did you really think the cattle mutilations, abductions, anal probes and crop circles were all done by the same little green men?"

"I'd never thought about it before."

"Space is pretty big. And everyone has their schtick."

I nodded. "Okay. That makes sense, I guess." Except for the part where I was still talking to a monkey and he was talking back. It was quiet now. The car rolled easy on the highway.

"Sure could use a cigarette."

"They're bad for you. They'll kill you."

"Jury's still out on that," the monkey said. "I'm not exactly part of your collective gene pool." He paused. "Besides, I'm pretty sure it doesn't matter."

"It doesn't?"

"What do you really think they're going to do to me in Roswell?"

The monkey had a point. The next truck stop, I pulled off and went inside. I came out with a pack of Marlboro's and pushed one through the little hole. He reversed it, pointing an end out to me so I could light it. He took a long drag. "That's nice," he said. "Thanks."

"You're welcome." Suddenly my shoulders felt heavy. As much as I knew that there was something dreadfully wrong with me, some wire that had to be burned out in my head, I felt sad. Something bad, something *experimental* was probably going to happen to this monkey. And whether or not he deserved it, I had a role in it. I didn't like that at all.

"Have you seen a monkey around here," the California Tan Man had asked me two days ago in front of the CARECO building.

I looked up. "Hey. I saw that guy. The one in Seattle. What was the gig he had for you? Witness protection type-thing?"

"Sort of. Lay low, stay under everyone's radar."

Where would a monkey lay low, I asked myself. "Like what?" I said, "a zoo?"

"Screw zoos. Concrete cage and a tire swing. Who wants that?"

"What then?"

Cigarette smoke trailed out of the holes in his crate. "It's not important. Really."

"Come on. Tell me." But I knew now. Of course I knew. How could I not? But I waited for him to say it.

"Well," the monkey said, "ever since I landed on this rock I've wanted to join the circus."

Exactly, I thought, and I knew what I had to do.

"I'll be back," I said. I got out of the car and walked around the truck stop. It didn't take long to find what I was looking for. The guy had a mullet and a pick-up truck. In the back of the pick-up truck's window was a rifle rack. And in the rifle rack, a rifle. Hunting season or not, this was Idaho.

I pulled that wad of bills from my wallet and his eyes went wide. He'd probably never seen a clown with so much determination in his stride and cash in his fist. I bought that rifle from him, drove out into the middle of nowhere, and shot the lock off that crate.

When the door opened, a small, hairy hand reached out, followed by a slender, hairy arm, hairy torso, hairy face. He didn't quite look like a monkey but he was close enough. He smiled, his three black eyes shining like pools of oil. Then, the third eye puckered in on itself and disappeared. "I should at least try to fit in," he said.

"Do you want me to drop you anywhere?" I asked him.

"I think I'll walk. Stretch my legs a bit."

"Suit yourself."

We shook hands. I gave him the pack of the cigarettes, the lighter and all but one of the remaining hundred dollar bills.

"I'll see you around," I said.

I didn't call Nancy until I got back to Seattle. When I did, I told her what happened. Well, *my* version about what happened. And I didn't feel bad about it, either. She'd tried to use me in her plot against a fellow circus aficionado.

"I've never seen anything like it," I said. "We were just outside

of Boise, early in the morning, and there was this light in the sky."
I threw in a bit about missing time and how I thought something
invasive and wrong might've happened to me.

I told her that they also took the monkey.

She insisted that I come over right away. She and her husband had a big house on the lake and when I got there, she was
already pretty drunk. I'm a weak man. I joined her and we polished off a bottle of tequila. Her husband was out of town on
business and somehow we ended up having sex on the leather
couch in his den. It was better than the last time but still nothing compared to a high wire trapeze act or a lion tamer or an
elephant that can dance.

Still, I didn't complain. At the time, it was nice.

Three days later, my phone rang.

"Merton D. Kamal?" a familiar voice asked.

"Yes?"

"I need a clown for my act."

"Does it involve talking monkeys?" I asked with a grin.

"Monkeys can't talk," the monkey said.

So I wrote Nancy a note, thanking her in great detail for the
other night. After putting it in her mailbox, I took a leisurely stroll
down to the Greyhound Station.

When the man at the ticket counter asked me where I was
headed, I smiled.

"The greatest show on earth," I said. And I know he understood because he smiled back.

HARLEY TAKES A WIFE

It CAME TO PASS THAT OLD HARLAN BOSCO SUSSBAUER, last of the Big Space Rock prospectors on the far edge of the Frontier System, found himself feeling quite alone, terribly lonely, and in dire want of companionship. And so, Harley took a wife, as one does.

Of course, it didn't happen in such straightforward fashion. And Harley was far too nervous and careful a man to *take* anyone or anything, so perhaps it is more accurate to say:

It came to pass that Harley bought a bride.

But truly, because Harley Sussbauer considered himself, above all things, a practical man, it also started, as these things inevitably *should*, with a plant. A cactus, to be more specific.

"Howdy, Pilgrim," the cactus said in a low, gravelly voice when Harley opened its shipping pod. "My name's Duke."

Harley blinked behind spectacles that made the world greasier and grayer than it really was. "Uh . . . howdy? I'm Harley."

"You'll always be Pilgrim to me," the cactus drawled. Then he rustled in his enviro-dome. "I'd offer to shake yer hand but I'm told I can be a bit of a prick." The cactus guffawed.

Harley looked down at the packing material and owner's manual, then looked back at the cactus. *Talk to your plant . . . AND YOUR PLANT TALKS BACK!* That's what the sales pitch had been. And it had been well on a decade since the last of the other prospectors had folded up and ceded their claims to Big Space Rock Mine Co-op, of which Harley was now the sole member. It had taken some time for the loneliness to settle in, but when it did, he sat down like an engineer to sketch out his options and draw a blueprint toward his happiness. And every fiber of his being agreed with that time-honored bit of sage counsel.

Start with a plant and see where it goes.

Within just those first few introductory moments, Harley suspected he'd made a terrible mistake. But he was the last prospector in the belt for good reason. Harley had a stick-to-itiveness borne of some patience and a good deal of pathological persistence in the face of contradictory facts. And so he committed fully to giving this new addition to his life a fair shake.

"Where are you going, Pilgrim?" Duke asked on their first morning.

"Down to the mine to check the mites."

"Alone?" Harley heard disdain in the cactus's voice.

"Well . . ."

"So why again," Duke asked, "did you buy me?"

And then suddenly, it was bring your cactus to work day. Every day.

His father had patented his Mighty Tiny Mining Mites™ but had never seen them spring to life in the Frontier System. And Harley had seen them bring home the bacon, even in a trickle, that let him outlast the others with their more conventional approach. But for Harley, going to work meant visiting a mobile monitoring station near whichever asteroid of the week happened to pay off. He watched ancient television reruns on one monitor and rat-sized drones on the others as they ran their course, bringing back small amounts of the various ores and minerals as they wandered.

One thing was certain: Harley no longer felt alone. Or lonely.

After a hundred "what's that's" and a few hundred "what's this do's," Harley started missing his loneliness a smidge.

And after a few weeks, he more became certain: The off switch on the AI-induced plant was looking more and more tempting and, at some point, his politeness was going to collapse in upon him.

At six months, to the day, he took his cactus to breakfast instead of work.

"I'm sorry, Duke," Harley said, "but it's not working out. I think I'm going to need something different."

Duke shrugged. "Remember how I told you I was a bit of a prick?"

Harley shook his head. "No, it's not you, Duke. It's me."

Duke nodded. "Well, that's a comfort at least. Have you considered therapy?"

Harley shook his head again. "I don't think therapy would help our situation." He sighed. "I think," he finally said, "I need to consider taking a wife."

"Whoa there, Pilgrim. That's quite a bit more of a mouthful than a prickly cactus," Duke said. "Are you sure that's where this here experiment-gone-wrong is pointing you?"

Harley wasn't sure. Not by a damned sight. But he nodded anyway and in that moment, everything changed.

Duke's drawl vanished and an overenthusiastic, very young voice—too loud for the large empty room they sat in—replaced the cactus. "Well then, Mr. Sussbauer, let's see about getting you into the soulmate of your dreams. Have you considered the benefits of a customizable artificial mail-order bride? Let's see what we have on the showroom floor. Everything—I'm sorry, every*one*—we have is fully customizable to your wants, wishes, and needs. And, of course, if you'll be returning Duke, we'll apply that refund to the cost of your new companion."

Harley sat back and rubbed his eyes. "Who is this? Where did Duke go?"

"Hi," the cactus said with more enthusiasm than its envirodome seemed designed for. "I'm Todd with Acme Artificials, Incorporated, the Frontier System's number one source for Labor, Love, and Other Mechanical Oddities."

It moved quickly from there. Todd remoted onto the cafeteria's holo-table and took Harley quickly through his options, then began building his perfect companion based on a series of questions a bit too similar to those that had led to Duke.

When they were finished and the loan was approved, Harley and Duke finally got to the monitoring station to check the day's work.

"I'm glad you decided to keep me, Pilgrim." There was something like affection in his voice now. "I'm going to do you and your blushing bride right proud."

And then for the next three weeks, while he waited for his bride's imminent arrival, Harley heard all about just what kind of family they would make together—and wondered again about just how large a mistake he might have made.

*

Harley wore his Sunday finest for maybe the third time in a decade for the big day and was pleased that it still nearly fit him. He even put a bow on Duke's enviro-dome for the occasion. Then they trundled off to the docking bay to meet the supply shuttle.

The crate looked like your standard cryo-pod for reasons of discretion—not that there were any prying eyes or nosy neighbors to consider. The NuFedEx lift-load-bots brought it down along with the rest of the quarter's supplies, then fastened themselves back into the shuttle for departure after Harley accepted the shipment on his e-tab.

He activated the co-op's mechanicals to haul the other items and then looked at the crate from Acme.

"It's your big day, Pilgrim. How are your feet?"

Harley looked down. "They're fine, I reckon."

Duke chuckled. "Mine are shaking in their boots for you."

"I thought you said this was a good idea?"

"I think that was Todd."

Harley shrugged and faced the crate, extended his finger, and pushed the single button on its control panel. With a pop and a hiss and a rainbow of lights, the crate started to hum. An LED started counting down from one hundred.

At zero, the lights on the crate went out with a click.

Harley found himself closing his eyes as the lid swung open. It was as if something inside him compelled him to give Mrs. Sussbauer just a bit more time.

He squeezed them shut and then after it had been too long, he forced them open.

"Well, I'll be a sassafras-assed sumbitch," Duke said.

Harley stared into the cold, blue, killer eyes of his new bride. Blue like steel, blue like gun smoke on high noon air. Harley watched the mouth curl into a sneer that pulled at the handlebar mustache, watched the rough hands move across ruffles and lace for a gun belt that wasn't presently worn.

"There isn't room in this one-hopper town for the two of us, Pilgrim," the mail-order bride said in a voice far too deep and far too familiar for his liking.

"Nope," the cactus finally said, "that's not awkward at all."

*

Unlike Duke, the gunslinger bride had no operating manual and no visible switch. But he was quieter than the cactus, settling into following Harley as he returned to the cafeteria where he could pace more comfortably.

Harley kicked himself. A private man, he'd not wanted to open the crate in front of the lift-load-bots. If he had, then it would've been simple enough to start a return. But now, he only saw one path forward.

"I'm sorry," he told his new bride, "but this isn't going to work for me."

The veil dropped and behind it, the eyes narrowed. The right hand moved toward the right hip. "Exactly what are you saying, Pilgrim?"

Harley sighed. "There's been a mistake."

"Shipping me without my six-guns," the bride growled, "seems the bigger mistake." The eyes widened quickly before narrowing slowly again. "Otherwise, I make a beautiful bride."

Harley felt his face grow hot. "It's not you. It's me." He exhaled and sat abruptly. "Maybe I should talk with Todd."

The bride looked around. "Who's Todd?" He sized up Harley, then sized up the cactus. "You named your cactus Todd?"

"My name's Duke," the cactus said.

"*My* name's Duke," the bride said.

"Todd's the sales rep who . . ." Politeness. "He was our matchmaker," Harley said. "And based on our conversation, I'm confident there's been a mistake."

"You believe I'm someone else's intended?"

"I do," he said.

"Saints be praised," Duke the bride said.

"I'll get Todd," Duke the cactus said.

"Unfortunately, Todd is no longer with the company," a flat-voiced woman monotoned when they finally got through. "This is Megan. Can I help you?"

"I'm having a problem with my bride," Harley said.

"Mr. Sussbauer, that just can't be possible."

"He arrived today. He's standing right here." Harley looked over at the bride. "Say something."

"Howdy, ma'am."

Harley could almost hear her eyebrows twisting. "You did not order a male bride."

"No," Harley said, "I did not. But I have one, nonetheless."

Megan was quiet for a moment. "Well, this is a pickle indeed. Because we haven't shipped your bride yet. She is right here. There was a last-minute problem with your credit application that Todd was supposed to take care of with you, but . . ." The way her words trickled out made it sound like Todd could have just as easily died a slow and terrible death as having been fired. "Is there any chance that you have friends playing a prank?"

Duke cut in and laughed. "Harley has friends?"

Harley scowled at the cactus. "I don't have any friends." He considered for a moment. "And wouldn't that be a terribly expensive prank?"

"I've seen everything in this line of work," she said. "What is the bride doing now?"

He glanced over to meet those piercing blue eyes. "He's staring at me. He reaches for his guns a lot even though he isn't wearing any."

"He sounds . . . potentially problematic." Now her voice became serious, conspiratorial. "Can we talk privately?"

Harley nodded for the cactus to follow him out of the room, then lowered his voice when they were behind a sealed door.

"There is another possibility," Megan said, "but I would need to examine your bride. We have no record of the shipment, and I doubt you have the biomechanical scanning equipment we would need."

"What do you think it is?"

"Dastardly Al might be up to something."

Harley felt a headache coming on and closed his eyes. "Dastardly Al?"

"Dastardly Al's All-Android Caper Gang. Surely you've heard of them?"

Harley had not, but she educated him. "Wanted on New Colorado and New Texas both. New Wyoming's marshals haven't been able to make anything stick, but Al's been active in the system for maybe a decade. Folk legend stuff."

Harley shrugged though no one could see him. He'd never heard of them but couldn't imagine what might bring them to his co-op. "What would they want with me?"

"Maybe they're looking to expand," she offered.

Harley laughed louder now. "I'm a prospector not a gangster."

"And that," Megan said, "brings us back to Todd's unfinished business. How would you feel about killing two turkeys with one shot?"

He waited while she explained. "Your father established credit with his prototype mites as collateral, but our understanding is that the Mark Two is a better machine, likely more valuable."

"It is," Harley said, "but they still only bring in a trickle. They just aren't designed for large production."

"Yes, we've heard. And Acme has some ideas around that; our CEO, Amos Anderson Acme, would like to chat with you."

Harley first felt his father's stubborn boot prodding him to close the conversation down. But he'd limped by on credit and scrimping, following a vision that had started in another system with another Sussbauer. There had been an initial buzz about his mining mites when they'd first arrived and started chewing their tiny tunnels. Of course, his father, Horace Sussbauer, had died en route to the co-op and his son had carried on, sporting his black armband for three solid years. "I'd be happy to schedule a holocon with Mr. Acme."

"Mr. Acme is old school and prefers to meet in person. And he's going to want to see the mites in action."

"Mr. Acme is coming here?"

She laughed. "Oh no. He doesn't have the time for that kind of travel. Two weeks and three days out from our corporate offices in Anarchy Territory, New Texas, by hop-shuttle . . . talk about the farthest edge of the existence. He'd like you to bring a mite and give him a demonstration here. At the very least, it should raise your credit limit sufficiently. At the very most, you could join Mr. Acme in becoming one of the wealthiest entrepreneurs in the system."

So after it was all said and done, Harley Sussbauer agreed to close up the co-op, secure all but one of the mites and a portable command dock and packed his bag into the co-op's seldom used shuttle. He would secure his cactus and bride in their respective shipping containers and put himself in stasis for the trip to New Texas.

Looking back, he'd later wonder what had compelled him to take his third trip "to town" and decided it must've been the combination of loneliness and the disappointment of having things go so surreally astray in his attempts to fix it. He'd never had any interest in making it rich anywhere but the asteroid belt, and he had less interest in wealth than he did in living the life he wanted to live. But the idea of meeting with a person, of sitting in a room and having a conversation . . . well, it sparked something in him.

It must indeed be the loneliness, he thought. Because now, how Harlan lived his life mattered less than not being alone. And the only thing worse than no company was ill-fitting company. And now he was getting ready to put himself to sleep for a few weeks—over a month if he counted the return trip.

And he couldn't stop thinking about the sales rep's voice. *Megan.* Todd's voice had not left such an impression.

Harley chuckled.

"What are you laughing at, Pilgrim?" his bride and his cactus both asked in stereo.

"First woman I've talked to in ten years," he said.

The gunslinger bride's eyes narrowed for the hundredth time. "Keep it up, and it'll be your last. I'm the jealous type."

Harley said nothing. He sealed his two companions into their crates, fired up the automatic pilot, and settled into his own crate for a little shut-eye.

In his dreams, Megan had blond hair and had also been oh, so lonely and—

"Mr. Sussbauer?"

The voice hung somewhere in a void, tiny and far away. But it was in a place no voice should be and the weight of everything pressed on Harley's eyes. He pushed back and opened them a slit, bright light flooding him.

Now he felt a hand on his shoulder. "Ah, you're awake."

Harley worked harder at his eyes, becoming painfully aware of how dry his mouth was. As if reading his mind, he felt a straw press to his lips. "Drink," the voice said.

Something sweet and cold flooded his mouth. *Apple juice.*

"Welcome to New Texas, Mr. Sussbauer. You had quite a trip."

The disorientation from stasis licked and bit him like a passive-aggressive tomcat and he shook his head against it. Then he opened his eyes. He was on a sofa in a reception area and a blond woman sat near him, an instacup of apple juice in her hand. "What happened?"

The woman leaned forward, her eyes wide. "There was an attempt on your shuttle. Marshal thinks it was Dastardly Al's All-Android Caper Gang. They ran them off and escorted your shuttle into our care. Mr. Acme offers his sincerest apologies for such a rude and unexpected awakening." She paused. "I'm Megan Miller."

Now Harley could smell her—it was a soft, clean, floral smell—and he suspected that it could intoxicate him given enough time. He sat up and blushed, hoping she wouldn't notice. "I can't imagine what they'd want with me."

"Maybe," she said, "they're interested in the mites. Mr. Acme certainly thinks it possible."

Harley scowled. He couldn't imagine what else it would be. "Does the marshal have any idea where they ran off to?"

Megan shook her head and then stood. "No, they're a slippery lot. But Mr. Acme is prepared to hire a security escort for your return trip, and he's already authorized repair work to your shuttle. He's quite distressed about this development."

Harley watched her walk around a large wooden reception desk beneath a simple sign that read ACME ARTIFICIALS. She was dressed in a pantsuit and loafers that were silent on the thick burgundy carpet. She was pretty enough to bring out all of his awkwardness, but if she noticed, she had the grace to overlook it.

"Our technicians are getting to the bottom of your gunslinger bride. It does appear to be one of ours, but it was reported as stolen several years ago." She glanced down at the desk, pushed some buttons. "And Mr. Acme is hoping to see a demonstration of your Mighty Tiny Mining Mites™ once you're feeling up to it. Are you ready for coffee?"

He nodded. "Thank you."

"And maybe," she said with a quick grin, "you'd like to meet Mrs. Sussbauer?"

Now Harley really blushed and stammered. "I-I reckon that would be fine." Then an afterthought brought the tiniest stab of guilt home. "And where's my cactus?"

"That particular model is a bit . . . vocal." He appreciated the politeness in her tone as she chose her words. "So we've left him crated for now. He's in the other room along with your luggage."

She went to the 3D-All printer, pressed more buttons, and returned with a cup of coffee. "With chicory," she said as she brought him the mug.

"Thank you." Harley took it and sipped. It was perfect.

Already, the stasis fog was lifting. He'd made three trips in a decade. The first, he'd stayed awake and killed the time with reruns and mining tutorials. But after that, he'd slept the time away. And each time, he'd been more than ready for the solitude of his solitary co-op upon his return. Of course, none of those trips had involved attempted space-jackings and law enforcement.

Megan returned to her desk and work. Harley sat and drank his coffee. A bright red, old-fashioned telephone jangled, and she lifted the antique handset to her ear. "Yes, Mr. Acme?" She smiled at Harley as she said it. "Yes, he's awake. I'll tell him." She put down the phone. "The marshal may also want a word later. But Mr. Acme is ready to meet whenever you are feeling ready. He's very keen to see your mite in action. And I imagine you're ready to meet the missus."

He felt the heat in his face again and told himself it was the coffee. But it wasn't. It was a strange mix of embarrassment, maybe shame, and an extra helping of a little more awkward. He'd gone most of his life quite fine with being alone and then some corner had turned, and he'd become one of_those people.

He'd bought a talking cactus.

He'd bought a gunslinger bride.

And now, he sat in a room with a real woman—the first he'd been near in years—who knew these things about him and continued to be polite and engaging anyway.

Of course, it was her job. And it made him curious about what took a person into the business of artificial love and labor. Gauging things from this single, spartan room, business was not booming despite his confidence that loneliness abounded in the Frontier System.

Harley swallowed more of the coffee. "I think I'm ready."

She opened the door, and he went through. This room was better decorated. Unlike the other, it had a large window that looked out on a salt flat beneath a blistering sun. It was an office, decorated with an antique Terran theme. In one corner, his bag, his mining kit, and his crated cactus were carefully arranged. Various mechanicals were scattered around the room: a canary in a jar; a chimpanzee dressed as a clown that appeared to be asleep in a cradle; a baby grand piano complete with a pianist dressed in period clothing; and, in the center of the room, a woman who took his breath away.

She was tall, blond, and like the gunslinger, her eyes were blue, but with the warmth of a summer sky. She wore a simple dress and held a bouquet of daisies. "Hello, Harlan," she said. "I'm Abigail. It's nice to finally meet you."

He stammered and blushed while a tall, older gentleman dressed in a bowtie, suspenders, and lab coat stood from the oak desk behind her. "Mr. Sussbauer, I'm so sorry for the way this has gone. And I hope it wasn't an overstep to have you wake up here rather than down at the spaceport in the marshal's care. Brady is an old friend and agreed to take his report from you here, later." His smile was narrow but sincere. "I thought this would be a more comfortable beginning."

"I appreciate your hospitality," Harley said.

"Abigail," he said, "would you wait for us with Megan?"

She nodded and flashed Harley a grin. Then left.

"Abigail," Harley said after she was gone. But as she passed, he noticed that, unlike Megan, she had no scent that went with her.

"You can change her name to whatever suits you, of course." The gentleman stepped forward and extended his hand. "Amos Anderson Acme," he said. "I'm a fan of you and your father's work."

Harley shook it. It was firm and dry. "It's slow going," he said, "but we get it done a little bit at a time."

"It was a shame he didn't get to see his dream come true. I'm sure he'd be proud of what you've done with his legacy."

Harley wasn't so sure. But he'd gotten his stubbornness from his father, and he'd inherited the life he lived now, fashioned from his father's lab-infused dreams. "I've tried to do right by him. And over the years, I've made some adjustments."

Acme rubbed his hands together. "I'm eager to see it. It'll dig through anything, correct?"

Harley chuckled. "Not anything. There are surfaces too hard, too hot, or too cold."

Acme pointed to the window. "How about salt?"

Harley shrugged. "Sure. But I'm not sure what it would find out there."

"And the Mark Two has more customization and programmable features than the Mark One your father showed me?"

Harley nodded. "Yes."

"And," Amos said, "I take it that Abigail is more what you had in mind in the way of a bride?"

He gulped. "Yes."

"Then I propose a test and, if it goes well, I'd like to talk with you about more than raising your credit limit."

Harley's eyebrows arched. "More?"

Amos nodded. "I think there are potentially multiple applications for a device like your mites. Shall we get started?" He rubbed his hands together again and this time, the gesture seemed off. But Acme smiled, and Harley let the smile reassure him.

"Sure," Harley said. "We can set it up right here." He nodded to the window. "We'll just need to put the mite out. What exactly are you hoping to see, Mr. Acme?"

Acme opened a drawer and pulled out a photograph. It was on retro-yellowed paper in black and white of an older man and a boy. He pushed the photo across the desk and tapped it with his finger. "That's me and my father," he said, "shortly after we crossed the gate. If you look closely, you'll see he's wearing a pocket watch. The same watch that his father and his father before him carried."

Realization dawned slowly for Harley. "And it's out there somewhere?"

Acme nodded and his face took on a sudden and dramatic weight of sorrow. "I took it from him without permission, and then I lost it racing around the salt flats with my friends as a boy." Harley saw the beginning of tears. "I don't have words for how much guilt I still bear, though my father's been gone decades now."

"What's it made of?"

"Platinum. Glass and steel, too, of course." Now Acme's right eye twitched, and Harley noticed that the left one seemed to be the only one making tears.

Harley pulled the mite and control dock from his mining kit. Then opened them both up and starting poking at the settings. He adjusted the range finder, loaded in the specs, and grinned as the rat-sized mite spun to life. "This should be easy enough. If it's still out there." He looked out the window again. "Worst case is that it might take some time. If I had the entire pack, it would go faster."

Acme was rubbing his hands together again, and it tickled Harley's imagination. He'd seen the move in a dozen ancient movies, and nearly always it was a villain move.

Maybe, Harley thought, *he has some kind of condition.* Trying not to notice, he forced a smile. "I think we're ready."

Acme picked up the red phone on his desk. "Megan? Can you come in here?"

The door opened. Harley saw the excitement on her face shift to concern for a moment when she saw Acme's face. Her eyebrow went up.

Acme was on his feet again, gesturing to Harley. "Can you put Mr. Sussbauer's Mighty Tiny Mining Mite™ outside?"

Harley tried to identify the look that passed quickly between them but couldn't. Megan smiled, nodded curtly, and took the humming mite into her hands carefully. "Yes, Mr. Acme." She held it at arm's length. "Do I need to do anything special?"

Harley shook his head. "Just set it on the ground. Point it toward the flats."

She took it and left the room. Acme went to the window and motioned for Harley to join him. Harley put the control dock on the desk, and stood near Acme.

Something was definitely wrong with the man's eye as it rapidly blinked. But once again, Harley forced his attention away and pointed out the window to a small object that moved quickly toward the salt flat. "There she goes."

Acme clapped and the clap turned into more hand-rubbing of the nefarious sort. Only this time, he seemed aware of it, and his leaking eye widened a bit as he watched his own hands.

The red phone rang, and Acme picked it up. "Yes, Megan?" He nodded. "I understand." He put the receiver down and turned quickly to the door, careful not to look toward Harley. "I am afraid," he said over his shoulder as he moved quickly, "that I have an unexpected and rather urgent matter to attend to. It shouldn't take long. I'm certain you can manage your mite for a few minutes without me?"

Harley opened his mouth to respond but Acme was gone, through the door, before he could say a word.

Maybe it was the coffee kicking in, or maybe it was that he was moving further and further past the initial fog of a stasis wake-up. Whatever it was, Harley found himself suddenly of the thought that perhaps things were not exactly on the up-and-up here at Acme Artificials.

He spent the first ten minutes checking his control dock, adjusting the programming on the mite as it established a pattern and began moving through the salt. Staring out the window, Harley wondered just how long his mite would take to track down such a specific item.

Then he started examining the mechanicals around the room. The bird was the only one functioning and all of them seemed older models.

Finally, at about twenty minutes, Harley went to the door and paused. He put his hand on the knob and that was enough to send him back to the mite controls, tweaking and adjusting. After another five minutes, the door opened, and Megan pushed her face through. It was red now with exertion or frustration.

"I'm so sorry, Mr. Sussbauer. Are you doing okay in here?"

He tried to channel nonchalance. "I'm fine."

She was gone before the words were completely in the air, and now the look on her face added to his rising questions. He waited and then returned to the door.

He put his hand on the knob again and willed himself to turn it.

Locked.

Harley pressed his ear to the door. Beyond it, he heard nothing and now he found himself digging into the hazy fog of his first memories waking up here. There was a front door, or at least he thought there was. A narrow door in, the ornate door into Acme's office. What else?

Harley paced and pondered. He'd been muddled at best upon waking up and then distracted by Megan and the tale she spun.

When Harley flushed this time, it was down into his boots, and not from a slight social embarrassment. This heat came from having been not just any fool, but specifically a damned fool. Whoever these people were, he doubted they were with Acme

Artificials, Inc. And the more he thought about Acme's hands and eye, Harley knew he was now using the term "people" loosely.

No, he was surely in the hands of Dastardly Al and his All-Android Caper Gang.

And I'm their current caper, it seems.

For some reason, apart from his embarrassment, Harley didn't feel the level of anger one might think normal for the circumstances. It was as if some part of him sat on the fence, willing to wait for whichever feeling made the most sense to feed in the moments sure to unfold on the trail ahead. He didn't feel really any anger and, at this point, if these were indeed captors they'd been nothing but polite and accommodating beyond the subterfuge.

No, instead Harley felt curiosity.

He looked around the room again, then listened at the door. Hearing nothing, he went to his luggage. His control dock wasn't finding a network to access and it had him curious about the cactus. What had Megan said? *That particular model is a bit . . . vocal.*

It was true. But he wondered now why they might not want Duke in the picture.

Harley went to the crated cactus and pushed its activation button, watching the indicator lights spin to life. The packing crate opened with a click and a hiss.

"Hey, Duke," he said, "we have a problem."

"You mean besides the other Duke showing up in a wedding dress and complicating our perfect little family?"

Harley nodded. "I think we have been and currently are being hoodwinked by Dastardly Al and his gang. Are you connected? Can you get the marshals?"

"I can get them, but it'll take a few days."

Harley looked out the window. "Aren't we on New Texas?"

Duke chuckled. "Sorry, Pilgrim. We are a *long* way from New Texas. We are currently on Nephi."

Nephi was the third moon of New Wyoming, known for being a bastion for the lawless and lost, high above the surface of the system's least policed planet. It had one small port and a scattering of unincorporated communities made up of people who didn't want to be easily found. It was also a leading source of salt in the system.

The control dock chimed, and Harley looked up. Moving

across the room quickly, he saw the mite had come within range of a target that lit up the board. The mite adjusted course to capture what Harley assumed must be the watch.

He glanced at the door and wondered exactly how this was supposed to play out once Al had what he wanted. He put the mite into a holding pattern, moving in a slow circle around its target, then Harley went back to the cactus. "They are after a platinum pocket watch," he said. "Acme—or at least the android pretending to be him—says it belonged to his father."

"So all of this has been to find a missing watch?"

"Seems so," Harley said.

Duke grunted. "They could've just asked you for a favor."

Harley nodded. Then he heard a voice from the other side of the door. "No," he heard Megan say, "I'll take care of it." He heard exasperation in her voice.

He shushed his cactus and closed the crate, hoping Duke would take the hint and not use this moment to prove the nature of his vocality.

He was back at the panel, moving levers and buttons, when the door opened and Megan stepped in. "I am *so* sorry, Mr. Sussbauer. Mr. Acme has taken unexpectedly ill and hopes you'll forgive his sudden absence."

Harley was never much of a gambler, but his best play now was clear, so he bluffed. "I am sorry to hear that. Perhaps we should reschedule? I would be happy to come back at another time." He moved a few buttons. "Let me call back the mite and—"

She was quick to interrupt. "Oh, there is no need for us to reschedule. It's such a long trip." He saw her eyes quickly calculating as she took him in. "Mr. Acme has asked that we complete the demonstration without him." Her smile was warm. "How is going? Has it found anything?"

"Not yet," Harley lied. "And Mr. Acme is certain it is out there?"

She nodded. "I suppose someone else could've found it, but that would be highly unlikely."

Harley scratched his head. "I don't recall exactly where the salt flats are in New Texas?"

Her eyebrow arched. "Southern hemisphere," she said quickly. "Obviously near our headquarters."

"Obviously," he agreed but noted the eyebrow.

He silenced the dock and took it out of its holding pattern. "So I get Mr. Acme his watch," he said, "and you send me and Abigail home?"

"After the ceremony, of course," Megan said. Her eyes met his. The blue seemed something closer to the gunslinger bride's shade now. "If, of course, you want a wedding." She smiled. "It is nonbinding and simply a part of the complete companionship experience. Makes sense if you've come all this way."

The mite had the object now, and he let it run in a loop. He put his body between Megan and the control dock. "And what happens if we don't find the watch?"

Her look was blank enough that Harley found himself unconcerned with failure. "Well, I suppose we'd just send you and your cactus home. I'm sure Mr. Acme would be disappointed, but if the mites can't be used for this type of work, his interest would be lessened considerably."

Harley nodded. "And if it does indeed work?"

"The beginning," she said, "of a potentially beautiful and profitable partnership."

Now Harley saw his moment for what it was and seized upon it. "Don't you reckon," he said, "that all of the best and most lasting partnerships are built upon the bedrock of honesty?"

Megan blushed.

Harley continued. "Just to add a helping of honesty to this casserole of untruth, you should know that the mite already has the watch—if that's what it really is." He moved out of the way to show her the button his finger hovered over. "This here fuses the whole mite into a useless scrap of metal."

Her eyes narrowed and they were now fully gunslinger blue. "What do you want?"

"Not to deal with lackeys," Harley said, in a firm voice that surprised him. "Go fetch your boss."

Her face flushed. Then she picked up the red phone. "Get in here." She paused. "No," she said, "just get in here. We're done."

The door opened, and Acme swept into the room, a screwdriver jutting from an empty eye socket. The left side of his face sagged. "Have the you watch, then?" The voice was as garbled as the words that jumbled together.

"I do," Harley said. "I assume I can call you Al?"

Acme rubbed his hands together and chortled in dastardly fashion.

But it was Megan who replied. "Yes, Harley," she said. "You can call *me* Al." She extended a hand. "Alyce Portman."

Harley blinked.

"And I'm hoping," she said, "that if you do indeed have my grandfather's pocket watch in that mite of yours, you'll do me the kindness of bringing it in."

And despite the earlier deception, Harley felt the sincerity in her words, saw it upon her face. He stared at her and she stared back.

Quietly, Abigail and the gunslinger bride both entered the room behind Acme.

"You've been properly introduced to Abigail," Al said. "This here is Tommy." The gunslinger wore a gun belt now, and his hands stayed near the pearl handles of his Colt blasters while his eyes stayed on Alyce for direction. Abigail watched Harley, a breathless expression upon her face that made him uncomfortable.

Harley looked back to the control dock, hit another button, and moved a dial. "It's on its way."

Alyce put a hand on his arm and the warmth was as discombobulating as her smell. "Thank you," she said. She looked at the breathless bride. "Go fetch, Abigail."

Abigail left, and in her absence, an enviro-dome drifted through the doorway. Tommy watched.

"What the happy horseshit is going on here?" The voice was rough but female.

"Hey," Duke the cactus said from his corner, "is that a cactus in your garden or are you just glad to see me?"

Harley's eyes narrowed. "You have a cactus in the gang, too?"

Alyce grinned. "No. Daisy is my relationship practice. I got her from Acme." Their eyes met briefly. "Just like you."

Harley watched the controls, then started the shutdown process once Abigail returned holding the mite. Harley moved his fingers over the unit and opened its cache.

The pocket watch lay within, scratched and dented. Alyce reached for it, then paused and met Harley's eyes. "May I?"

He nodded, and she lifted it out. Carefully, she turned it over in her hands, then opened it and squinted down.

"There it is," she said. She held it out to him, and he saw the engraving. *For Cedric Acme*, it said, *03/11/97*.

"So it really was Acme's watch?"

She nodded. "Follow me."

They left the office and passed through the reception area to the only other door. Everyone followed them in procession as if on parade. Duke took up the rear.

Beyond the reception area lay what appeared to be her workshop: tables, bins of body parts and other bits of electronic detritus, toolboxes, shelves, and racks crammed full of props and costumes. And in the far corner, ancient and rusted, stood a small antique safe.

She spun the dial, and he watched the left right sequences as she paused at 3, 11, 9 and 7.

Harley could feel the anticipation in the air as it clanked open, and Alyce slowly swung its heavy door. There was a pause and then a muted gasp.

Empty.

"Well, that's a fine howdy-do," Duke the cactus said to the empty safe.

"That's a fine howdy-do, indeed," Daisy the cactus agreed.

At the end of it all, they sat around the empty safe on chairs gathered from around the three-room prefab.

"Well, most of it went well enough," Abigail said.

"I wish my eye had been more cooperative," Roger said.

"I wish I'd gotten to use my six-guns," Tommy said.

Dastardly Al shrugged. "We *did* find the watch and the combo for the safe."

"But," Harley said, "I'm guessing I am back to the proverbial drawing board when it comes to matrimonial bliss."

Abigail reached over and patted his arm. "Sorry, sugar."

Tommy reached over and did the same. "Truly sorry, Pilgrim."

Alyce chuckled. "But you *do* get to keep the cactus." Her blue eyes held his and she offered an apologetic smile. "For what it's worth, I'm sorry."

Harley shrugged. "If you'd just asked, I'd have likely said yes."

She nodded. "Lesson learned."

"So what's next?"

"Oh, I reckon we'll get you pointed toward home, get the prefab torn down and loaded, and get on to the next thing." Alyce waved her hands in the direction of the wedding gown now placed back on the rack. "And, you know, your credit with Acme was fine. And I'm sure Todd will be glad to hear from you."

Harley shook his head. "An android bride may not be in the cards for me," he said. "No offense," he said to Abigail.

"None taken." She and Tommy were in stereo and everyone laughed.

"What's this I hear, Pilgrim?" Duke's voice was heavy with sarcasm. "You having second thoughts about taking a wife?"

Al's eyes went wide with mock outrage. "Taking a wife? Who talks that way anymore?"

"Exactly," Daisy the cactus said.

"Harley does," Duke said. "As in Harley takes a wife."

Now Abigail joined in. "Oh no. That won't do."

"Nope," Harley said. "I surely don't see me taking a wife."

Alyce grinned. "Maybe," she said, "Harley takes a girl on a date?" She paused, let her eyes meet his again. "Sometime? If you want to?"

Harley looked at Duke, then looked back at Dastardly Al and her gang. He was already here. And it might just be the oddest way to meet someone, but he felt this meeting all the way down in his boots.

"Well," he finally said, "there's no time like the present."

And so it came to pass that Harlan Bosco Sussbauer, the last prospector of the Big Space Rock Mine Co-op, did not take a wife after all and, instead, took a girl—Ms. Alyce Portman of New Wyoming specifically—on a date.

It was, as they told their grandchildren many years later, nice enough as first dates go. And, of course, Mrs. Portman-Sussbauer would add quietly for their waiting young ears, that despite the empty safe, her biggest caper had gone exactly as planned.

OF ANCHOR CHAINS AND SLOW REFRAINS AND LIGHT LONG LOST IN DARKNESS

THE FIRST BELL CHIMED SOFTLY IN THE DIM-LIT ANDRO-francine lobby, and Gregoric looked up from the corner where he waited. The sky had been a predawn purple when the Grey Guard had admitted him to the Office of Acquisitions and Travel thirty minutes before.

The early hours of these offices astonished Gregoric. He'd spent his twenty years living in the Ninefold Forest, set apart from the rest of the Named Lands in the distant northeast, where customs were far more relaxed. In the Forest, no business was transacted until well after sunrise.

And now I'm waiting on an arch-something and a king before my first cup of chai, he thought.

Gregoric had half expected to find his king snoring in one of the lobby's plush chairs, reeking of peach wine and perfume, grinning at having proved his friend wrong.

"These ladies," Rudolfo had told him last night in one of the city's less restrained quarters, "only require my attention for a few short hours." Gregoric had protested both the practicality of the proposed venture and the underestimation of the time available before dawn, but Rudolfo was king and general, after all.

Of course I'll be on time for the meeting. Of course I will have slept and bathed. The offense upon Rudolfo's face at the mere suggestion that he might not be either of these things had Gregoric's eyes rolling even in memory.

But Rudolfo hadn't been waiting, and so his first captain had initially paced the room, then finally succumbed to the chair, where he fidgeted and fussed at a state uniform he'd worn only once before.

At the next bell, Gregoric sighed and stood. He'd made his second turn in a new round of pacing when the doorknob rattled. Beyond the door, he heard a familiar voice.

"Thank you, good sir," Rudolfo said as the door opened to the Grey Guard captain stationed at the building's main entrance. "Oh, *Captain*, is it? Yes. Then sir seems certainly apropos. Ah. There he is." Rudolfo strode into the room, met Gregoric's eyes, and laughed, the Grey Guard just behind him in the doorway. "My own captain, whom I assume you've met?"

Rudolfo, Lord of the Ninefold Forest Houses and General of the Wandering Army, stood a full head shorter than most of the men of the Named Lands. Barely nineteen years, his beard was coming in wispy and thin. That, combined with his own state uniform and the green turban of office, lent him a comic quality that he seemed at ease with.

Gregoric saw it as a possible blind spot—not taking things seriously and then not being taken seriously—but then again, he saw blind spots everywhere.

Because it's my job to see what he can't see. It's what you did when your best friend was also your king. And if he stumbled, you picked him up and carried him if you had to.

The Grey Guard captain's face betrayed the slightest bemusement as he pulled the door closed and Rudolfo crossed the room to clap Gregoric's shoulder. "Well met, First Captain Gregoric," he said with a wink. "And good morning."

Gregoric smelled the faintest trace of perfume but little of the wine he'd expected, and his friend's uniform was surprisingly well put together. He raised an eyebrow and opted for the military title. "Good morning, General Rudolfo." He lowered his voice. "You've slept?"

Rudolfo chuckled. "After a manner."

Gregoric let his curiosity lift his eyebrows even farther. "And?"

"It seems the Androfrancines do not tend to all of their flock with equal grace and magnanimity," Rudolfo said with a grin. "Our assistance in certain earthly matters was long anticipated and greatly . . . appreciated."

His words would've been more suave than boastful except that he blushed as he said it; Gregoric pretended not to notice.

"Good then," he said. He wouldn't say more beyond that and hadn't any of the other times.

Rudolfo, Lord of the Ninefold Forest Houses and General of the Wandering Army, had come late to his awareness of his body and the bodies of the young women around him. Far later than most young men, and Gregoric saw its arrival over the last year as a welcome change.

It seemed a much healthier activity than brooding on the observation deck while listening to the screams of repentance beneath the Physicians of Penitent Torture's knives. Not that Gregoric blamed his friend for that streak of darkness. Nearly all of the penitents had been followers of the Heretic Fontayne and those who'd harbored or aided them—those responsible, directly or indirectly, for the murders of Rudolfo's parents.

They had grown up together, Rudolfo and Gregoric, mostly in the vicinity of Rudolfo's father's Seventh Forest Manor and the unnamed town that had sprung up around it. Gregoric's father, Aerynus, had been Lord Jakob's first captain, and from his earliest memory, Gregoric had assumed he would serve Rudolfo in the same way. But no one had expected it might happen so soon.

The sudden memory ambushed Gregoric. His closest friend, covered in his parents' blood, eyes red but fierce, as Rudolfo barked his first commands. He'd gone from twelve to thirty in seconds, and Gregoric still saw it in his eyes some days. Wrath and sorrow twisting and turning to find a purpose. They'd both gone with Gregoric's father to hunt Fontayne down, but only Rudolfo had participated directly in the interrogations led by Chief Physician Benoit.

No, Gregoric thought, the stream of dalliances was a welcome change. *Let him chase pleasure for a season rather than pain and penitence.*

Rudolfo dropped himself into one of the chairs. "How are the men?"

Gregoric snorted. "They're sleeping, I'll wager. But they'll be ready to ride at your command."

Rudolfo nodded. "Excellent." He opened his mouth to say more, but a smaller bell chimed and the inner door opened to admit a young man in a long white robe lined with threads of blue that marked him as an acolyte.

"Lord Rudolfo? His Excellency Arch-Archaeologist Tobin will see you now."

Gregoric watched his friend incline his head and then made to follow him as he left the waiting area.

"I'm sorry, Lord," the acolyte said, raising his hand. "But it is more appropriate for your aide to wait here."

Gregoric felt a flash of anger and gritted his teeth. Rudolfo chuckled. "Actually, it would be utterly inappropriate," Rudolfo said. "But if my first captain is not permitted beyond this door, I'm happy to receive His Excellency here in the lobby."

The acolyte turned purple and said nothing. Rudolfo winked at Gregoric as the acolyte turned to lead them into the office.

Swallowing that moment of anger, Gregoric followed his king.

The walls of the Office of Acquisitions and Travel were largely undecorated. Tobin was third in command, and that gave him a lush office on the ground floor with a window overlooking a meditation garden now gray with morning.

The arch-archaeologist waited by a small table set with chai. "Good morning, Lord Rudolfo." He glanced disapprovingly at Gregoric and then to the acolyte, whose face still looked flushed. "Will your officer be joining us for chai?"

"Certainly." Rudolfo looked to Gregoric and raised his eyebrow. "You've not had your chai, I'll wager?"

Gregoric knew better than to say anything and instead sized up Tobin. He was portly but powerfully built, his hair close cropped and iron gray. He wore spectacles—something Gregoric had only seen once before, on another Androfrancine passing through: pieces of glass fit into wires and worn for vision by those whom the various powders and magicks available in the Named Lands could not heal.

The arch-archaeologist gestured for another chair, and the acolyte fetched it before pouring out chai in three spotlessly shined silver mugs.

Once each had sat and taken a first careful sip of the steaming liquid, Rudolfo dug into his pocket and drew out a letter. "This is a Letter of Credit from the Tam Banking Concern that I've had drawn up for your consideration. It is the Forest Houses' honor to serve the Order and to underwrite our service to the light, as is the custom of kin-clave."

Tobin took the document, opened it, and scanned it. "This is a liberal Offer of Underwriting, Lord Rudolfo."

"I am very specific in the offer I am making."

Tobin nodded, and Gregoric waited. They'd spent years talking about this moment, in their boyhood. It was around the same time that they'd discovered the secret doors and hidden tunnels that networked the Seventh Forest Manor. And not just the Seventh, but all of the manors they'd visited before the day that Rudolfo's childhood burned down.

"When I'm king," Rudolfo had said in those lighter days, "I'll get the Order to help us find him, and we'll join his crew."

Gregoric couldn't remember the circumstances, but he remembered the words with absolute clarity. They'd spent the entire summer pretending that houses were ships and sticks were swords.

He forced his attention back to Tobin, who'd handed back the letter. "We have valuable work for you to do, but we have no control over some portions of your offer."

Rudolfo nodded. "But he *is* available for hire, and the Order *does* have the ability to contact him?"

Tobin returned the nod. "Yes. And your letter may underwrite half of the offer you propose."

Gregoric waited and held his breath. *Now you surprise him.*

Rudolfo drew the small box from his sash and placed it on the table. "I think he will be interested in this portion of my offer." Opening the lid, he slid it toward Tobin.

The Androfrancine's eyebrows went up behind his spectacles. "It's a brooch," he said.

"No," Rudolfo said. "It's *the* brooch."

And Gregoric smiled when he saw the recognition upon the arch-archaeologist's face. It had taken some work to figure out the details, but Rudolfo's intelligence officers had earned their promised lands and titles.

Tobin swallowed. "*The* brooch?"

Rudolfo nodded. "The same."

They'd read about the brooch in Hyrum's *Pirate Lord of the Ghosting Crests.* Certainly much of Hyrum's tales scribed during the scholar's year with Merrique were embellished, but the brief conversation about regrets during the seventeen days they spent shipwrecked in the Ghosting Crests seemed starkly real. And the pirate lord's singular regret, voiced to the Androfrancine in a moment of raw honesty, was a brooch. There was no additional explanation. But over the course of this last year, Rudolfo had put himself and his kingdom's vast resources to determining what the brooch was and how to acquire it as bait.

And now, Gregoric thought, *we catch ourselves a pirate with it.*

Rudolfo smiled. "Did you know that it was an heirloom that had been stolen from the Merrique family?"

Tobin held the brooch up to the light. "Yes," he said. "I do not know how you came to possess it, but I'm certain the Order could . . ."

His words trailed off at Rudolfo's upraised hand.

"No, Your Excellency, I'm afraid it's specifically for Rafe Merrique, and we intend to deliver it to him personally." His grin caught Gregoric off guard with its ferocity. "It's my gift to him for his service to the light."

For a moment, Tobin said nothing, then he placed the box on the table. Looking up, he met Rudolfo's eyes. "We'll make the arrangements. Captain Grymlis will have the Letters of Introduction for you once they're executed by the office clerk. By then we'll also have instructions from Captain Merrique, should he accept your offer. It will be a simple retrieval from the Churning Wastes if he is inclined to serve as transport."

Rudolfo inclined his head. "Thank you, Your Excellency."

He slipped the box back into his sash. "And please forward our gratitude to Pope Introspect for his hospitality and endorsement."

Now the arch-archaeologist inclined his head. "I will tell him." He stood. "Now, gentlemen, please finish your chai. I've another matter to attend to."

Once he and the acolyte left, Rudolfo grinned again, and Gregoric tried to resist doing the same. His king and best friend raised his eyebrow, and only then did Gregoric notice the lip rouge on his neck. "What say you, Gregoric? Are you ready to test your sea legs?"

Gregoric shook his head against the sudden ache in his stomach. "I guess we'll know soon enough."

Then Rudolfo drained his chai with one gulp, stood, and broke out in the one song they'd memorized as children. "Far into the Ghosting Crests and beyond the Emerald Sea, I swear my sword to the pirate lord and a life of piracy."

Gregoric blushed, and Rudolfo smiled and sang all the louder. He was into the third—and raunchiest—verse when a Grey Guard, face red with restraint, arrived to escort them out.

And Gregoric quickly covered his embarrassment at the spectacle of it all. The look of delight upon his friend's face was like time turned back by magick, like light brought back from darkness, and for the briefest moment, Gregoric let himself rejoice in it.

The ride south and west onto the Entrolusian Delta was a wet and cold affair with autumn moving closer to winter. The staunch Gray Guard officer they'd met at the main doors had shown them to a quartermaster for re-outfitting, given them a map, Letters of Introduction for Rafe Merrique, and generic letters that proclaimed the Ninefold Forest engaged in service to the light on behalf of the Order. The Order also sent birds ahead requesting discretion and non-interference for a kin-clave nation's traveling retinue in service to the light, including the promise of any and all appropriate fees and taxes for such discreet passage. These of course being carefully accounted for in Rudolfo's offer.

Once they were out of Windwir, Gregoric sent half the squad back to the Forest. Those who remained turned their horses toward the Delta.

They made good time to Dandylo Terrace, dressed in the nondescript clothing of lumbermen on leave from the evergreen forests that blurred the border between the United City States of the Entrolusian Delta and the Protectorate of Windwir to the north.

The city states were united under an overseer—currently a pompous man-child named Sethbert—and were Windwir's largest, closest neighbor. They had kin-clave with the Ninefold Forest, as well, though the two nations had little to do with each other. The Ninefold Forest was largely self-contained and its Gypsy Scouts seldom rode farther south than Windwir—and even that was rare. So Gregoric turned his three scouts loose to gather intelligence on their immediate vicinity while exploring and experiencing Dandylo Terrace. Even this smallish town, here on the southern tip of the Delta, was a metropolis to the wide-eyed Foresters. Still, he trusted them to enjoy themselves properly while at the same time maintaining their presence.

Only the best became scouts of the Ninefold Forest, and these were the best of Rudolfo's Gypsy Scouts.

With the men left to their own devices, Gregoric and Rudolfo found a quiet corner in a tavern where they could wait for Rafe Merrique to make contact.

Time away and unknown, in a tavern full of a variety of food and drink that defied Gregoric's imagination. Time spent hunkered over a table with his best friend, listening as he predicted their future at sea. It was a good enough time together. At least, it was when Rudolfo wasn't trying too hard to engage the various ladies of the establishment. Still, even one day in a tavern would be too much for Gregoric, and three was becoming unbearable. He closed his eyes against Rudolfo's latest attempt, with a woman who looked maybe five or ten years his senior. "Stab me in the eye with a fork," he muttered to himself.

The woman smiled sympathetically at Gregoric, and he blushed at being overheard. "He's not that bad," she said. "Just too young." She raised an eyebrow, pouted. It was the first time Gregoric thought of her as pretty. "And too poor."

Rudolfo winked. "I may be that book that is on the wrong shelf of the library."

She returned the wink and leaned in. "An unfinished book, I fear, in a rather small library." Then the woman leaned even closer, her hands moving down the front of Rudolfo's shirt toward his waistband. "On, I suspect, a rather short shelf," she finished.

The woman flashed a smile at them both and bolted for the back door.

Rudolfo's face turned crimson even as he leapt up. "She took it," he said. "She took the brooch."

Gregoric was on his feet and whistling for his men by habit. He doubted any were within earshot. Then he was out the door and in the alley behind the tavern in the gray of midafternoon. His hands ached to draw his knives, but he resisted and focused instead on the woman. He could hear the splashing of her feet in the puddles as she ran, and he followed.

A low whistle reached his ear, and Yaric, one of the older scouts, slipped in beside him. "First Captain?"

"Stay near the general," Gregoric whispered and stretched his legs into a run. He felt the pouch of scout magicks beneath his shirt and was tempted to take them for the burst of strength, speed, and clarity they would give him. But scout magicks also rendered one nearly invisible, and they were expressly forbidden by kin-clave except during time of war. Gregoric wasn't about to violate the Forest's kin-clave with the Delta.

Instead, he ran. He heard Rudolfo and Yaric following.

The alley spilled out into a wider paved street still awash with puddles. Overhead, a dark sky drizzled rain on the tired city. The street was largely empty, and the few stalls along it were closed. The woman ducked behind one and then down another alley. Gregoric willed speed into his feet and raced after her, entering the alley as she leapt through an open door.

He was two sword spans behind her when the door closed behind her, and he hit the oak with outstretched hands full force before it had time to latch. Gregoric's momentum carried him through the door, and he had a moment of stark panic that caught his breath as his feet found no floor beneath them.

As he fell, he heard the door close and latch above.

When he struck the water, his entire body felt the penetrating cold of it, and his mouth and nose flooded with salt. As he sank, Gregoric felt ropes grabbing at him, and a net closed over him and lifted him from the water.

"Ho there," an amused voice said. "Look what we've caught."

Gregoric took in his surroundings as his net began to move. It was a large stone room stacked with barrels and sacks and crates, and a single canal that exited toward a distant slit of light. A long boat loaded with supplies was tied off not far from where Gregoric hung, and he saw a system of ropes and pulleys. A slender, middle-aged man with salt-and-pepper hair tied back behind a colorful scarf stood at the levers, a cutlass at his hip, as Gregoric swung toward him. A pirate. The pirate. Rafe Merrique. Gravity and the tightness of the net made moving difficult, but Gregoric's hand found the hilt to one of his knives and he started quietly working at the netting behind him.

The woman from the tavern entered the room from a door that Gregoric noted as the exit up and out. She crossed the room, her face flushed, to stand beside the pirate. She held up the box she'd stolen from Rudolfo. "He had it, Captain. Like you said." Then she nodded toward Gregoric. "This one has two knives. Might be a third in his boot."

The pirate raised an eyebrow and yanked the lever another direction. Gregoric stopped moving toward the man, instead swinging back out over the dark water he'd fallen into. "Is that true?" Rafe Merrique chuckled. "I invite you into my home and you bring weapons? I thought your king wanted to parley with me, Forester."

Gregoric gritted his teeth and saw Merrique work another lever as the rope released and he plunged back into the icy cold.

He came up sputtering a minute later as Merrique hauled him up. This time he left Gregoric hanging over the water.

"Let's start over," the pirate said. "I'll ask some questions. You can answer or you can keep trying to cut your way out. Either way, the water is quite cold, and I truly have all the time in the world." He smiled, and Gregoric growled. "What does the Gypsy King want with me? Why has he spent a dozen fortunes to compel the Order to summon me?" He held up the box, now opened, and the stones sparkled in the dim light. "And how in the nine hells below did he find this?"

Gregoric glared and said nothing. Rafe Merrique laughed and hit the lever. There was something in that echoing peal of laughter that touched spark to some deeper anger, and Gregoric didn't feel the water this time. Instead, he felt heat and a throbbing in his forehead.

He came up roaring his rage at the pirate and his accomplice. They both laughed all the louder.

He was still bellowing when the water closed over him again. He wasn't sure exactly how many more times the pirate asked or how many more times he was dunked.

Finally, he hung limp in the nets, coughing and shaking.

"Well?" The pirate raised his hand above the lever.

Gregoric tried to shake his head. "We read Brother Hyrum's book as boys," he finally said. "And he did spend a dozen fortunes. He would've spent more to find it; he knew you wanted it."

Rafe Merrique grinned. "And now I have it." Gregoric's anger flared at the sight of that grin, but this time, Rafe's voice took on a gentler tone. "But why?"

Gregoric's frustration gave his voice more urgency and edge than he'd intended. "You're his hero. For the life of me, I don't know why," he said. "Especially after sampling your generous hospitality."

The pirate looked dumbfounded. "His *hero*? The King of the Ninefold Forest Houses?"

Gregoric nodded and met Merrique's eyes. "He wanted to meet you and sail with you."

Rafe Merrique stroked his perfectly sculped beard. "Well I'll be d'jin-and-crested," he muttered. "It's as they said it was." His eyes narrowed. "Did you really get tossed out of the office singing that damnable song of Hyrum's?"

Gregoric said nothing.

Finally, Rafe looked at the woman beside him. "What do you make of all this, Jasper?"

The woman shook her head and gave Gregoric a sideways glance where he dripped above the water. "I make of it whatever you tell me to make of it, Captain."

He worked the levers, and Gregoric lurched forward to slowly settle on the dock. "Then I reckon we're taking on servants of light," Rafe said as he slipped the brooch into his pocket and tossed the box aside. "I will get you dry clothes and send you back to Rudolfo. I'll take you around the horn and back, but I have a condition, and the ship has rules."

Gregoric waited as men slipped out of the shadows to pull him from the nets and stand him up.

Once he was standing, he bit back anger again. "I'm certain Lord Rudolfo will be eager to hear your condition himself."

Rafe Merrique laughed again. This time it was loud and long, and the others in the room, suddenly more of them than Gregoric had realized, were laughing with him.

"Oh no," Rafe Merrique said. "The condition is yours to meet, First Captain Gregoric."

The merriment in his voice and the twinkle in the pirate's eye told Gregoric that whatever condition it might be, one thing was assured.

It could not possibly bode well for him.

*

Gregoric put one foot in front of the other and avoided eye contact as the handful of people at the dockside market whispered and gawked. He felt more heat in his face as a child laughed, and he pretended not to notice the pointing finger.

They'd given him the choice of dressing himself or being dressed. But they were clear on what he would wear for his walk to the tavern. So now he walked quickly, head low, and followed the directions they'd given him. Supposedly, Merrique had sent word to Rudolfo that Gregoric would return shortly bearing instructions.

The colors he now wore were not so much the issue. His own uniform bore the colors of the kin-clave rainbow. But these silks, and the laces and the buckles and bells, made him the caricature of a pirate. Gregoric couldn't help but notice how similar the outfit was to the one worn by the pirate lord on the cover of Hyrum's book.

"Now that you're an honorary member of the *Kinshark* crew," Merrique had said, "go tell your king we sail at dawn. You know what door to find us at."

And so Gregoric walked and endured the growing noise of being noticed until he reached the tavern and the last humiliation of his day.

"Gregoric!" At first Rudolfo's face was concerned, but the weather shifted quickly. The amusement there looked too much like Rafe's expression for Gregoric's liking.

Their eyes met, and he fought the anger down again. He strode into the room in the midst of more laughter and kept walking, past Rudolfo and up the stairs to the room they all shared.

He was digging through his pack for new clothing when Rudolfo entered. His friend and king was quiet for a moment, and Gregoric swallowed against a sudden lump in his throat as the day caught up to him.

"How are you?" Rudolfo finally asked.

"Worn," he answered. "But it's done. We sail at dawn."

"And how was he?"

He looked at Rudolfo. "He's a bastard. I'd tell you this was a mistake but I know you won't listen."

Rudolfo nodded. "You're right."

Gregoric looked away. "You never listen."

"Sometimes I do, when you're not looking. But you're right about the other. It might be a mistake." Then he shrugged. "Mistakes," he said, doing his best impersonation of Gregoric's father's gravelly voice.

They finished the saying together. "Those that don't kill you just might teach you something."

Rudolfo turned away and sat on the bed as Gregoric peeled out of his costume. "We've had birds from home," he said. "You've a message from that girl you've been seeing. The one with the big brown eyes."

"Adela?" Gregoric wasn't sure why he was asking. She was the only one of late he'd spent much time with. She'd not been happy about him leaving for a few months but had understood well enough why he needed to be with their king. And she'd found the whole notion of going to sea both terrifying and elating.

But why would she write? It was a surprise and the first time he'd received a personal bird while out and about with Rudolfo.

He pulled on the sturdy woolens of the northern wood and dug a pair of soft slippers from someone else's pack, after looking long and hard at the brightly shined and brightly buckled boots he'd pulled off. He'd get his own boots back in the morning according to Jasper, Rafe's first mate.

Rudolfo offered up the scrap of paper and Gregoric took it.

The note was brief, and it dropped him to the bed beside his friend.

"Sorry, Gregoric," Rudolfo said. "I didn't mean to read it but . . ." His words trailed off, and Gregoric felt a hand on his shoulder. "Congratulations are in order."

He looked at the note again and blinked. The anger and humiliation of the day melted away into a wonder he'd not considered but found welcome.

"I'm going to be a father," he said. "The River Woman says it will be a boy."

Rudolfo squeezed Gregoric's shoulder then dropped his hand. "Yes. I know. And I also know that you'll have the biggest, most audacious Firstborn Feast that the Seventh Forest Manor has ever known. A week, I think, and perhaps even a traveling celebration."

He heard excitement in his friend's voice, and it took some of the fear out of him. He stared at the tiny scrap and read the coded words again.

"So," Rudolfo said after another two minutes had passed, "if you need to return, I'm prepared to forgo this voyage and send Captain Merrique our regrets."

Gregoric wasn't sure he'd heard correctly and looked up. "Forgo this voyage?"

Rudolfo's eyes were warm. "Of course. You're becoming a father. There's much preparing."

He looked back to the paper. "It's months away," he said.

Rudolfo's eyebrow arched. "That is true. Or at least I'm told that it works that way."

Gregoric nodded and gestured to the boots. "And I've endured much to secure our passage."

"You have indeed," Rudolfo said. He leaned over to examine the boots. "But these are actually a bit fantastic." His eyes lit up. "They look like the ones on—"

Gregoric cut him off. "They're meant to."

Now Rudolfo nodded. "Then to sea?"

Gregoric took a deep breath against the ocean of fatherhood that threatened to flood him. "To sea," he finally said.

Rudolfo had them all awake well before dawn, and the enthusiasm in his eyes and grin were too much for Gregoric's pre-chai capacities. To make matters worse, his king had decided to dress himself in the ridiculous garments—and the boots—that Gregoric had returned in.

"How do I look?" he asked with a flourish.

Gregoric grunted and pulled on his boots. Yaric and Bryn were already dressed and packing. Gerundt fussed at the sheaths tucked beneath his oversized shirt, adjusting the knives so that they were within reach.

Gregoric stood and did the same, slipping a fresh pouch of magicks over his neck once his blades were in place.

When they were ready, Gregoric opened the door to lead them out. He'd expected the tavern to be dark at this hour and was surprised to see a lantern lit and a small group gathered in the common room below. He picked out Jasper and Rafe Merrique immediately, and he paused long enough that they looked up at him there at the railing.

And Gregoric finally found something in the morning worth smiling over. Rafe wore the same outfit—or at least the original that the model was based on—that Rudolfo now wore. Only his bore the marks of time and were obviously made from the finest silks. His black boots were decorated with polished seashells of deep burgundy and bright silver buckles. His feathered hat was deep purple, and he bore twin rapiers at his waist.

"Captain Merrique," Gregoric called out in a gruff voice. "Allow me to present to you Lord Rudolfo of the Ninefold Forest Houses, General of the Wandering Army."

Then he stepped aside for Rudolfo, who leapt forward and bowed deeply. "Well met, Captain Merrique," he said.

Rafe Merrique stood. "I am at your service, Lord Rudolfo," he said. Then he returned the bow. There were snickers and chuckles. Jasper rolled her eyes. Gregoric noted it all with suspicion.

"I had thought we were to meet you at dawn," Rudolfo said as he took the lead and moved toward the staircase. "Has something changed?"

"Only my heart," Rafe Merrique said. He moved toward the stairs as well and glanced to Gregoric. "I was unkind to your first captain and owe amends. I thought I would apologize in person and escort you myself."

They clasped hands at the foot of the stairs. Then Rafe offered Gregoric his hand as well. "I apologize, First Captain."

Gregoric nodded and shook the hand, then moved aside. Jasper joined him.

She tipped her head toward Merrique and lowered her voice. "He reread the Hyrum book last night over a bit of rum," she said.

Gregoric glanced to her before nodding toward Rudolfo. "He retold bits of it from memory last night, and there was chilled peach wine involved."

The two were complimenting one another's boots now, their voices becoming louder as they sought to out-grace each other. "This is going to be an insufferable day," Jasper whispered.

"Aye," Gregoric agreed.

They left the tavern, Rudolfo and Rafe in the lead as they strode into the predawn gloom. As they walked, the two continued their upbeat chat and pulled ahead, a few members of the crew falling in behind them. Gregoric tried to move past them, but Jasper was at his side with a question.

"So have you sailed before, First Captain?"

He shook his head. "I've been on lakes but nothing like an ocean. Our ocean is grass."

"I've always wanted to see the Prairie Sea and visit the forests," Jasper said.

"It's a long way from the Ghosting Crests."

His half squad moved in behind them, carrying Gregoric's and Rudolfo's packs along with their own.

"One day," she said, "I'll get there."

They left the main avenue and slipped into an alley. Rafe and Rudolfo stopped at the door, and the others gathered around. The pirate gestured to the door. "Welcome to my home, Lord Rudolfo. We will breakfast and then board, if you concur?"

Rudolfo smiled. "I look forward to both, Captain Merrique."

Rafe opened the door. "After you," he said.

Gregoric glanced at Jasper. The expectant look on her face brought his mouth open, but he closed it when Rudolfo spoke.

"Oh no, Captain Merrique, after *you*."

"I insist," the pirate said, extending a hand toward the door.

Rudolfo seized the hand. "We'll go together then," he said and then tugged Rafe toward him as he tipped himself back and through the doorway.

Rafe howled all the way down even as Rudolfo laughed, and Gregoric found a second reason to smile on a pre-chai morning. The splash followed by more splashing, the spluttering, the cursing—it was all music to Gregoric's ears, especially mixed with the raucous laughter of his closest friend.

"You ridiculous fop," Rafe yelled below.

"You damnable pirate," Rudolfo yelled back.

Music indeed, Gregoric thought.

Three vessels that might or might not have been Merrique's *Kinshark* sailed out of Dandylo Terrace that morning, and between the decoys, the bribes, and the administrative fees, Merrique's actual crew slipped quietly out of the harbor in a ship that no one would've suspected carried a pirate or a king. It looked like a fishing schooner, and it ran low and sleek in the water, most of the crew hidden below deck as they put the Delta behind them.

Once they'd stowed their gear and toured the ship in Jasper's care, Rudolfo and Gregoric met Rafe in his stateroom. The room had a small wardrobe and a narrow bed, and those were the only evidence that anyone lived in it. Otherwise, it held a table strewn with papers and shelves crammed with books and charts in no order whatsoever. A long iron tube fixed to a wooden stock—some kind of weaponry Gregoric didn't recognize—hung above one of the room's portholes. A telescope hung over the other.

Rafe gestured to stools that waited and unrolled a map over the scattered pages of his worktable. He pointed to an area that Gregoric didn't recognize. "We are here," he said. Then he drew his finger south and east slowly until it stopped at the far end of the parchment. "We need to be here in two weeks, but we are already four days ahead of schedule."

Rudolfo glanced at Gregoric then back to the map. "Then we arrive early?"

Rafe shook his head. "It doesn't serve to be early with the Androfrancines. Their caravans are never early . . . sometimes late . . . and those aren't waters to lay anchor in for long."

Rudolfo leaned over the map. Gregoric was gradually orienting to it from where he sat. Windwir was at the center of most Named Lands maps, which helped, but in this case, the world's largest city wasn't noted. But the Keeper's Wall, that north-south border of impassable mountains stood out, and that gave him some perspective.

"So what do you propose then, Captain Merrique?" Rudolfo asked.

Merrique pointed to a large island south of them that seemed to have been split in half. "A pit of piracy," he said. "Down here. An estate that needs breaking into."

Gregoric sat up. This wasn't what they'd planned, and he already saw a dozen reasons why this was a bad idea. First, Rafe was from the Divided Isle, and no longer welcome there. Second, there was an awfully big leap between setting sail in service to Androfrancine light and robbing a manor. Rudolfo noticed the look on Gregoric's face and raised an eyebrow but looked back to Rafe. "Please continue, Captain."

Rafe smiled. "These hauls around the horn are nothing. There and back quickly without incident nearly every time." The smile widened. "If you want to experience the life of a pirate lord, you won't get it running crates and robes. That's the least pirate-like thing I do, sir."

Rudolfo glanced at Gregoric again before speaking. "And you think we can do this with the spare time we have?"

Rafe nodded. "I do, Rudolfo. Though it may involve a bit of running under magicks. But I'm told that's something your people are quite good at." The pirate looked at Gregoric this time. "Is that true, Gregoric?"

Clever now to use our first names and not our titles. Gregoric found himself answering, "Rudolfo's Gypsy Scouts are the best of the best."

"I'm counting on that," Rafe said. He looked at them, and in that moment, Gregoric thought the older man almost seemed fatherly. It evoked a kind of trust that was unexpected—something else for Gregoric to keep his eye on. "We change course, do a bit of piracy, make haste around the horn, and have you back with the Order's trinkets, hale and whole, in no time at all. What say you? Shall we?"

Gregoric's hand found Rudolfo's shoulder and pressed scout code into it with fumbling fingers. *This is ill-advised.*

But before Gregoric finished, Rudolfo grinned. "Aye, Captain," he said. "We shall indeed."

That night, after a much better dinner than he would've expected on a ship, Gregoric found a quiet place above deck and settled in to watch the sky at sea.

He and Rudolfo were sharing a small room, and the three scouts were in a similar room directly across the passageway and near the galley. Two of them had spent most of the day vomiting in pails and sleeping against the seasickness that gripped them. Even Gregoric had felt twinges of nausea those first few hours, but by dinnertime, he was ready for the salmon steaks served in a bed of chilled, pickled sea vegetables he couldn't possibly name, with warm black bread and cold rice wine.

And now this sky.

It was painted in colors he had no adequate words to describe and against a horizon that defied his comprehension. He'd thought the line of horizon over the Prairie Sea was vast, but it was nothing compared to this.

He sat and watched the sky deepen toward dark and didn't notice Rudolfo until the Gypsy King was already seated beside him. "What do you think, Gregoric?"

Gregoric saw concern and curiosity on his friend's face. "I think we violate a dozen articles of kin-clave with the Independent Counties of the Divided Isle and risk war if the Lord of the Ninefold Forest Houses is caught in a criminal act," he said. He could hear the matter-of-fact nature of his tone.

Rudolfo grinned. "Getting caught is definitely not optimal, so I'm recommending that we not." He dangled his scout powders from their string around his neck.

Gregoric felt his eyebrow twitch. Use of magicks during a time of peace was one of those violations he had anticipated.

"But," Rudolfo continued, "that's not what I meant." His eyebrows furrowed. "I mean about becoming a father. That was a bit . . . unexpected."

Gregoric shrugged. It was the thought he didn't want to have but kept having regardless. "It happened to my father. It happened to your father, too. It doesn't seem so very unexpected."

"Yes, but not so young."

Gregoric could tell Rudolfo wanted to ask, thought he shouldn't, and then moved forward with his next question anyway. "Weren't you using the powders? Your father and Kember both have been pretty insistent about them with me of late."

Gregoric sighed. No, he'd not used them, and neither had she. But they'd also been clear-eyed on the possibilities no matter how rare. And it was none of Rudolfo's concern. Deflecting was easy here. "I think they've good cause for their concern of late," he said.

Rudolfo smiled. "Regardless. I've no heir, and you've one on the way. I meant what I said about the Firstborn Feast. But how do you *feel* about becoming a father, Gregoric?"

It was a serious question. Gregoric smiled. "I feel like I'm meant to."

"And how is that?"

"A mix of fear and delight, a stuttering and stammering heart full of love," he said. "And like I'm meant to . . . like I'm *meant* to be a father." He looked back at the sky. Pregnancy was rare enough in the Named Lands—a leftover of the Age of Laughing Madness studied and unsolved by millennia of Androfrancine research—that most couples did not marry until after their first child was born. "And I don't feel like starting a war over a bit of piracy here in the shadow of my impending fatherhood."

Rudolfo smiled. "Then we must stick to the plan of not getting caught." He stood. "I think fatherhood will suit you well, Gregoric."

Gregoric inclined his head, and Rudolfo did the same before he slipped aft and below deck.

He'd always assumed he'd have a family just as he'd always assumed he'd be Rudolfo's first captain. It was all starting sooner than he'd thought, but then again, Adela had also surprised him when she'd shown up. She'd fit into his life easily and quickly, with grace, sass, and ferocity. *And those big brown eyes.*

She drew out aspects of him that Gregoric wouldn't let others see, and he could only imagine what their child would draw from him.

He took in a great breath and held it, watching the faintest stars grow brighter against the falling night. The wind in the sails and the sound of the water against the hull were a driving pulse in a refrain that declared this journey and the salt air more intoxicating than any rum.

Gregoric sat there for a goodly while taking comfort from a wide-open sky at sea and wondering how his life would unfold.

He was still wondering when the moon rose blue and green and full of promise.

Piracy, Gregoric decided, was nothing at all like Hyrum described it in his book. A day and a half after his first night at sea and he'd exchanged the rocking of a ship for the jostling of a wagon. And hours of bumping along rutted County roads had left him bruised and brooding.

Merrique had been vague about their target, but during the

hours they'd spent planning the heist, he'd talked them through his plans.

Three parties, all magicked, would approach from three entry points onto the property, would make their anticipated acquisitions, and would then retreat. That was all well and good, but Gregoric had flinched when he'd first heard the words.

"And no weapons," the pirate had said. "We're going in magicked; we're not fighting."

Jasper and Merrique's own men had nodded. Rudolfo, Gregoric, and the half squad did the same.

And now we're about our piracy, Gregoric thought as the wagon jerked.

They were stretched out beneath a false bottom in the wagon, side by side like felled timber at the river's edge. For the first few hours, he'd fussed at the powerlessness he felt, then made a reluctant peace with it.

Closing his eyes, he turned his focus back to the plan and to his and Rudolfo's part in it. "Your room is *here*," Merrique had said, pointing to a map of the manor. "The window will be open. There is a book—leather bound and without a title—and a jade statue of a long-finned kinshark." His eyes were fierce for his next words, and Gregoric sensed a quiet threat in their tone. "Touch nothing else."

"It seems quite specific," Rudolfo said. "Is it always so?"

Rafe had shrugged. "Not always. But sometimes it is better to sip than to gulp."

Gregoric heard something in those words that resonated and he noted it.

Rafe continued. "In this case, the dividends of this venture will be invaluable."

The wagon, after so many hours at a steady straight-ahead pace, now slowed as they navigated a series of turns. They came to a stop, and a few minutes later, he heard voices and felt the creaking of the wagon as men unloaded the cargo. It had been quiet for maybe thirty minutes when Gregoric heard a low whistle that someone in his wagon returned. Then, fingers from outside unlatched the false floor and swung it up and open.

Gregoric sat up slowly along with the others.

Moonlight, blue and green, washed the yard where the three

empty wagons sat. Beside them stood a barn, its doors closed against the night. Beyond it, a scattering of trees and, farther away, the lights of a large town.

"We're close," Rafe said. "We'll run from here."

They wore dark clothes now along with their scout boots. Gregoric felt naked without his knives. He'd strongly resisted this decision to forgo weapons, and his attempt to change Rudolfo's mind had left him with an ache in the pit of his stomach. Still, Merrique had been most insistent, and even now, he raised the point again.

"We are in and out without touching a hair on anyone's head," he said.

Gregoric couldn't resist his question. "And what if something goes wrong?"

A voice cleared to his left. "I see no reason," Rudolfo offered, "for anything to go wrong."

Rafe's face was sober. "No matter what might go wrong," he said. He held up a handful of small silk pouches from their slender cords. "You'll be wanting fresh magicks, I'll wager."

Rudolfo reached for them, and Gregoric spoke up. "We have magicks, Captain Merrique."

"You do," Rafe said, "but they are from the north through one of your medicine makers. They don't always work well after being in the salt air."

Rudolfo shrugged and took the pouches, handing them out.

Gregoric slipped the cord around his neck with the other.

"You know your window and your target," Rafe said. "Keep your men in the garden. I'll take the vault; I have the Rufello cipher for it. Jasper and Uke have the library. We meet back here and run for the coast with a bird off to the *Kinshark* for our rendezvous."

Then he held up his pouch, opened it and sprinkled it into his hand, and licked it. Rafe vanished even as he sprinkled the powders onto his shoulders. "Let's run."

Rudolfo and the scouts followed the forest ritual, touching the powders to their foreheads and shoulders, tossing some to their feet, before licking the palms of their hands.

Gregoric watched them fade from sight and then followed the same steps. Only instead of using the new powders, Gregoric used his own powders. He was far from home, far off course from their Androfrancine-sanctioned mission, getting ready to violate their kin-clave . . . and without his knives. And Rafe Merrique, the prankster pirate, was the common denominator here. Gregoric had given over as much control as he was going to and would use the magicks he knew and trusted and trained under his entire life.

Gregoric felt them take hold, felt the strength surge through him as his stomach twisted into a knot and his head began to pound. The smell of the horses in the barn, the maple trees beyond, rushed his nostrils as the night became less dark.

And as he ran after Rudolfo and Rafe Merrique, his hands bereft for knives he did not have, Gregoric thought this bit of piracy felt much like the forest run of a Gypsy Scout.

They left the forest for the stone-walled fields that marked the lands and delineated the various manors on the outskirts of the city. So far, the maps and the hours spent poring over them were paying off, and whoever was in the lead knew exactly where they were going. Gregoric heard the low clicking of a tongue ahead and adjusted his course and pace as they crossed a road and approached a gated wall.

He heard the softest scrabble ahead of him as someone—Rudolfo, he suspected—scaled the wall. Gregoric followed after, dropping lightly to the ground on the other side.

A cobblestone drive nestled in the midst of fruit trees went perhaps a quarter league ahead to end in front of a large, two-story building. They stayed to the trees, skirting the large courtyard and moving into the gardens at the rear of the main house. Once they were on the other side, Gregoric saw their window on the second floor and the trellis beside it that they were to climb. And thanks to the magicks, he could also pick out the guards—two of them—both by scent and by their hazy outline in the dark.

He and Rudolfo broke away from the others now and moved in closer to the house. Gregoric was approaching the trellis, now ahead of Rudolfo, when he felt the first muscle spasm in his left calf. It slowed him, but he checked the trellis and then climbed it to the windowsill.

Another cramp, this time in his forearm. Gregoric winced and could've sworn he saw his hand and arm before him for just a moment. He blinked at it and felt a wave of nausea as yet another cramp seized his stomach.

He felt Rudolfo's hand on his shoulder and translated the coded words pressed there with his friend's fingers. *What's wrong?*

I don't know, Gregoric answered. He took a deep breath as the clenching subsided and then checked the window.

Moonlight etched the room in soft shades of green and blue, but Gregoric found his vision coming and going with the onset of a sharp pain behind his temple. A desk stood before the window, its surface tidy in a way that suggested it was never used. It was a smallish room, and apart from the ordered nature of it, it looked a great deal like Rafe Merrique's stateroom. A narrow bed piled in blankets, bookcases crammed with books and charts, a few objects here and there—including the jade kinshark, within reach on the corner of the desk.

Gregoric slipped onto the desk and dropped to the floor, then put his hand on the kinshark and waited for the magicks to work their way onto it. It guttered and flickered in and out of focus, but the magicks didn't hold. More than that, Gregoric's hand came in and out of focus along with the jade statuette.

"Who's there?"

Gregoric jumped, and the jade statue grated against the desk. He backed into the shadows and looked in the direction of the bed.

The pile of blankets had become a young woman sitting up in bed staring directly at him. "Rafe? Is that you?"

The name and the familiar way that she used it was as shocking to him as the cold water he'd been dropped in over and over again by the man attached to that name. Gregoric looked to the door and back to the bed. His first impulse was to flee, and his second was to reach her and silence her before she called for help.

Except it is almost as if she expected us. And Rafe specifically.

And before he could do anything, another cramp seized him, and he fell over this time. He closed his eyes against the sudden onset of it as his entire body clenched in pain.

"We are affiliates of Rafe Merrique," a low voice confided from the window. There was fear underneath Rudolfo's voice but Gregoric was confident that the girl could not hear it. "It appears perhaps we were expected?"

Gregoric squinted up at her as she looked to Rudolfo. "No," she said in a careful voice. "*You* were not expected. But *he* is hoped for *every* day." There was an emotion there that spoke to some kind of longing Gregoric couldn't fathom, followed by a bitterness he could. "At least some of us around here feel that way."

And for whatever reason, those words were the spark that, combined with the layout of the room, gave it all enough sense that Gregoric could solve the Whymer Maze before him.

This is Merrique Manor. This was Rafe Merrique's boyhood room, organized in the likeness of the stateroom of a pirate ship he'd yet to steal and sail. An imagined future he had crafted for himself.

The realization was lost to more cramping, and Gregoric groaned as his legs and arm shifted in and out of focus beneath the moonlight.

Rudolfo hopped to the floor beside him. "What's happening?"

Gregoric bit his tongue against the tremors that now rolled over his body.

"Something's wrong with his magicks." The young woman was up out of bed now, wrapped in a blanket, and reaching for her lamp. "Who are you? You still haven't answered my question." She paused and her next words weren't convincing. "I'm not above screaming for help."

"I hope you won't," Rudolfo said. "As I said, we are affiliates, and Captain Merrique would be quite unhappy with any mistreatment we might receive at your hands." He was thinking fast on his feet, and Gregoric was glad. His own ability to think shrank the longer his body shook against the magicks.

They both knelt over Gregoric, and he felt her hand, cool against the heat of his skin. "So you are part of his crew then? I saw him lifting up Rafe's kinshark statue."

"Of a fashion," Rudolfo said. "We are sailing with him in service to the light."

She snorted. "That explains little." Gregoric felt her hands probing his neck and armpits. "How are *your* magicks holding up?"

"Fine." Rudolfo paused and Gregoric felt his fingers suddenly pressing words into his shoulder. *Did Merrique's magicks do this to you?*

Gregoric couldn't keep the shaking still enough to code his

words. "I used my own," he said through chattering teeth.

"I know little of these things," Rudolfo said, "but Merrique told us to use the powders he provided. He said the salt air could have an impact on ours."

She sniffed Gregoric's breath. "Fortunately, I know a bit about these things. And I have what I need in my workshop to treat him."

The trembling and cramping stopped for a moment and Gregoric tried to climb to his feet, only to find his legs now unable to hold his weight. He buckled.

"And where exactly is that?" Rudolfo asked.

"It's in the basement," she said, "but I can be there and back quickly."

There was no hesitation in Rudolfo's reply as he squeezed Gregoric's shoulder. "We are at your mercy, Lady," he said.

She grinned. "Yes. You are."

She slipped into a robe and slippers but didn't leave by the door. Instead, she ducked into the closet.

The kinshark lifted from the desk and Gregoric blinked at it as it gradually disappeared. "What was the book he told us to take?" Rudolfo asked.

Gregoric found his voice. "You're not planning to—"

"Save your voice, Gregoric," Rudolfo said. "And yes. I do not know exactly who she is or where we are, but I intend to complete the task and escape even if I have to carry you out of here on my back."

"It's his own house, Rudolfo." Gregoric's voice was raspy. "He's had us break into *his own house.*"

"To be fair," Rafe Merrique said from the closet, "I didn't think anyone would be at home apart from the staff. But I see you've met my sister, Drea." A wall of clothing rustled as his magicked form entered the room.

There was an edge in Rudolfo's voice. "This doesn't appear to be quite the act of piracy we discussed, Captain Merrique."

"No," the pirate agreed. "Not at all." His voice was closer now. Gregoric felt a boot nudging his side, and too weak to snarl, he groaned. "And the stubborn baboon used his own magicks despite my warning."

"Aye," Rudolfo agreed.

Gregoric felt Merrique's hands, strong and firm, taking his

ankles. "Grab his arms then. We need to be gone before she returns."

The hands tugged at him but no others joined in. Gregoric saw the young woman was back now, postured in mock outrage in the open closet with her hands upon her hips. "Do you now?" she said. "I think you've spent enough time gone, Rafe Merrique."

Her brother chuckled. "I thought you were *all* going to be at the summer lodge on Lake Elsyn?"

"I decided to stay home when I saw the bird from Simmons." Drea Merrique smiled and Gregoric saw a strong beauty in the line of her jaw. "I know which people you correspond with when you're going to be in the area."

"Yes," Rafe said. "But I time my visits for when everyone's away. I didn't expect to find you here. Neither at home nor in my room. I sent them for my journal and my statue from Grandfather. Why aren't you in your room?"

Drea shrugged. "I like it in here. Not everyone's big brother is a famous pirate." Then she smiled. "Besides, I was hoping you'd be back and thought this would be the best way to catch you. The oily-voiced one already has the statue, I'll wager." She pointed to the drawer on the desk. "The journal is still there. They've kept it all the same since you left . . . only cleaner . . . which has always struck me as odd." She stepped from the closet and knelt over Gregoric, drawing a satchel up from the leather strap it hung by. Drea rummaged through it, drew out an envelope and tore it open.

"Give me a canteen," she said, then her warm breath was near Gregoric's ear. "Open up, sailor."

He complied and tasted the bitterness of the powders she tipped onto his tongue. She closed his mouth, opened another envelope and mixed those in as well. He felt foam building as the powders hissed and bubbled. Drea uncapped the canteen and pressed it to his mouth, the cold water pushing the powders down his throat. He felt the softening of all his edges as the kallacaine relaxed his muscles. His eyelids were heavy, and he could see his hand clearly now when he held it before his face.

Drea Merrique pushed his hand away and down. "This one is going to need some rest before he can be re-magicked."

"He can rest on the ship," Rafe said.

Drea ignored her brother. "Help me get him into the bed," she said.

This time, Gregoric felt hands half lifting and half dragging him across the room and he did his best to help until he rolled into the bed and hands pulled the blankets over him. Behind them, he heard Rafe protesting. "We don't have time, Drea. This was supposed to be a quick in and out."

"Next time," she said, "you should have the civility to plan a longer visit."

Rafe smiled. "I might be able to now, and you've these men to thank for it."

Then Gregoric was in a warm tunnel. The room, the bed, and their voices were all growing farther away.

"I asked them who they were," she said. "They wouldn't say."

"How rude of them," Rafe Merrique observed. "These men have acquired the brooch and brought it to me at great expense." His voice was sober now, and Gregoric heard Drea gasp as the words took hold. "We've brought it back tonight. Tell them that it's back in the family vault."

Their act of piracy had been breaking into Rafe Merrique's family estate to return the brooch Rudolfo had spent a dozen fortunes to acquire. There was some aspect of this that made Gregoric want to laugh and not stop laughing, but he was too tired. There were more words, and he could've sworn he heard his friend introducing them with great flair and embellishment. But everything melted into warmth and darkness as Gregoric slid into a deep and welcome sleep.

At some point, Gregoric awakened to the lurch and lope of being carried across a meadow in the gray of predawn. He was certain he must be dreaming, strapped to someone's back as they ran.

"What's happening?" His mouth was dry as cotton and his voice raspy.

"Easy, Gregoric," Rudolfo panted. "We're nearly there."

He's carrying me. Gregoric tried to move but found he couldn't. He'd been tied over Rudolfo's shoulders with belts, and they were both wet from the sweat of Rudolfo's exertion as he ran.

Every word was an effort, but he forced them out. "You should not be carrying me, General."

And Rudolfo's words silenced him for the rest of the run and long after hands had lifted him up and pulled him aboard the waiting ship. He took those words with him back into sleep. "You've always carried me, Gregoric," his king and closest friend said between ragged breaths, "and across much rougher landscapes." His hands squeezed Gregoric where they held him across his shoulders. "From time to time, when it falls to me to return that favor, I will carry you, my friend."

Gregoric smiled as the rocking of the waves replaced the rocking of their run and sleep carried him back down the warm well of Rudolfo's echoing words. They were a slow refrain to a song that soothed him and flooded him with an unexpected gratitude.

I will carry you, my friend.

Gregoric watched his second sunset at sea from a hammock they'd rigged for him on deck, and Rudolfo sat nearby and watched it with him. He'd been nearby most of the time Gregoric had been awake, and according to Jasper, he'd stayed by while Gregoric slept.

"We tried to help him carry you," she had told him during one of Rudolfo's brief absences, "but he insisted upon doing it himself."

Rudolfo said nothing about it, and Gregoric wasn't about to bring it up.

They watched the setting sun paint a wide-open sky in colors so overpowering that he simply watched slack-jawed in wonder. Rafe Merrique approached, raising a bottle of rum.

"How are you feeling?" the pirate asked, offering Gregoric the bottle.

Gregoric took it. "Much better," he said. He drank from the bottle and passed it to Rudolfo.

The Gypsy King took a long drink and handed the bottle back to Rafe. "And how are you, Captain Merrique?"

Rafe's face was a mix of emotion, and he tried to hide it with another swig of rum. He smiled, but his eyes held something closer to sadness in them. "I've seen my sister a handful of times in twenty years. She was five when I left." He leaned back against the mast. "I was at odds with my parents and the life they planned for me—the life planned for them by their parents. But Drea—she was the innocent caught in the wake of my departure." He took another long drink from the bottle.

"Regret," Rafe said, "is a curious thing. Our Androfrancine friends would tell us the only useful regret is the variety that is more akin to guilt—feelings of remorse that lead to a change in one's path." He used the bottle to conduct the next words as if he were in front of a choir. "Because as we all know, 'Change is the path life takes.'"

"I aim to regret nothing," Rudolfo said.

Rafe Merrique laughed. "Good luck."

Jasper poked her head out of the hatch and looked around. Gregoric saw her eyes meet with Rudolfo's and suppressed his smile. It seemed that sometime in the last twenty-four hours, Merrique's first mate had decided Rudolfo's library was perfectly adequate, shelf, book, and all. Which of course meant Gregoric would be staying up on deck long into the night.

The coded looks between the two of them weren't lost on Rafe either, but like Gregoric, he pretended not to notice.

"You're certain," Rudolfo asked, "that you want to proceed, Gregoric?" He looked up at Merrique. "When is our last chance to change our minds?"

Merrique chuckled. "We're pirates. We can always change our minds."

Rudolfo stroked his beard and considered Gregoric carefully. "And you're quite comfortable here for, say, a few hours?"

Now Rafe's chuckle was the bark of a laugh. "Best not keep my first mate waiting, Lord Rudolfo. She brooks no dissent."

Gregoric smiled as Rudolfo blushed and disappeared quickly.

Rafe settled into the chair he'd left and handed the bottle back to Gregoric. "Your king is a fine young fellow. He's on the way to becoming fierce and sharper than sharp." Their eyes met. "And you, too. I'd have not trusted me on the powders, either, especially with the paces I've put you through."

Gregoric shrugged and was surprised at how easy his next words were. "I should've listened." He took a drink and passed the bottle back. "So explain to me what we did?"

Rafe smiled. "You and your king helped me lay a regret to rest. I've returned the brooch I stole to finance the first *Kinshark*. I knew the moment I had it in my hands that I needed to take it home immediately. And you not listening to me gave me a few hours with my little sister that I didn't know I needed to have." He finished the bottle. "So there's nothing there for you to regret. Learn your lesson and move on."

Gregoric nodded. "Aye."

Now Rafe regarded him and raised an eyebrow. "You also have family. A father and mother?"

Gregoric nodded. "And a son on the way." He paused. "A bride, too."

"And Rudolfo," Rafe said.

"He's more than family. He's my king and my closest friend."

"Yes and what are you to him? Do you know?"

Gregoric hesitated, and Rafe continued.

"You're his anchor, Gregoric. You ground him."

He nodded. *Yes.* He could see that.

"And he is your chain. When you're buried in the muck of doing your job, he can lift you up if you let him."

Gregoric looked from Rafe back to sky and sea that had become indistinguishable from one another. The pirate was right, of course. As much as Gregoric focused on Rudolfo's need for grounding, he needed to let the tie that bound their fates pull him up when the ground he was so good at going to swallowed him whole. Chains kept anchors from being lost and stuck.

For a moment, he was drugged and hazy on Rudolfo's back and he heard his friend's words again—that refrain that he suspected he'd go back to for the rest of his days as one of the more surreal assurances life had ever granted him. *I will carry you, my friend.*

Gregoric wasn't sure what to make of their bit of piracy, but he knew it had changed him. And that more change lay ahead as they sailed for the Churning Wastes. There, men in dusty robes would pass over to them whatever bits of light long lost in darkness they had dug up in the ruins of the Old World. And then, they'd sail for home and fatherhood and Firstborn Feasts. If he had his way, he'd raise his son in peace among his family in the Ninefold Forest and in service to his friend. And one day, he'd tell his son all about the time he sailed with a pirate.

Rafe stood up and stretched. "Rest well, First Captain."

"Aye, aye, Captain," Gregoric replied.

And after Rafe Merrique slipped down the hatch and after Gregoric had checked to be certain no one was within earshot, he turned his eyes upon the stars that guttered to life above him.

"Far into the Ghosting Crests and beyond the Emerald Sea," Gregoric sang softly to that sky, "I swear my sword to the pirate lord and a life of piracy."

Gregoric, First Captain of Rudolfo's Gypsy Scouts, smiled and wondered what tomorrow might bring.

STUCK IN BUENOS AIRES WITH BOB DYLAN ON MY MIND

I'VE READ ALL ABOUT THAT OTHER GUY, LAST SON OF A dead planet flying around in tights to save the world. Let me tell you something: Not everyone who crashes here was sent, not everyone gets adopted by a kindly Midwestern farmer and your little yellow sun in this backwoods corner of the universe sure didn't dole out any superpowers.

No, that's not how it went for me at all.

My first taste of your planet was the Seine. Not a wonderful start. I woke up choking and clawing my way toward gray light in a body that felt clunky and wrong.

Aren't you forgetting something?

I heard the voice clearly in my head and it was familiar to me.

I should leave you. What were you thinking? It was all coming back to me now and I was, as you might put it, mad as fuck. I forced myself to turn downward, scanning the river floor. *Over here.* A brief flash of light and I saw it. *And I was thinking with my—*

Yes, I cut him off. *There you are.*

My ship flashed silver at me and I grabbed it, kicking upward again. I felt its shame radiating through the handle I clutched tightly with an oddly effective four-fingered hand complete with an opposable thumb.

My ship sighed. *It was a Dothari Belt-class Schooner. I couldn't say no.*

I broke the surface and felt the slow tug of the river as it moved me between stone bridges in a gray twilight lit by the lights of a city. Of course, at the time I had no idea it was the Seine. Or Paris.

Actually, you could've said no. You really could've. But he hadn't. And he'd caught something from his port tryst eight days now behind us. So here we were.

More shame. *I'm sorry.*

I thrashed my way onto a cobblestone ramp and flopped over, staring up at the evening sky. The smells of the city overpowered the smell of the river and I lay there panting alien air into alien lungs. I looked over to my ship. His name isn't pronounceable with these vocal chords of yours. Let's call him Carmichael.

He'd disguised himself as a guitar case, buckled closed, with a pearl handle. It was worn, dented metal and covered with stickers. Some of the markings were familiar to me but most weren't. *Wow. You're small.*

Use your vocal chords, Carmichael answered.

"Wow," I said. "You're . . . small."

Actually, I'm the same size. The dominant sentient species here is significantly larger than the galactic standard. You've been up-sized to avoid drawing attention to yourself.

I continued testing my vocal chords. "Where's here?"

Earth, he said. *Buenos Aires, to be precise.*

The city's name registered and I started accessing my memory of its streets and skyline. "Hey, I know that place."

Yes. I was able to upload several data packets that will hope-fully enhance your chances of survival here.

I stood and looked around, checking my knowledge of the city against what I saw around me. "I don't think it's likely to en-hance my chances," I finally said.

Why not?

"Because I don't think this is Buenos Aires."

No, Carmichael said. *I'm quite certain this is Buenos Aires.*

I knew then that things were about as bad as they could be. Until I started up the ramp and met my first humans. Then things got worse. It took me a minute to figure out why they looked at me the way they did. Or didn't look at all.

"I'm naked," I said.

A white-haired male human winked at me as he passed by. "Oui, Monsieur," he said. "Vous êtes en effet nu."

See? Carmichael said. *They're speaking Spanish to you.*

"But I don't seem to speak Spanish. And public nudity ap-pears to be frowned on here."

A brown-haired female human in a blue uniform made eye contact with me. She said something into what I guessed was a radio.

You better run, Carmichael said.

And so I ran.

Morning found me huddled against a stone wall in the back of an alley, my body covered in pages from a newspaper I couldn't understand.

I squinted at it. "I thought you programmed me with Spanish?"

Carmichael sighed. *I did. After all, Spanish is the most spoken language in Argentina.*

I glanced at the guitar case and wondered how I knew what it was. "What other helpful information did you upload into me?"

A plethora of skills and knowledge necessary to survive undetected in a hostile environment.

I smelled something pleasant on the air for the first time since arriving. Whatever it was made my stomach growl and I associated it instantly with being hungry. "What kind of skills?"

Well, Carmichael said, *let me out of this case and I'll show you.*

"I thought you *were* the case?"

That's just silly. What good is an empty guitar case?

I thumbed the clasps and opened the lid. A stringed instrument shone dimly in the morning light. "I don't see how—"

Just pick me up. You'll see.

Papers crackled and crunched around me as I lifted the guitar. It had a strap made of what appeared to be the hide of a pink, fuzzy creature and a silver pick tucked between its strings. It felt as familiar in my hands as a kermauchoof—which you've never heard of. I took the pick in one hand and curled my fingers around the neck. Something tickled at my brain and music happened as I picked at a series of strings with my right hand while pressing them with my fingers of my left hand.

See?

I gave myself over to the song and when I opened my mouth to reply, strange words poured out. "Once upon a time you dressed so fine," I sang, "you threw the bum a dime when you were in your prime—"

Didn't you? Carmichael chimed in.

I stopped. "What is *that*?"

It's Dylan. Part of a wide variety of uploaded chords, notes and lyrics covering several decades of popular music.

"I don't see how this is going to help me survive in a hostile alien environment."

Try it again. Play more this time. Sing louder.

So I did. And when I finished, I jumped at another voice in the alley.

"Bravo," it said and I looked up. A man in a white hat stood backlit by an open door. He held something that smoked in his fingers and he sucked at it as he watched me. He dug into his pocket and pulled out what looked like a coin. "How do you say it? Threw the bum the dime?" Then he laughed and tossed the coin at me.

"Oh," I said. "I get it."

Then I gathered up my ship, my newspapers and my first bit of currency and set out to sing my way off this desolate backwater rock.

By noon, I'd earned myself rudimentary clothing—a pair of gym shorts, a Grateful Dead T-shirt and flip-flops—along with an assortment of breads, cheeses, chocolates, and coins.

I took a break and stretched out in the dirty sunlight, feeling the ache in my fingers and throat. As I'd sung, I'd continued integrating what I could of my surroundings with the data packets Carmichael had uploaded into me. My knowledge of Buenos Aires told me it should be warmer than it was but the infection that had crashed us here had likely glitched the upload. Apart from watching the people around me, seeing how the music impacted them, I was left with the music itself to educate me.

Her cheating heart had told on her so bye bye love, there goes my baby. And bye bye Miss American Pie, for that matter, because we've all come to look for America with Carolina on our minds and a heart in New York. Wearing blue suede shoes and a long black veil.

So what do you think?

I nibbled at a pastry. "It's good. A little cold. They take themselves and their reproductive drives a bit too seriously in their music." I paused and frowned. "Then again, look who I'm talking to."

"Pardon?" a white haired female asked. My blank stare kept her walking by.

Yes, yes, Carmichael said. The shame was gone now. *I crashed us here.*

I opened my mouth to speak and thought better of it as young blond male in a blue uniform walked by. It was occurring to me rapidly that people who spoke aloud to voices in their head may not be regarded in high esteem here and that these other people in blue uniforms might find such behavior noteworthy for their little radios. So I went silent. *How about you get us uncrashed?*

I'm working on it.

And?

Carmichael paused—an equivalent of taking a deep breath before delivering bad news. *Our options are . . . limited. Earth is a bagged world.*

"Great," I muttered. Bagged meant it was being monitored for its social evolution and kept in the dark about the rest of us just down the way. If you wonder why, go watch how my kind is typically portrayed in your popular entertainment. We blow up your big important buildings, messily kill people and then succumb to some ultimately silly end in a triumph of the human spirit. Or we show up as your pals, cure cancer and give you a sneak peek at our cookbook as we start measuring you for our frying pans. Or this one is especially good: After traversing millions of light years, we arrive completely incompetent and need someone from your species to help us return to our intergalactic culture.

Notice a pattern? You all don't treat each other much better, truth be told.

Bagged also meant that the technology necessary to eradicate my ship's infection wasn't going to be found here for a long, long while.

I sighed and watched more of the primates move around me. Many of them held communication devices to their ears. Or held them in their hands. *We could try to get a message out,* I suggested. I nodded to a young male, his opposable thumbs earning their keep on the tiny device he held while an even tinier device jutted from his ear. *Hijack a satellite and call for help.*

We could try, Carmichael agreed. *But did I mention that this world is bagged?*

I didn't need him to explain. Anyone who heard our message would be obligated by law to hand us over to the authorities. Captains were responsible for the health and safety of their vessels . . . and for where those vessels landed willingly or otherwise. My ship would be recycled and repurposed and my license revoked for the foreseeable future.

The man with the devices paused to pick his nose and examine what he found there. I looked away and thought perhaps the loss of my career was a small price to pay for rescue.

I changed locations three more times before sunset cast the streets in a red, warm light. Twice, those blue uniforms had shown up and taken an interest in me. Each time, I'd finished up my song and slipped away. Finally, I'd settled into a spot near the river and as the city moved into its night life, I started drawing a small crowd. A young male with a tattered backpack sat beside me and pulled a small metal object from his pocket and looked at me with raised eyebrows. I was singing about good times never seeming so good with someone named Caroline and didn't understand whatever non-verbal language he used. Smiling, he put the object to his lips and made music of his own that joined perfectly with mine.

It had taken me most of a day to relax enough to study the effect of music on you primates. Music, of course, is common throughout most of the galaxy. There are some civilizations that managed to emerge without it but they are few and far between and the rest of us think they lack something. The simplicity of your music—and the obsessive, extreme nature of the lyrics—is one of your better qualities. And with just my fingers and my vocal chords, I'd watched what it did to those who stopped. Flushing skin, flaring nostrils, tapping feet, swaying bodies, knowing looks. It would've been fun if I weren't stranded on a planet full of xenophobic barbarians.

The young male played with me through the rest of the set. After nodding his head to the scattered bits of applause, he grinned at me. "Vous êtes plutôt doué."

"I'm sorry," I told him. "I don't speak Spanish."

He laughed and now I understood him. "I do not speak Span-ish either. I was speaking French."

"Spanish is the dominant language in Buenos Aires."

"Yes," he said. "It is. And *French* is the dominant language in *Paris*. Which is where we are." He blew and pulled a few notes on the harmonica. "But now I am speaking English to you."

I closed my eyes. *I told you this wasn't Buenos Aires.*

Carmichael was nonplussed. *This primate could be mentally deranged and unaware of its present location.*

I looked around. "This is Paris?"

The young human nodded. "Oui." Then he grinned. "You must be American." He dropped the small metal instrument into his shirt pocket. "I am Claude." He extended his hand.

I watched the hand with caution. "What is *Claude*?"

"I am. It's my name." He extended the hand again. "And you are?"

"I'm . . ." I paused hoping Carmichael would save me. He didn't. "Dylan," I finally answered. "Dylan McLean."

Claude laughed. "Good one." Then, he took my hand in his and squeezed it in too brisk a fashion to be mating protocol. "So, Mysterious American, are you here to play the ex-pat open mic then?" He nodded in the direction of a building with a red door.

I patted Carmichael. "I only play guitar."

"You're funny," Claude said as he stood up. "Come on. I'll show you."

I crammed the contents of my guitar case into a plastic bag with the rest of my day's earnings and buckled Carmichael in. Claude was already crossing the street. I hesitated, noticing the line that formed and the humans who stood in it. There were several other guitar cases, and though I was the least elaborately garmented, I was still less scantily clothed than some of the fe-males. One of them—tall with dark hair and long legs—made eye contact with me.

I caught up to Claude and he noticed the woman, too. He grabbed my arm and moved me down the line past her. "You'll do best to—how do you say it? Steer clear of her, mate. She hates Americans."

"But I'm not American."

Claude guided me through the line. When we reached the dark clothed man at the door, Claude said something to him in French. The man nodded and ushered us inside. The room was crowded and stank of humans and the things they drink and smoke. There was a small stage toward the back and a bar on the far side. My guide moved me across the room to another man, this one dressed colorfully and wearing paint on his face. Claude pushed me to him. "This is my friend Dylan," he said. "He's American. Really good."

"Sergio," the man with a nod. He held up three fingers. "Three songs," he said. He glanced at a sheet in front of him. "Fifth up." Then he went to scribbling and Claude moved us over to the bar.

I don't think this is a very good idea, Carmichael said. *You're supposed to be laying low.*

"No," I muttered quietly. *I'm supposed to be finalizing my delivery to Goral's Reach right about now and then taking a little vacation. But someone crashed us here over a bit of shiny new hyperdrive schooner.*

Carmichael said nothing.

We stood at the bar as the room filled and Claude—with help from some coins and bits of paper from my bag—introduced me to my first glass of beer. It was cold and sweet. I was part way into it when the woman from outside slipped in between me and Claude. She tipped her very plump mammary glands—barely restrained by her red dress—in my direction and batted her eyes. "Who's your friend, Claude? Did I hear you tell Sergio he's American?"

"Leave him be, Annie." Claude tried to switch places with her but she held him at bay with a glance.

Then her eyes went back to me. She finally seemed to take in my clothing. "So did you come from the gym or the beach?"

Her question was gibberish to me so I took a hint from the others I'd met so far and extended my hand. "I'm Dylan," I said.

She snorted. "I'll bet you are." Then she got in close and the smell of her was sweet and crisp like the beer I sipped. "So you're from America. I'm from your neighbor to the north."

Human faces, it seems, are exceptional at transmitting sub-verbal messages like confusion. Her smile widened at the look on my face and over her shoulder I saw Claude shaking his head and mouthing the word 'no' over and over again. I decided to err on the side of caution and say nothing.

Annie continued. "You know it?" She paused and waited for me to answer.

I didn't.

She raised her eyebrows. "A little place called Canada?"

Now the look on my face seemed to annoy her but it didn't last long. She smiled again and took a sip from the glass of red fluid that had appeared in front of her. She drew closer and now Claude was rolling his eyes over her shoulder.

Annie leaned even closer now, her mouth near my ear. I felt heat from her breath as she spoke. "I'll give you a blowjob if you can tell me the capitol of Canada."

I suspected that gainful employment would be useful here though I wasn't sure how much her job paid. I decided to err on the side of honesty and see if that served me as well as caution had. "I need the blowjob quite badly, but I do not know the capitol of Canada." I paused. "But Buenos Aires is the capital of Argentina."

She sniffed and for a moment she looked like Multon gusp spawn deprived of its marpy at the last moment and angry over the wasted effort. "You just lost yourself a blowjob."

Annie took her wine and pushed off into the crowd. Claude watched her go. "It's Ottawa," he said. "In case you're wondering."

I wasn't. I was still trying to piece together how a human female on Earth could look so very much like something from the planet Multon. I opened my mouth to reply but the music started. Slender greasy bits of fried and salted starch arrived with more beer. Claude and I ate quietly and listened to the music.

Most was guitar with vocals—male, female, and at one point, one of each. And there were other instruments I did not recognize. Still, I knew most of the songs from my own repertoire. None of them especially impacted me and I was pondering the overpowering obsession with reproductive activities when the fourth musician took to the stage.

Sergio spoke into his own microphone off to the side as she strapped on her guitar.

"Cecilia Dumas," he said. She was not very tall, but sturdily built and compact. Her hair and eyes were blue and her hair was brown. She had a metal harness that held an instrument identical to Claude's—small and silver. She hid behind the guitar, blowing a few notes as her fingers moved over the strings and her eyes wandered the room.

This song wasn't one I recognized but I felt it instantly. "I'm just a poor wayfaring stranger," she sang, "a-travelling through this world of woe." The room did not erupt in applause but something inside me resonated with her mournful tone. She moved from it seamlessly into a soulful rendition of a song I did know, only she'd cleverly altered its lyrics to be about a Rocket Girl instead of a man. "It's lonely out in space," she crooned and her eyes met mine.

What was that? Carmichael's voice was panicky in my head.

Nothing, I said. *Go back to sleep.*

The second song gathered up a smattering of applause when she finished and she launched into her last, one she told us she'd written herself.

I was entranced and felt my new body doing things it hadn't done before. The light around her softened and my pulse quickened. My stomach felt oddly light. I looked down and saw my foot was tapping in time.

Then Claude was pushing Carmichael into my hands and shoving me toward the stage. "You're up, you're up."

Sergio waved at me, said something in French that I didn't understand, and the audience chuckled. Then he winked at me and smiled. "Dressed in the latest American fashion for his Parisian debut: Dylan McLean."

There were snorts and giggles and chuckles as I strapped on Carmichael. Sergio handed me a wire and I looked at it blankly.

Don't you dare plug that into me, Carmichael said. *I don't know where it's been.*

That's never stopped you before. I examined the guitar's body and found where it went. Then I pushed the cord in and twisted it. As I did, static burst from the speaker followed by a warbling, high pitched squeal that settled down as I started to play.

My fingers knew what to do and so did my mouth. "I got my first real six string," I sang. "Bought it at the five and dime." And from there, I let the song carry me away.

I wasn't alone. The mood in the room shifted as I sang. People swayed, tapped their feet, even clapped and sang along. And after

I moved them along through that summer of '69, we were suddenly slip sliding away, slip sliding away, and I watched the music take us all nearer to some destination where only music could carry us. When I finished the second song, the room exploded into applause and I paused to scan my audience.

I saw Annie first. She was up in the front of the crowd and the look on her face had changed now. It was flushed. Her eyes were wide. Her nostrils flared. When our eyes met she smiled at me. I kept that eye contact and started playing again, and a slow melody built as I picked out the notes on Carmichael's strings. The look on Annie's face was something I'd not seen on the humans yet and I found that I liked it. So with eyes locked, I leaned into the microphone. "You fill up my senses," I sang to her, "like a night in the forest . . ."

But even as I sang it, the words felt false to me. I found myself wanting to look around the room to find the other female. Cecilia. Still, I held Annie's gaze and let the show go on. The subtle and not-so-subtle physiological responses played out in her posture and on her face as I brought the song around into its final chorus.

The bar went wild when I finished. I waited for a moment then broke eye contact with Annie, looking around the room. What I felt was hard to explain. Something about the enclosed space, the press of warm bodies, the glasses of fermented fruits and brewed grains and distilled starches had given the music more power and even I felt the rush of it in my body. This was nothing like a street corner or park.

Sergio waited for the applause to die down but it grew.

This is the opposite of laying low, Carmichael said.

"Encore," someone shouted. I looked out and it was Cecilia, grinning up at me. Claude stood beside her and shouted the same.

Others picked up the word and it became a chant.

Sergio stepped back and leaned close to me. "This never happens, mate. Got one more in you?"

I nodded.

"One more!" Sergio shouted to the room and my fingers took off, my voice jumping in after.

When I wrapped that there was more applause and a dark skinned woman approached Sergio. "Give him my set, Serge." she said. Then she winked at me and slipped back into the crowd.

"You heard her," he said.

And that's how it went that first night. We were free-falling through Darlington County with Penny Lane in our ears and in our eyes and in the early morning rain, guessing we'd rather be in Colorado. Turn, turn, turn.

I found myself moving to the music I made, moving with the humans in the room, and I realized suddenly, mid-strum, that I was experiencing a profound sense of community. A room full of people far from home brought together by melody and poetry.

I lost track of time but finally, the ache in my fingers and rasp in my voice settled in. "Last song," I said into the microphone.

I looked around the room and found Claude. "Get up here, Claude." He blushed and shook his head but Cecilia laughed and pushed him. Then she smiled at me.

I smiled back and then knew what song I needed to sing. I flipped my guitar and started banging out a rhythm on it with my hands. I countered each slap with a stomp and Claude began clapping in time. I met Cecilia's eyes and her smile widened as she recognized the song. Then she was clapping and stomping too. Gradually, the rest of the room joined her and when that pulse reached its inescapable crescendo I shifted into the chords and leaned into the microphone as Claude's harmonica wailed.

"Cecilia," I sang, "you're breaking my heart," and then let the music sweep us into ecstatic connection.

And then, on the last note and the last chord, Carmichael sparked and I felt it shoot through my body and out through my feet.

We have to go.

But—

WE HAVE TO GO.

That's when I noticed the blue uniform in the door talking into her radio. Carmichael's urgency finally registered and I yanked the chord from him as reached for his case. They were still clapping, whistling, chanting but I pushed everything out of my mind.

What happened?

We've been pinged. We have to get out of here now.

Claude was beside me and Cecilia was near. "What are you doing?"

"I'm sorry, Claude. I have to go. Right now."

Now the look on his face was new to me, but it was clearly less pleasant than the other expressions. "But you can't. We just—"

"I'm sorry," I said. Then I pushed past him and Cecilia and Sergio and through the others as I went looking for the back door.

I thought this planet was bagged? How can we possibly get pinged?

Carmichael didn't answer.

I looked over my shoulder and saw that two men in suits had joined the blue uniform. They picked their way through the packed room. I found the back door and went through it into the alley, moving into an awkward run with Carmichael clutched in both hands.

"Dylan!" It was Annie.

I stopped. "I'm sorry, Annie. I really have to go."

"No," she said. "I'm sorry. I was just being a bitch earlier. I don't like American boys so much." She paused. "Thank you for the song."

"You're welcome," I said and then got back to running. Until a new voice stopped me in my tracks again. This one from inside my head.

You should save us both some pointless effort and just stop right now.

It wasn't Carmichael.

Now. Slowly put down the guitar and turn around with your hands up.

This wasn't my first Carlucci milking toad rodeo. I did what I was told.

An older male human in a long gray coat stood there. He was the last thing I saw before a bright blue flash spun the world away and turned out all the lights.

Okay. You can wake up now.

I forced my eyes open and blinked into bright sunlight pouring through a window.

I sat in a chair in front of a desk that the older male sat behind. Carmichael lay in his open case, upright in the chair beside me.

The man cleared his voice. "First," he said, "I'd like to welcome you to Earth. You seem to have made quite a splash." He looked at me for a minute then glanced at his desk.

I wasn't sure what else to say so I aimed for gratitude. "Thank you." I glanced at the guitar next to me. *Carmichael, what's going on?*

The man smiled and blinked. *Your ship is in stasis.*

I stared. *How is it that you have the technology for direct cortical communication?*

He chuckled. "I'm not from around here." He looked at the papers again. "We've extricated your vessel's system core from the instrument it was concealed in and placed it in quarantine."

"Do you have antivirals to upload so—"

The man raised his hand. "No more questions, Dylan."

"My name's not Dylan. It's—"

"I don't want to know your name." He leaned forward. "I don't want you to speak. I just want you to listen."

I listened.

"As you no doubt realize, Earth is a bagged world. Your presence here violates no less than two dozen Division of Developing Planet laws." He paused, letting the words soak in. "Obviously you are not alone here. There are actually quite a few of us living on Earth quietly. Some came for science. Some have fetishes for backward living and less developed species. Others are in hiding. You're the first shipwreck in a while but it's happened before."

I opened my mouth to speak again and he raised his hand again. I closed my mouth.

"We thought we picked up a technological anomaly when you crashed but it was plugging your vessel into the power grid that really gave you away. Unfortunately, by doing so, you've infected the human power grid, and I've had operatives working all night to smooth that over." He rubbed his temples. "So you are starting out at deficit with me, I'm afraid."

"What does that mean?"

The question didn't seem to annoy him. "It means you owe me. A lot."

"If I can get off this rock, I'm certain I can—"

He shook his head slowly. "I'm afraid leaving with that debt unsettled will not be possible. As you can imagine, none of us here are interested in bringing down the Imperial Division on our heads. I can certainly arrange for your quiet departure but you'd also need to have your time here expunged. Memory alteration and transport alone are hefty sums."

I did the math and wondered just how many bits of metal and paper it would take to get out of here. "And my ship?"

"Your ship, too, of course. But also for a price."

I doubled the math. "That's . . . a lot."

He nodded. "But still cheaper than what happens if you're caught here."

"What are my other options?"

"Well," he said, "I can euthanize you today. I'd have to eat your current debt but you'd not incur any other. And my problem is effectively solved. Dead men, as they say, tell no tales."

Now it was my turn to nod. "Less appealing to me, actually," I said.

"Yes." He studied me. "Or," he said.

"Or?"

"Or you go ex-pat like the rest of us. Make a life for yourself here."

"What about Carmichael?" He looked at my blankly and I elaborated. "My ship."

"In stasis until you leave. That stunt at the Red Door left you pingable in a twenty light year radius. We can't risk another incident like that. So if you decide to stay, we'll wipe the core and dispose of it."

"And I'll be compensated for the cost of my ship?"

Now he laughed. "No. You'll be billed for the disposal."

I sighed. "Can I have some time to think about it?"

He shrugged and stood.

"And can I talk to my ship?"

I could tell that he wanted to say no. And his face had all the signs of exasperation squeezed into it. "Five minutes," he said. Then he left the room.

I felt the hum in my skull when Carmichael woke up. *I told you not to plug me into that primitive electrical device.*

I looked around but had no idea where exactly they'd stored Carmichael's core. *Do you know what's going on?*

Yeah. I've been told.

So what do you think?

Carmichael was faster at the math than I was. *I think earnings based a single twenty-four hour planetary rotation indicate that it will take four hundred and eleven cycles around the system's sun to raise the funds necessary to extricate us from this predicament.*

That, I said, *is a long time.*

And I don't think euthanization suits you.

I sighed. *Agreed. Or you, for that matter.*

Sorry I gakked that schooner.

I reached out by habit and patted the guitar even though he wasn't there. *I know. I'm sorry I yelled at you about it. I do think the survival skills are working out.*

You did, as they say, rock the house.

I'm not sure why I said it or why I said it the way that I did. But it came out: "Thank you. Thank you very much."

Carmichael laughed. It was going to be a long time before I heard that laugh again—if ever—and I savored it. We'd spent most of a decade stomping around the stars together and I would miss him. *I'll be back soon, Carmichael.*

Rock on, Dylan McLean.

I waited until the hum left my skull.

Okay then, I finally said. "I'm ready."

The door opened and the man came back in. Now he had an envelope with him. "So?"

"It looks like it might take some time to raise the funds. Long enough to see the sights, it seems."

"And then some."

"And I can keep the guitar?"

"Of course. It's harmless without the core."

Remembering the faces, the clapping, the chanting as I played, I wasn't so sure I agreed with him.

I decided to go out on what you call a limb. "And can I visit my ship from time to time?"

The man scowled. "Maybe in a decade or so. I don't want to see you around Paris for a goodly while, Mr. *McLean.*" Our eyes met briefly before he continued, "Speaking of which, I've taken the liberty of establishing the background and necessary documents for one Dylan McLean." He handed me the envelope. "There is an

American passport in there. I hope you'll use it. Today even. I've also included account information for the payment of your debt and an emergency contact number that I sincerely hope you will not use." He paused. "We'll let you know when you've accrued enough credit with us for a visit with your ship."

"Understood," I told him.

This time, I extended my hand. He shook it.

Then the blue light flashed and I was gone again.

"Hey there," a voice said and I opened my eyes. It was Claude. "Where did you go?"

I was sitting on a bench not too far from where I'd met him. I could see the Red Door down the street. It was late morning now. I wasn't sure what to tell him. "I remembered an appointment I was late for."

His face beamed. "It was quite a show. They were talking about it all night." He dug a communication device from his pocket. "I'll tell Cecilia I found you. I'm running late."

The mention of her name increased my heart rate and made my stomach feel odd.

He took off his backpack and opened it, digging around. "They always take up a collection after the show and then divide it among the musicians. I think your attire convinced them you were down on your luck and they all insisted that you receive the full amount."

It was my day to collect envelopes. This one was thick with bright colored bills and he pushed it into my hands. "It's a lot," he added looking around. "Keep it safe."

Not nearly enough, I thought and felt a twinge of sadness that Carmichael couldn't hear me. "Thank you."

He nodded toward the bar. "And Sergio wants you back."

"I may be leaving town soon."

His face brightened and that surprised me. "We are, too. Cecilia will tell you all about it." Then he kissed each of my cheeks and rushed off.

I pulled out Carmichael—the name stuck—and started picking at the strings. It wouldn't be the same without his voice in my head but he had fashioned himself into a fine instrument and my hands knew just what to do with it.

"I'm just a poor wayfaring stranger," I sang to passersby who paused to listen, "a-traveling through this world of woe."

When Cecilia arrived she hung back until I finished, then set her own guitar case down beside mine and joined me on the bench.

"So my brother found you?"

"Claude is your brother?"

"Well, half-brother. Same Mom. She's French. But I grew up with my father in Oregon. I busked my way over here to meet him a few years back and decided to stay."

I looked around. "Not a bad place."

"What about you?" Her eyes were dangerously blue and I wanted to fall into them.

"What about me?"

"Where are you from?"

I remembered the other envelope and pulled it from the guitar case where I'd tucked it away. I opened it. "I'm from . . . California, it seems."

She sniffed. "That explains the outfit."

I laughed and looked at the other envelope filled with money. "I suppose I should take care of that."

"And then what? Claude texted and told me you're leaving town."

"Yes. Someplace warmer."

"We've been saving up for South America. We're getting close."

"Argentina," I said, "is quite nice I hear."

She grinned. "I've heard that, too." Then she looked at me. "But meanwhile."

"Meanwhile," I answered.

"Wanna play with me?" She bent down to open her guitar case.

I did. Very badly. And for the next two hours we crooned about the giant steps we took walking on the moon, losing our religion as we went under the dancing spell cast our way in a big top world behind green eyes. And when we finished, we stood and bowed to the gathering crowd.

"That," she said, "was a lot of fun."

It was. And more than fun, that feeling from the bar had followed us here, and I felt the spark of ecstatic connection, the roots of belonging.

Maybe, I realized, shipwrecks weren't so bad. I would take what Carmichael had given me to survive and I would learn how to thrive. I'd see Buenos Aires and every other place on this rock. I'd eat the foods and drink drinks and sing the songs. And maybe I would travel with Cecilia and her brother for a while. And maybe later I would travel alone.

I'd make the money I could. And maybe I'd find a way to square my debt with the secret, hidden ex-pats in this place. Or maybe I would stay.

Maybe I would even start to write my own songs, like Cecilia did—or maybe even write some with her—and sing them in front of hundreds, or thousands, or maybe even millions. And maybe then, I'd tell my story—the whole story—about how I came to this backwoods rock and found joy and purpose bigger than I'd known as a space jockey. And maybe that song would be part of their preparation for the great unbagging that lay ahead of humanity on the trail.

I knew what I would call my song when I wrote it, and I whispered the title aloud as I smiled at my new friend here. "Stuck in Buenos Aires," I said, "with Bob Dylan on my mind."

"Is that a song?" she asked.

"Not yet," I said. "But it will be."

Then we packed up our guitars and set out for the next park or corner to conquer with our songs.

THE GREATEST GUNS IN THE GALAXY

with *Bryan Thomas Schmidt*

JOHN SELMAN HAD SHOT JOHN WESLEY HARDIN, THE deadliest gunman in the West, in the back, you're damn right. He'd done what had to be done to take down a monster. To some, including Selman himself, that made him a hero. To others, it made him a target.

So when the two odd-looking strangers with distended eye sockets and peculiar, orange-tinted skin walked into the ACME Saloon and called his name, Selman knew they had come for one reason: to challenge him. He downed his latest shot in one gulp and left his cane resting against the bar as he whirled to face them. "You two must be the ugliest strangers to walk in here in months," Selman said with a cocky smile.

The saloon's swinging doors let through dust and sand from the desert outside. The usual scents of El Paso—cowtown, dry heat, mixed with human and animal waste from the sewers just below the streets. Selman was almost used to it by now. But tonight, the winds seemed to bring it out.

"Is that the sewers or you?" Selman asked, sniffing the air, and the bartender and a few familiar local faces chuckled around him. But the strangers showed no reaction.

"They say you killed the greatest lawman in the West," one of them said, its overly large, beady eyes scanned the room.

Who was this—male or a female? It ain't no human. Its limbs looked stretched, overly long, hands resting just below the bumpy knees. Its companion looked just as odd, only slightly chubbier, and both of 'em stank worse than Mexicans from across the border in Juarez. *Just more foreign scum wandered into another Western town.* Well, Constable John Selman was intent on cleaning up

El Paso, and he'd damn sure clean this mess up.

Selman's adrenaline spiked, his heartbeat racing, as his hand hovered over his Colt .45, flexing and ready. "Yeah, I shot him. Three times. Son of a bitch threatened my son." Selman's eyes narrowed.

"That makes you the champion," the other stranger said, flashing oddly sharp teeth in what might be a smile.

"Champion of what?" Selman scoffed. The way the two strangers looked at him made him feel cold and he hesitated, fear rising for the first time.

"We are the best in the universe," the first stranger said.

Selman laughed. "Not the humble sort, are ya?"

In an instant, Selman had drawn and the two strangers did, too, pointing oddly long, wide barreled pistols of a sort at him while the bartender shouted for them to "Take it outside!"

They all fired simultaneously, Selman's hand so used to the Colt, it barely bucked at the recoil. His stare locked on the strangers, cold, hard, and sure.

Selman felt the wind sucked out of his lungs as a searing hole opened in his chest. There was a burning pain as an invisible forced caused his body to buck.

"Son of a bitch!" he cursed as he fell. They'd shot him. Suddenly, he couldn't move. His hands were clammy and sweat dripped down off his forehead to sting his eyes.

"That was too easy," the first stranger said, shaking its oddly shaped head. "Maybe it's true he shot John Wesley Hardin in the back like a coward."

"I ain't no coward," Selman whispered, choking on blood. He spat and tried again, but the strangers paid him no mind.

"Shot him in the back? Too afraid to face him. This is no great gunman," agreed the other.

Selman's anger rose at the insults, but they were the last words he heard before he slipped into darkness, the bartender calling for someone to get his son and the town doctor .

Everyone in the ACME stared at Jailak and Mairej as the two Andromedans holstered their blasters. They stood over Selman's body on the floor in a widening pool of blood.

"He was supposed to be good," Jailak said. "We traveled back in time for this?"

"He was not," agreed Mairej. The man who shot the greatest gunman in the Old West had been a pure disappointment. John Wesley Hardin was legendary. John Selman had become famous for shooting him. Mairej saw no other reason why such an unexceptional human being should be remembered. The man was skinny, almost like he'd barely eaten, a bushy mustache over his lip, gray streaks in his blondish hair.

They turned to the bartender. "Is this not the man who killed the great John Wesley Hardin?" Mairej asked.

The bartender nodded. "Shot him in the back right over there." He motioned down the bar a few feet. Mairej could still see the stain on the floor where the great gunman must have fallen.

The two aliens exchanged a look and headed for the front door.

"Wait! The sheriff'll be coming!" the bartender called.

"We are done here," Jailak said, ignoring the man, and followed Mairej through the swinging doors, dodging blowing tumbleweeds—some of them bigger than the aliens themselves—as they stepped onto the smelly, dusty Old West street. Sand clouded their eyes and made them water a bit as the sounds of saloon music and laughter resumed, filling the night air.

The Andromedans returned to the chrono tag and ported back to their ship, leaving 1895 behind them like the dust of that El Paso street. The familiar warmth and clean smell of home greeted them, and once they were orbiting Earth again, they took lunch in the observation deck cafeteria and watched the demolition of the eastern seaboard. The various time crews wrapping up their exploitation of the planet's past would witness the treat of its demolition prior to the development fleet's impending arrival.

"That," Jailak said, "was a waste of time and budget."

Mairej nodded. "It was . . . unsatisfying. And not nearly enough footage."

Raiding the timelines of inferior species for entertainment purposes was considered the bottom of the duggha trough in the new Andromedan economy. Anyone with CNS mapping could capture the experiences. And then the record of it could be re-sold in small rapidly consumable experiences—even several at a time. The sample (in a neat handful) that Jailak fed him after the first interview had Mairej under the moons of Garglex killing Charlobundix III, their greatest warrior, with a blowgun. Only he'd done it while sampling the finest Dambril wines and having sex with three of the four poet sisters of Telpaz Prime. It was four minutes and thirty seven seconds (Andromedan Standard) that boggled his mind and convinced him to join Jailak's small compa-ny on the brief break between Garglex and Earth's assimilations.

Jailak's eyebrows went up and he nodded at the glass wall and the burning planet below. A bright light flared and then collapsed upon itself. "That was Boston I think."

"New York," Mairej said. "So what is our plan?"

Jailak took a bite of his Glomboli sky bat salad. "Well, we have to go back. I think maybe we need to kill John Wesley Hardin ourselves."

Mairej nodded. "Kill him before Selman does?"

Jailak thought about it some then clapped and pointed. The cafeteria wait staff saw and started moving their direction. "That is New Jersey I'm sure of it."

"Miami," the waiter said as he re-arranged a bat wing. An-dromedan cafeterias were known intergalatically for their fine dining and apt help.

"No," Jailak said.

"I'm pretty sure it is," Mairej said.

Jailak waved at the screen. "Not that. No, we don't do it before Selman. Can't. It violates all kinds of rules." Jailak took another stab at the bat on his plate. "For starters, Hardin wasn't killed by aliens in the original timeline. He was killed by Selman."

Mairej blinked, his partner was talking in circles. "But Sel-man wasn't killed by aliens in the original timeline either. So haven't we already violated all kinds of rules?"

Jailak shook his head. "No, not really. Just one rule. But if we do it to Hardin, too, then it's *all kinds of rules*."

"Or two," Mairej said. But he was fairly certain that it didn't matter what he told his new boss. "Then what are you thinking we do?"

Jailak leaned forward and smiled. "I think we go back, bring

John Wesley Hardin back from the dead, and kill him all over again ourselves." He waved his hands around like they were six shooters in a flurry of bad pantomiming.

Mairej pointed. "That was DC there."

Jailak laughed. "No. Seattle."

"Seattle is on the west coast." And that was when Mairej experienced the first inkling that things might not work out.

The dust and stink of the 19th century was a shock after the cool green mist of the restaurant when they slipped back to work. Mairej noted that El Paso had changed during lunch and it baffled him.

"Where are the horses?"

Jailak shrugged. "I'm not sure."

"The buildings are different, too."

"We're in a different part of town," he said. He pointed. "There's the cemetery."

The night air was hot and quiet other than the sound of automobiles slipping past beneath the gray light of buzzing streetlamps. Mairej took it all in. "We are not in 1895 El Paso. This isn't the Wild West."

"No," Jailak said, already moving toward the gates of the Concordia Cemetery. "Just a bit later."

Another internally combusted engine rumbled past. This metal beast had a "1968: Nixon's The One" sticker on its bumper.

"But our license is for 1895," Mairej said.

"A brief stop. Then 1895." Jailak was over the gate now and moving off into the dark. As he counted paces, Mairej followed at a distance and kept an eye out.

The Concordia Cemetery was in the center of city near several busy roads and an interstate highway that rose above it on stone pillars—dust, exhaust, and debris raining down from passing vehicles above. Stone grave markers of various colors, shapes, and sizes were lined up in neat rows. A couple had buildings or shelters around them. The cemetery's owners seemed to have made an effort at grass and flowers, but most were dead or dying from being beat down by the desert. The place was open with a nice breeze and so smelled no different than most of El Paso.

Mairej thought humans had odd burial rituals. The stones were rather plain, no valuable minerals had been used. What kind of respect did they have for their dead?

Jailak stopped at a flat marker and fished a tube from his coveralls. "This is it."

"What are we doing?"

Jailak had the look on his face that said he hated working with amateurs just before he rolled his eyes. "We're resurrecting John Wesley Hardin so you can gun him down on the streets of El Paso."

"So much for the rules."

Jailak sighed, then squeezed the contents of the tube onto the grave. "A minor violation at best. We're not going to gun him down here. We'll take him back to 1895."

"1895," Mairej said raising his eyebrows as he watched a puddle of black goo twist itself into a slender work and squeeze itself into a crack near the marker. "And why aren't we just bringing him back in 1895?"

"We're not licensed to perform resurrections in 1895."

Mairej decided against pointing out that they didn't even have a license to be whenever they were now. Instead, he watched the ground. Something was happening. A distant hum as the ground vibrated beneath their feet. He'd not seen a resurrection before. "So it's bringing him back to life underground?"

Jailak shook his head. "Just watch."

The goo was back, only it was a mottled gray instead of black. First a slim tendril, then another. And then another. Until there was a gray puddle growing large enough to make them step back.

Mairej glanced up at Jailak and saw concern on his face. "What is it?"

He shrugged. "Usually it's pink, not gray. But see? It's working!"

The goo was spreading out in the form of a human body there on the ground above the grave. Mairej took another step back. "It smells."

Jailak wrinkled his nose. "That's not normal either." The smell was something akin to gundar carcasses left in the sun too long before cooking, only much, much stronger.

The body was taking on more definition now but it looked decayed and unhealthy, as rotten and barely hung together as the suit it wore. They both jumped when the eyes popped open, black and full of nothing. A pale worm crawled from one socket and disappeared back into another.

"Good evening, Mister Hardin," Jailak said as he offered the man a hand. "Time is short, so if you'll come with us."

John Wesley Hardin took the hand and stood, growling as he did.

Mairej finally found a question that he suspected he could handle the answer to. "How many times have you resurrected humans?"

"Oh this is my first human," Jailak said. "But it was pink on Orthon V."

Their new traveling companion seemed bewildered but willingly led. He said nothing, groaning and growling instead. As he walked, the top of one ear flopped up and down, hanging off his head.

When they slipped into the time pod, the bio screen filter paid John Wesley Hardin no notice at all as Jailak dipped them back into 1895.

It was approaching High Noon on Main Street when they gave John Wesley Hardin a pair of loaded Colts and a gun belt. He wouldn't take them and strap them on so Jailak had finally given up and buckled them around the man's moldering waist himself.

Mairej moved upwind of the gunslinger. In brighter light, the man looked even worse for wear. Whatever the goo had done, it didn't look like any kind of healthy. And Hardin didn't like the sunlight or the people who stopped and stared. It wasn't clear which he was growling at but he sniffed at the growing crowd of horrified onlookers.

"Is that John Wesley Hardin?" Mairej looked and realized it was Jailak who had said it. "Get ready," he said in a lower voice. "Are you rolling?"

The sensory capture bug clicked in his ear as Mairej checked his blasters. "We are."

"Me too," Jailak said, tapping his own ear. "Go."

Mairej checked his distance from Hardin, spread his legs, and held a hand over the butt of his pistol. "John Wesley Hardin, you are the most notorious gunslinger in the homosapien American Wild West, and I aim to gun you down, you murderous son of a bitch."

He reached for his gun and when John Wesley Hardin did nothing, Mairej paused.

"Say that last part again," Jailak said.

"I said, 'I aim to gun you down, you murderous son of a bitch.'"

Still nothing.

"Shoot him, then."

Mairej drew, convinced that any moment the rotting hand would slap leather and beat him to it.

Hardin sniffed at a woman near the edge of the crowd.

Mairej took aim and fired, watching the shot tear into Hardin's side. The resurrected gunslinger howled but it wasn't pain or fear—it was something else—and when he did, he leapt at the crowd.

Jailak pulled Hardin kicking and flailing off the woman. Her leg was bleeding and a huge lump of flesh tore off, clamped between Hardin's teeth. The stinky bastard chomped it down as quick as he could, whimpering and whining the whole time. The crowd screamed and hollered as they scattered in panic, some fleeing as fast as they could down the street, others backing away, but still watching and chattering.

"Well, as Dylan said, 'He ain't no friend of the people.' This is a mess." Jailak looked around. "We're going to need a different plan."

Suddenly, every implant in Mairej's body went off in instant alarm. "What is that?"

"It's a chronoalert," Jailak said. "Some idiot has damaged the timeline. We're being recalled." Hardin was struggling even more now and his howls sounded hungrier than Mairej wanted to allow. Jailak pulled him away from the crowd. "This isn't working anyway. Shoot him again so we can get out of here."

"Don't we need to take him back to where we got him?"

Jailak rolled his eyes again. "No. He was dead there, remember? And with whatever else is going on, we don't need to add to the problem."

Mairej shrugged, shot John Wesley Hardin once through the head, and helped Jailak move the body off the dusty street.

*

Back in the cafeteria, it was more of the same but this time, Europe. They were detonating Paris, London, and Rome simultaneously as part of the early dinner show. And by tomorrow, Earth and all of its resources along with its rich history would be safely tucked into the Andromedan Expansion Plan.

They found themselves at the same table with a waiter who looked unexcited to see them so soon. This time, Mairej tried the bat. It was dry but adequate. "So what do you think happened?"

"Hard to say. I'm just glad we wrapped up before anything else could go wrong."

Speaking of things going wrong, Earth below was dark now and that seemed odd. They'd left the lights on, after all, so it could be seen. And the show should've started but didn't.

There was whispering.

A waiter slipped by and Jailak grabbed his sleeve. "What's happening?"

"I'm certain it will be resolved shortly."

Mairej leaned in. "Is it serious?"

When the waiter spoke, it was with a low voice. "There was a timeline disruption in the late 19th century."

Jailak met Mairej's eyes. "Really? Somewhere in Europe or Asia, I'm guessing?"

"American West, actually," a new voice said. This Andromedan didn't wear gray like the rest. This one wore black. And there were only three black uniforms in this particular Expansion fleet. "But I think you know that already, Jailak."

"Chronogeneral Terflex," Jailak said, his face turning red, "I didn't realize you were with this fleet."

"No," he said, "but I knew *you* were. And I knew just whose license to pull when I saw humanity wink out of existence. The origin point of the disruption is El Paso, Texas, 1895. Sound familiar?" No Andromedans were particularly tall or intimidating but Terflex pulled off both. "So come along. If you're lucky, you only have some questions to answer."

"What if I'm unlucky?" Jailak asked.

"Then you get to help fix the mess you've made before it costs us our work here."

Mairej kept his eyes on his plate and worked on finishing the bat as Jailak stood.

"You too," Terflex said, looming over him.

Sighing, Mairej left another unfinished meal, having no idea just how grateful he would be for his empty stomach when he smelled what the late 19th century had become.

El Paso stank before but now it was out of this galaxy. Mairej and Jailak wore masks to cover their faces, and the stench was still almost unbearable.

"Son of a Taglothomri gundar," Mairej hurled a classic Andromedan epithet at the ground as he spit, "don't worry about the rules, you said. Minor violation. Does that smell minor to you?"

"It smells dead," Jailak said as they looked around. The creatures were everywhere—formerly human but like rotting flesh, falling apart, worm infested, and moaning and growling instead of speech. "This is odd. We killed Hardin."

"Maybe we just wounded him," Mairej suggested.

"I keep telling you, take your time and aim first," Jailak complained.

"Your mother mated with three Orthonians," Mairej snapped. "This is not my fault. The whole thing was your plan."

"Well then you come up with a plan to fix it!" Jailak said, ducking and jumping aside as one of the creatures grabbed at his arm, chomping its teeth in a clumsy attempt to bite him.

Howling, another grabbed Mairej from behind, nibbling at his neck.

Mairej felt a sharp pain and stiffened his skin, a protective instinct, then loosened his joints, bowed, and flipped the creature up over his back, slamming it down onto the dirt street. Gooey, stinky flesh rubbed his back as it slid, moaning and chomping the whole way. The thing smelled even worse up close, which was almost hard to imagine.

Jailak turned and shot it with his blaster. "You're welcome," he said.

"Terflex said 'it's all your fault,'" Mairej repeated. "He can't mean this?"

"We're gonna have to do a lotta killing if it is."

With that, they began aiming and shooting at every formerly human creature they could see, one after another, but more showed up as quick as they dispatched them. They quickly discovered that shots through the foreheads worked most effectively. Those creatures shot there fell to the ground and didn't get back up. Those shot anywhere else just kept on coming, even if they lost a limb or huge wads of flesh. One creature crawled across the ground with one arm and no legs, chomping and moaning at them the whole time. It almost made Mairej feel guilty, then he looked at Jailak and got pissed all over again. His partner had caused this and was enjoying the carnage far too much.

"What?" Jailak asked, seeing Mairej's glare.

"You're enjoying yourself."

Jailak grinned. "We're hunters and the greatest shooters in the galaxy. This is what we do."

"My mother warned me throwing my lot in with you was dumber than a gundar, but I didn't listen," Mairej said, shaking his head.

"This street's clear," Jailak said. "Let's go find another."

It turned out no street stayed clear for long, and it took them hours and hours to kill all the hundreds of creatures wandering around El Paso. But when they went back to their ship, Terflex's angry face filled their comm screen.

"You're not done. There are creatures like this all over the planet. You've got a lot more work to do. Get busy!"

Mairej scoffed. "He's got to be kidding."

"You know the policy. Our mess, our problem."

"Your mess, my problem," Mairej muttered.

Jailak rolled his beady eyes. "Just stop complaining. I got an idea."

"It's your ideas got us into this in the first place," Mairej pointed out.

Jailak punched a code into the communicator, ignoring him.

"Who are you calling?"

"Jonnapit, my cousin," Jailak said.

"For the love of the stars, don't involve anyone else!" Mairej warned.

"Meh, he has lots of friends in his hunting club," Jailak said. "They'll get a kick out of this. Besides, we're stuck here until we're done."

Mairej sighed and stopped complaining. Despite his anger at Jailak for getting them into this, help would be welcome and sounded like a good idea. Mairej was already exhausted.

Jonnapit did more than bring his club. Word spread to every flesh hungry, gun thirsty Andromedan on the planet, and soon, hundreds showed up with blasters to lend their aide.

"These creatures are too damn easy, like insects or Orthonian remars," Jonnapit complained. "I thought you offered us a challenge."

Jailak shot another and rolled his eyes at his cousin. "Cleaning up an accident. Good target practice. Stop complaining. It's the most shooting you've done in months."

Jonnapit blasted three creatures with one bolt of his rifle and cackled. "Yippeee kayay, motherfucker! You're right about that, and it's still fun."

"What the hell does that mean?" Jailak asked.

"Something I heard on a human broadcast once," Jonnapit said, smiling.

Then the two cousins opened fire again together, looking delighted as they sliced down more creatures.

Mairej left the two cousins by themselves and wandered off on his own to clear another street. They'd finished El Paso and Las Cruces long ago and were now across the border in Mexico, clearing the streets of Juarez which made El Paso look like a rich man's paradise by comparison.

"How do these humans live like this?" Raijah asked. She was one of the better shooters and far less annoying than most, so Mairej hadn't hurried off when she'd joined him.

"Well, this is how they lived a couple centuries back, but you're right," Mairej agreed. "Very primitive, not very intelligent."

"That thing they call tequila is delicious, though," Raijah said, taking another sip from a flask that hung around her shoulder on a strap and belching. "I'd like more of this."

"Once we wipe them out, maybe you can search the planet," Mairej reminded her.

She bounced and twirled, taking down five more creatures

with a stream of laser fire as she did. "If we bring enough back, we might get rich."

"It's all yours," Mairej said, shaking his head. "I want to forget this place ever existed." His body tensed at the thought of ever returning to El Paso or Juarez again, especially with Jailak. It was time for him to find a new pastime.

Raijah shrugged. "There's a reason the Andromedan Expansion Plan is so successful. We are far superior to most of the galaxy. I almost feel sorry for them. But mother of a bat do they stink!"

It took two weeks to clear the rest of the planet, but between the hundreds of hunters, spread out, they managed it. The bigger chore was burning the bodies, which Chronogeneral Terflex insisted they do before they returned home. Raijah even managed to find a beverage she enjoyed more than tequila—vodka, made by some creatures in a very cold, rugged land to the northeast. Raijah brought back an entire ship just to transport it, and in the end, she did grow quite wealthy. She even found an Andromedan chemist who could replicate the formulas.

Terflex was waiting for them both in decontamination when they finished, taking no risks with the 19th century homosapien undead. "I suppose you've seen the value of correcting your work?"

Jailak and Mairej both nodded. "We did."

"Good," he said. "You'll be needing to trade in your grays then."

Mairej wasn't surprised. Purple was the color he expected. Penitentiary purple. He was surprised when Terflex nodded to two black uniforms hung up in their lockers. "Raijah's uncle is a highly placed colonel and she's recently lauded your economic development strategy in facilitating the introduction of a new beverage that may indeed be an intergalactic hit. Further, Andromedan scientists concur that ending the human industrial revolution in 1895 has increased the property's current value due to less wear and tear upon the planet. There is even talk of establishing a theme park here around this new drink." He smiled wryly but his eyes showed clearly that he knew they didn't deserve it. Still, he managed to say the words. "So you've both been promoted to special ops." The smile widened. "Under my command, of course."

Mairej looked to Jailak then to the uniform and the chrono-general. They both managed to say, "Yes, sir!" in unison and he furrowed his brow at it.

"First things first," he said, "uniform up and meet me in my office. You've one last thing to do."

John Selman had shot John Wesley Hardin, the deadliest gunman in the West, in the back, you're damn right. He'd done what had to be done to take down a monster. To some, including Selman himself, that made him a hero. To others, it made him a target.

So when the two odd-looking strangers with distended eye sockets and peculiar, orange-tinted skin walked into the ACME Saloon and called his name, Selman knew they had come for one reason: to challenge him. He downed his latest shot in one gulp and left his cane resting against the bar as he whirled to face them. "You two must be the ugliest strangers to walk in here in months," Selman said with a cocky smile.

One of them looked at the other and then at Selman. "Actually, Mr. Selman, I think we look rather resplendent in our new uniforms."

He squinted at them, certain they were Canadians or maybe French now that he pegged their accents. Still, his hands itched for trouble almost as much as his throat itched for a drink. "What exactly are you?"

One of the strangers stepped up to the bar and plunked down a stack of shiny new silver dollars. The stranger looked uncomfortable with the words that came next. "I'm someone who is terribly sorry to have inconvenienced you with my poor choices, Mr. Selman, and I am sincerely hoping this round of drinks will make amends."

Selman looked down at the dollars and licked his lips. Then he looked back up to discover the strangers were gone.

In the end, he decided they must have been French. And there was a fancy French word for thinking you'd been in the same shitter before, after all. Only he'd been certain when those ugly fellers came into the bar that they were gunning for him. The drink—and everything else he could buy with the small fortune they'd left—was a nice surprise after a long, thirsty August.

"Viva la France," Selman said as he knocked his whisky back.

THE MONSTERS UNDERNEATH HIS BED

HE'D ALWAYS KNOWN THEY WERE THERE BUT THEY WERE easier to ignore before the hand. Benjamin Brown climbed out of bed for a three o-clock pee, placed his feet squarely into his slippers, and felt the cold hand grip his left ankle. Shrieking, he yanked away and fell backwards into the safety of his blankets. Clenching his thighs together, he waited for dawn. He needed to act on this.

Later that day, he walked to the library. The pretty girl was behind her desk and she smiled at him. He blushed, averted his eyes, and kept walking. He'd never been one to draw the pretty ones. Benjamin knew he was plain himself, and that like draws to like. He went to the computer and started his search.

An hour later, he left as empty handed as he'd been when he had arrived. Except for the smile that the pretty girl sent with him as he passed by again.

Benjamin cashed his unemployment check, picked up some frozen dinners, and went home nervous. By eleven that night, after eight hours of mindless sitcoms and volatile shock shows, he'd convinced himself it was a dream at least a dozen times. Of course, he *knew* they were there. But he knew it in a way that a person in a cave knew the sky was blue somewhere. Until this morning there had been nothing tangible to prove it other than his odd habit of wrapping his head in blankets and sleeping with his back to the door. But now: the hand.

He slunk upstairs, paused in the doorway, and leapt for the bed. He left the light on, he and pulled the blankets over his ears. Nothing had happened. He sighed, allowed the bed to absorb his body as the tension drained from him. Conviction number thirteen registered: It had been a dream.

Then, the monster underneath his bed farted loudly and chuckled low.

After that, it was a long night.

Two nights after the hand, one night after the flatulence, the monster spoke.

"Benji."

Benjamin, his head cottony from lack of sleep, his body trembling, waited. Then it started—a low whisper, a rush of words, a litany that built in the darkened room.

"Benjibenjibenjibenjibenjibenjibenjibenjibenjiben-jibenjibenji."

Screaming, he bounded to the floor, dodged the groping hands, and tripped over a shoe. He fell hard, smacking his head on the doorframe on his way down. He scrambled, hands and knees pushing and pulling, into the hallway.

He finished the night on the couch. Upstairs, his bed thumped time to the chanting voices.

The pretty girl's desk was empty at the library. Benjamin paused, trying to remember her face, eyes, long hair pulled back into a pony tail. Then he continued past the bank of computers and let the rows of books swallow him. His finger traced the call numbers of the paranormal, the philosophical and then: Psychology. He loaded his arms and found a table by the window. Outside, a gray sky spat Autumn rain.

The pages blurred and in the end, a hand on his shoulder jolted him awake, a shriek near his lips. He looked up. The pretty girl.

"Are you okay?" Her voice sounded like music. "Are you finding everything?"

He shook his head.

"We're closing soon."

Benjamin fought back tears that she must have noticed. Concern filled her eyes and voice. "Are you *sure* you're okay?"

Something about her squeezed his heart and he started to cry. "I know they're there," he said. "I *know* they are." He looked up at her, sniffling. "I'm not crazy."

She shook her head slightly. She should make an excuse now, he thought, walk quickly away, make a discreet phone call. But she didn't. "Who?" Her hand came back to his shoulder. "Who's there?"

He looked around, lowered his voice. "The monsters underneath my bed."

She should laugh now, he thought, cover her mouth with a fist. Walk quickly away and tell others so they can point and laugh and whisper. But she didn't. Instead, she leaned in, her mouth close to his ear. "I know all about them."

"You do?"

The pretty girl nodded. "I can help you." She looked at her watch. "We close in ten minutes. Wait for me?" Then she smiled a sweet smile at him and walked quickly away.

Benjamin waited near the door as she stepped out into the rain. "I'm Elizabeth," she said.

"Benjamin."

She shook his hand. "Nice to meet you. Let's go."

"Where are we going?"

She grinned. "To rent a movie. You live near here, right? I see you in the library all the time."

"Just over there." He pointed. His sleep-fuzzy brain hadn't registered exactly what was happening yet. As she started walking, her short legs carrying her at a deliberate pace, he fell in behind her and finally caught up. They rented a movie and went back to his place.

He microwaved two small lasagnas and carried them into the living room. Elizabeth had taken off her coat and shoes and now bent over the VCR. "Now pay close attention, Benjamin."

Outside, the light began to fade.

The movie was the one about the boy who saw dead people everywhere. Benjamin had seen it with his wife a few weeks before she'd left him. Back before The Downsizing. He tried to pay attention but the girl on his couch, cuddled up against him, filled him up with strange thoughts and alien feelings. Every so often he turned his head so that he could smell her hair. He felt a little drunk.

"There," she said. "Did you hear that?"

"What?"

She growled and it was a playful sound. Then, she grabbed up the remote control, rewound, and pushed play.

The child psychologist was telling the boy something. It sent chills down Benjamin's spine. Upstairs, the bed began to thump and Elizabeth looked up. "There they are, Benjamin. You know what to do."

He swallowed and nodded.

"Good. I'll wait here. If I fall asleep, wake me up when you're done." Then, she kissed his forehead.

His legs shook as he stood. Slowly, he climbed the stairs. Below him, he heard the channels change as Elizabeth surfed the stations. He went to his bedroom door and cleared his voice.

The bed stopped thumping.

"Hello?"

He heard a scampering, then a stifled giggle and a harsh whisper: "Shh. He's here."

He stepped into the room. "I know you're there."

Another voice. "He knows we're here." Another stifled giggle. Then a fart and laughter.

"What do you want?"

"Come to bed, Benji."

"I will. But tell me what you want."

"We're . . . hungry. Benjibenjibenjibenjibenjibenji."

"What would you like?"

"Apart from you?" one asked.

"Yes . . . apart from me."

More whispers. "Surprise us."

He started with what was left of the popcorn he had made earlier. He pushed it under the bed slowly and fell back when it shot out, showering the room with kernels. Then, he tried the bag of Oreos, the loaf of bread, and the package of bologna. The bedroom floor looked like a tornado-strewn lunchroom.

He went downstairs and saw Elizabeth was asleep, curled into a bright ball on his dark couch. Something dropped into his heart.

Benjamin went to the hall closet and pulled out boxes and shoes until he found the one box he hadn't looked in for three years. He hauled it into his bedroom and dropped it to the floor. Then, he opened it.

There on top, a wedding picture of a woman with a rose. He looked at it, thrust it under the bed. Something snatched it from him. He waited for it to fly back at him, but it didn't. Next, a bundle of poems and letters. A pair of dog-tags from a brother dead now thirty years. A yearbook with smudge marks on a marked page and forgotten face. More letters, one a Dear John from his army days. He pulled each item from the box, felt each item yanked from his shaking hands, and somewhere in the midst of it, his tears began to flow. When the box was empty, he sat back.

From underneath the bed, a satisfied belch. And then silence.

Benjamin sat there for a long time.

He woke the pretty girl, Elizabeth, sometime after midnight. Her eyes opened and he fell into them as he stood above her. She yawned and stretched. "Did it work?"

He nodded. "Yes."

She sat up. "Let's go make sure."

Elizabeth led him by the hand up the stairs, somehow knowing the way. She walked into the room and leaned over to look underneath the bed. He joined her.

"Feel better, Benjamin?"

"I do."

"Good." She dropped to her hands and knees. "Come on then." She scooted under the bed and waited. He paused, looked at the empty box, and then crawled under the bed with her. They lay there on their backs looking up at the underside of the box springs. In the gloom, he saw her eyes were shut and her breathing easy. In that moment, he loved her.

She rolled towards him, her arms pulling him closer and kissed him slowly on the mouth. "See? It's not so bad."

He kissed her back. No. Not so bad.

Her teeth elongated. A patch of hair sprouted above her third and fourth eyes. He only noticed it in part, though, because he felt his own mouth filling with fangs. The hair on the backs of his hands, growing in wild tufts, itched furiously. His fingernails became talons. A single horn pushed its way out of the top of her head.

Laughing, they kissed again. Then they feasted on each other long into the night.

And it wasn't bad at all.

LET ME HIDE
MYSELF IN THEE

SAMIRA BASHAR OXHAM BREATHED DEEPLY TO HOLD her profanity at bay, then let it loose when she remembered the empty work pits around her. No one to be offended or distracted by it here in the empty subbasements beneath J. Appleseed. That, she reflected, was the joy of working the weekend.

She'd spent weeks chasing down discrepancies in her employer's records, layers uncovered while chasing a bug in the heavy lift mass budgets and now, just as her leads became promising, data was vanishing like rats from a sinking ship.

And then there's my father.

She never heard from the man, never knew from moment to moment if he was dead or alive, and then suddenly, he's calling to warn her out of Seattle with veiled threats of death from above.

Near as she could see it, the occasion called for more profanity and she offered it up on the altar of her Saturday.

As if summoning Old Scratch himself, Sabo's ear phone chirped. She sent it to voicemail with a blink. It chirped again and she did the same again. On the fifth attempt, she clicked in, her voice sharp and cold. "I'm busy right now, Dad."

"Not Dad," the voice answered.

"Mom?" Something in Charity Oxham's voice tickled Sabo's ear. *When was the last time she had spoken to them both on the same day? Or within the same ten minutes?* She recognized the tickle for what it was: Apprehension. "What's going on?"

"Listen to your father, Sabo."

The words found their intended button and Sabo sucked in her breath as dozens of past conversations flooded the moment. She couldn't remember the substance of those conversations—they were about whatever argument-of-the-week a head-strong teenage daughter might fall into with the likely genetic source of her stubborn nature. Still, she remembered her mother's laugh and the words that always followed after. "Don't listen to your father," she would say. Then, the smile would fade and her eyes would go hard. "But someday, Sabo, you're going to come to me and I'm going to tell you to listen to him. When that happens, you'd *damned well* better listen."

Now, her mother's voice took on an urgent note. "Do you understand me, Sabo?"

"Leave Seattle?"

"Immediately," Charity Oxham said. "Go. There's a ride waiting on the roof."

The roof? Sabo opened her mouth to ask but her mother continued. "I'm sending you a present from your father. You know where to go to pick it up."

She did. Being raised by green wolves in the new world order had given Sabo an edge that most of her friends and colleagues lacked. She'd spent the bulk of her childhood moving among the hidden cities, living from backpacks and learning her reading, writing and arithmetic from a portable AI tutor provided by the Foundation while her parents did work she knew little about even to this day. But part of that work was a family-wide brutal form of know-your-neighbor security that they had meticulously trained their daughter in, with safe houses and drop sites. And before Bashar had gone off even his extremely limited version of the grid a decade earlier, there'd even been a close network of people through which Sabo knew she could always find her parents and vice versa if ever there was a need.

Of course, her father had dismantled that network before disappearing. And now, suddenly, he was back.

Sabo forced her attention once more to the voice in her ear. "Is Dad okay?"

Her mother's voice was unreadable. "Your father can take care of himself. Now get the fuck out of there. Get off their network and make your way to the roof." She paused and Sabo thought she heard indecision in her mother's voice. "Quietly, Sabo. Eyes wide open."

She nodded even as her hands moved over the light screen

suspended above her desk, logging herself off of a dozen systems as her eye moved to the door. "Okay, Mom. I'm going."

"Good." Charity's voice was distant, distracted. "I love you."

"I love you, too." Her father had said the same—another rarity in the Bashar-Oxham Tribe of Three. And one that spoke of something Sabo couldn't fathom but had to respect.

Her parents were afraid.

"Call me when you get the package," her mother added.

"I will." Then, when the line hiccupped into quiet, Sabo hung up and started moving files from her desk into her i-Sys.

Something flashed behind her left eye and she paused, her hands at the corners, ready to collapse the shimmering screen. It was an IM on a messenger program old enough that she didn't recognize it, asking her to approve a file transfer.

She looked to the door again and then back to the screen. "What is this?" she mumbled to herself.

She approved the transfer and, a second later, pulled the audio file into her server along with everything else. Then she closed the screen, blinked her pit-lights off and made for the center aisle and the door that waited at the other end. She was in the hall moving toward the elevator when the file opened.

A simple line of music played in her left ear. It was unfamiliar and crackling with age. Something preserved from as far back as the vinyl years, she suspected. It was a gospel choir accompanied by an organ and piano.

"Rock of ages, cleft for me," they sang, "let me hide myself in thee."

An IM window opened behind her left eye. *Y OR N?* appeared in bright blue font.

She crooked her index finger to enter 'Y' then paused. *I don't understand*, she sub-vocalized.

The file played again. Louder now in her earbud. *"Rock of ages cleft for me, let me hide myself in thee."*

More words reproduced themselves in the window beneath hers.

I HAVE INFORMATION REGARDING GREEN SPACE MASS BUDGET DISCREPANCIES. There was a pause. Then: LISTEN TO YOUR FATHER, SABO. Y OR N?

Fuck. Sabo stood at the elevator now and pushed the button. She needed to be leaving. Her ride was waiting, whatever her mother had meant. She sighed. *Yes.*

The response was instant. L2 SERVER ROOM STACK 7.

The doors whispered open and she slipped inside the elevator. She pressed the button for L2 and tapped her foot impatiently as the elevator whispered upward.

The floor was quiet and Sabo approached the server room quickly. Its hatch was a security wet dream, with bioptic scanners, thumbprint locks and an old fashioned numeric code sequencer.

And it was open. Just a crack, but open, nonetheless. That kind of security lapse was unheard of.

Unless I was meant to find it open, she thought. Convenient. Or perhaps not, given that she needed to be on the roof right now.

She pulled the hatch wide, a wash of cold air rushing outward. Her i-Sys accommodated for the dim light by dialing up her ocular implants. She scanned the large numbers above each stack until she found the seventh.

Sabo slipped into the cage and looked around. She didn't recognize this particular server though from the case design and the relatively clunky power supply she suspected it was older than the others nearby. The machine hummed quietly, its diagnostic cable hanging loose.

The instant message window flashed to life again. UPLOAD FILE SMA.EXE. Y OR N?

"Who is this?" She watched her voice-rec translate the words into an orange flashing font. The audio clip replayed, then its single line of lyrics appeared in the same orange font.

ROCK OF AGES CLEFT FOR ME, LET ME HIDE MYSELF IN THEE. Y OR N?

She took hold of the cable and tipped her head to the side, brushing her hair away from the small jack at the base of her skull. External bio-ports were rare—a throwback to earlier times—but sometimes old tech was the most reliable and discrete. One trip to an underground wetware hack shop and she could move data in and out of her i-Sys without touching the grid. Still, that also meant whatever she brought in would also dodge the normal safety protocols that kept her—and the online world—protected on the net. Whoever brought her here knew she had the port. And had left the hatch ajar.

Nothing about it smelled right.

I should leave, she suddenly thought. *I should drop the cable and run for the elevator.*

In the midst of her hesitation, the earbud crackled to life again. "Listen to your father, Sooboo," Bashar's voice whispered from far away.

Fuck. She held her breath, ported in and checked the connection. "Yes," she finally said and watched the letters appear behind her eye.

The data package hit her i-Sys like a shovel to the head. White light spider-webbed her vision and a loud roar brought vertigo upon her that threatened nausea. She fell forward against the server rack and gasped, her hand scrambling to disconnect the cable.

What the fuck? Whatever was being pushed into her personal system didn't fit cozily and her internal neural safety protocols were trying to push back. Of course, they weren't nearly as robust as the net's protocols and it was a losing battle. She found the cable but couldn't make her fingers work. They kept slipping over the surface of it and when Sabo finally did have a grip, she didn't have the strength to pull it free. Her arm fell limp to her side.

Sabo slid to her knees, a roaring pulse pushing at her temples from within her skull. Her vision morphed from white lace to gray and she gave in to the nausea, vomiting onto the cage's plain metal floor. When she went the rest of the way down, the cable snapped loose from her neck. The edge of the server cabinet clipped the side of her head, sending the gray light spinning into dark.

She came around to the smell of coffee, sour milk and bile in the puddle beneath her cheek. Her head ached and she sniffed again, now aware of the strong reek of iron. She touched her nose and looked at the blood that smeared her fingers. The IM window was open behind her left eye, the orange font flashing at her:

UPLOAD COMPLETE.

She blinked and pulled herself up to her knees slowly. Her ear bud crackled and popped to life. "We have to go, Sooboo."

Dad? She touched the sore spot on the side of her head and winced. "I know," she said.

"Then get up."

Sabo closed her eyes against the ache and climbed to her feet. "Okay. I'm up."

But her body felt sluggish, her eyes wanting to close as she leaned against the server cage. Now, her father's voice was firm, the tone of command she once feared and more recently loathed. "Get going, soldier. You're out of time."

She cast one guilty glance at the mess in the bottom of the server cage, then let herself out carefully. Her legs were rubber but she forced them to carry her through the server room's hatch and back to the elevator.

She pressed the button for the roof and settled against the wall as it began to climb. She was halfway to the top when she remembered her father. "Are you still there, Dad?"

No answer.

Sabo pulled the log with the twitch of an eyelid and scanned it for a callback number. Of course, he was smarter than that. Neither his earlier call nor the most recent appeared in the log.

The elevator whispered open onto the roof and she stepped into the wind that her ride kicked up. It was long and dark and silent, its gyros making a high pitched whine that tickled her inner ear. The passenger door folded up and a man wearing a Patriot, Inc. uniform leaned toward her.

"Ms. Oxham?"

"Bashar-Oxham," she corrected. "You must be my ride." She took in the unmarked copter. It was one of the new McDonnell Douglas four-seaters, designed primarily for urban combat support. She climbed into the passenger seat and fastened her belt. "I'm glad Mom still has some friends at Patriot, Inc."

The pilot nodded. "She has plenty of those. I'm Carmichael."

She opened her mouth to say something but the words were lost when her father's voice filled her ear again. "Go, Sooboo, go!"

"Let's fly," she told the pilot.

"Where to?" The engine's whine built as the copter lifted and moved over the edge of the roof. Beyond the tinted matrix-spun transparent sapphire she saw Seattle spreading out beneath her, bathing in an uncharacteristically warm winter sun. To her right, Puget Sound reflected back the sunlight.

"South," she said. "There's a Hawking Grove there I need to visit. Shadows-In-Line-With-The-Moon."

"I know the place." Carmichael got busy being a pilot.

As they accelerated south, she felt the slightest change in the atmosphere. There was a sudden burst of noise on the pilot's headset and she heard him gasp even as lights started flashing on his console. "Hang on," he said, casting a glance up and behind them. She found herself pressed back into the chair as their speed built even more and she twisted herself to see what he was seeing.

Fuck.

Behind and above, the sky was filled with fire as something massive fell upon them. She felt the copter shake as a hot wind tore at it as they shimmied to the left and dropped suddenly. The pilot regained control over the aircraft as they sped away south, climbing as they went.

She felt the impact down in her teeth, the sound of it a roaring like nothing she'd ever heard. The winds were stronger now and Sabo was distantly aware of alarms going off in the cockpit as the pilot's hands scrambled over the control panel. The copter bucked and twisted against the wind as her stomach turned with the sudden turbulence that shook them like a rat in a dog's unrelenting jaws.

Fuck.

She looked over her shoulder and gasped. Smoke and fire choked out the horizon to their rear where a city once sprawled and the weight of it settled upon Samira Bashar-Oxham's shoulders.

Seattle was gone.

And, somehow, her parents had known what was coming and warned her away.

The pilot gave echo to the voice in her head and when he said the word, his voice was cold and hollow. "Fuck."

They set down near the Hawking Grove. Sabo studied the small group gathered near the trees. Already, people wore bandanas tied around their mouths, breathing through the wet cotton as they shuffled into the grove with empty eyes.

"I'll be right back," she said.

The pilot looked up from the console and nodded. "Hurry." She could hear the rush of static in his headphones and knew the channels had to be choked now as they tried to ascertain what exactly had struck Seattle and how much of that city it had carved away.

And as they tried to figure out where to start pulling survivors out of the rubble and seawater.

Sabo slammed the hatch behind her and made her way quickly to the grove's single cobble-stone path. She couldn't help but look north, watching the cloud that continued to rise there where a city had been. In the distance, she heard disaster alert sirens.

What have the two of you gotten into? She couldn't remember exactly when it was that she first felt a parental impulse toward her parents. It might've been around thirteen or fourteen, and they'd largely laughed at her attempts to assume that role but they'd never corrected her.

"Worrying about what we're up to," her father had told her back then, "will only make you tired, Sooboo."

She moved into the grove, letting its security and network protocols tickle her as it read who she was as she inhaled the scent of pinesap and old needles. Of course, her parents being her parents, she also had to offer up answers to a half dozen other questions before the grove granted her access.

Even still, she was unsurprised that they'd paid for the deep-down security only afforded by the grove's expansive root system, which meant a hardwire data transfer. She moved to the tree that flashed the implant in her left eye, studying its branches for a port cable, even as her right eye took in the other people moving beneath the grove's canopy of sheltering branches. Most were haggard, their faces drawn in lines of worry, their eyes darting north despite the view being blocked.

How many lost? At its peak, the city had boasted maybe a population of three million, its citizens packed into massive strato-rises tethered to an already crowded downtown corridor. But the city was shrinking again as people moved inland, joined the seasteads or went abroad. The seawalls were keeping up with the rising Pacific but the cost of holding the future at bay was translating into higher taxes and an overall higher cost of doing business for the green industries that had helped rescue the coastlands to begin with. Even her own employer, the J. Appleseed Foundation, had started looking into relocation. Those vanishing companies and their payrolls had cut that population easily in half. Still, the city would typically be full of people during the middle of a workday, despite telecommuting mandates and quotas. It would be harder to calculate a typical Saturday population.

Fuck. There had been an impact but no blast that she was aware of beyond the relatively minor wave of heat that had pummeled the chopper as they'd fled south. The 'net buzzed with the news but she didn't have time to scan more than headlines. First glance, an asteroid strike had taken out downtown Seattle.

Sabo found her own eyes drifting north until a familiar orange font caught her attention.

TRANSPORTATION BEING RE-DIRECTED. ATTEMPTING COUNTERMAND. Her ear bud crackled, her father's voice suddenly filling her head. "Hurry, Sooboo."

She blinked and glanced at the copter. "Dad?"

"Get what you need. We need to go."

She stood before the flashing tree now and reached up into a leafy branch, her fingers closing around the data jack. She pulled it down and held it to the back of her neck, starting at the sudden memory of vertigo and vomit that ambushed her. Closing her eyes and crossing her fingers, she plugged in.

Sabo went through another layer of security with the grove and initiated the download. It wasn't a large packet—certainly within her wetware's limits—and she was surprised when the download terminated due to lack of memory. She ran it again, not believing the results even a second time. Perplexed, she still refused to believe it until she checked the memory level and saw it, then checked for the program that had consumed every bit of space on her i-Sys, extending deep into the wetweb that served as overflow.

SMA.EXE.

The executable file she'd downloaded from that J. Appleseed server. She blinked voice-recog on. "What is SMA?" The words appeared, flashing in orange, as she spoke to them into the chat window.

Her father's voice answered even as his own words appeared. "I am, Sooboo. But there isn't time for that now. We need to go."

"Mom thought this was important; she sent the helicopter.

Whatever is going on, I'm sure we need this." Even as she spoke, something tickled at her memory. What had her mother said?

I have a present from your father. "She said it was from you," she added. Of course, now she couldn't be sure of that. Or sure that it was actually her father whispering in her ear.

But she was sure of one thing. Something had gone wrong in that last download. Her implants were malfunctioning . . . or worse, her mind was. Her phone hadn't been able to dial out since the impact and she knew she couldn't be hearing her father's voice. She'd checked her call log and there had been no calls since her mother's warning what seemed hours ago.

"I will analyze the packet and save any relevant data," her father told her. "Steady yourself."

She opened her mouth to protest even as she leaned against the tree. Her body spasmed. Then her head tingled, building to a sharp, hot ache.

All of the trees were flashing now and she was vaguely aware of a dozen sirens going off both internally and externally even as she pieced together what her father's voice told her. She didn't have the memory to store, let alone analyze, the data but someone or something else had something better. It was using her connectivity to hack the grove, bending the grove's vast memory resources to access and analyze her mother's packet.

It didn't take long. The orange font appeared: SALIENT DATA RECOVERED.

Sabo pulled the jack free, aware again of a nausea that flooded her. She steadied herself against the tree. The sirens still blared around her but there was no evidence of any security presence. Of course, that didn't surprise her. Whatever happened up north certainly trumped a suburban grove-hack of less than three minutes.

She followed the path back out, scanning ahead for the copter. She held her breath until she saw it waiting ahead. The pilot watched her through narrow eyes when she climbed back inside. "Someone out there loves you," he said. "I was ordered back. Then, just as I was lifting off, it was countermanded by the White House."

Sabo nodded. "Someone out there *does* love me."

At this point, she had no idea who. Neither her father nor her mother had anything close to the level of skill required to hack a grove. They were both hellaciously talented people, but not in that direction. She couldn't think of anyone she knew that could pull that off, even with the best equipment, much less through her i-Sys by way of a file transfer cable.

And with results in under three minutes. An impressive level of skill.

Sabo didn't realize Carmichael was speaking until he touched her arm. She looked at him. "I'm sorry?"

"Where to next?"

She blinked. "I don't know."

"Chelan Heights," her father whispered in her ear.

Mother, of course. "Chelan Heights," she told the pilot.

Carmichael banked the helicopter east. The ash and debris fell now, pelting the metal skin and the tinted sapphire canopy. She closed her eyes against the wave of grief that struck her again and settled in for the ride.

She pulled up the instant messenger window, activated her embedded optical communication wizard and blinked her words. *I know you're not my father,* she sent.

"You're correct," his voice whispered in her ear. "His voice samples were on file in your i-Sys and in the J. Appleseed Foundation security cluster. I thought his voice would facilitate a more effective working relationship for us."

"Boy, you got that one wrong," she muttered. *So who are you then And what is this working relationship you speak of?*

"I am SMA. And our working relationship began the moment you agreed to download me."

What was the choir singing in that audio clip that started this? *Rock of ages, cleft for me, let me hide myself in thee.* She pondered a moment, then sent the question that she so carefully shaped. *You hid something in me to avoid it being destroyed by Dad's asteroid strike?*

"Almost, Sooboo," the voice whispered and she understood the truth of it before it continued. It settled into her belly with a flutter. "I hid *myself* in you to avoid being destroyed by the asteroid strike. So that we can prevent a much greater catastrophe."

Let me hide myself in thee. She released held breath as she realized more fully what she had agreed to. And this time, she whispered the words and her voice recog picked them up, dropping them into the chat window in bright orange font. "AI, then?"

Carmichael glanced over. "What?"

"Yes," SMA answered.

She ran back over her knowledge of J. Appleseed. They had well over a dozen AIs involved at various levels in the org, including the triumvirate of Heinlein, Hubbard and Kornbluth, left to the Foundation by William Silas Crown. She knew of those but she'd not heard of SMA. *I am not familiar with you,* she sent.

I am not a part of the organization's stated IT inventory, the AI answered. *My existence is unacknowledged; it was a secret my parents hoped to keep.*

Badly enough to drop a rock on you, she thought. She opened her eyes and saw that they flew over the foothills now, making their way east. To the south, Mount Rainier rose up stoic and white with snow. To the north, Mount Baker did the same. She didn't need to look behind her to see the smoke and desolation there. She closed her eyes again, satisfied with their course.

Easily a dozen questions vied for preeminence but something SMA had said earlier brought her back around. *And what is the greater catastrophe we're going to prevent?*

"Watch and see, Sooboo," her father's voice whispered.

The data began to scroll behind her closed eyes.

Sabo watched and saw, her anger rising as she did. The missing mass accounting data was here—bioware smuggled into orbit, for God only knew what purpose—and more. A tug of the single thread of those mass budget discrepancies exposed even more threads and the new threads unraveled the fabric of deception quickly. Executive session notes going back to the transition of human members off the board—forty years ago—and still more financial shell games for the creation of facilities she assumed must be intended to house the Appleseed AI beyond humanity's exit stage left. And medical research—lots of medical research— for a Foundation primarily committed to community and economic development.

Zero population re-wilding, managed by AIs of our own making, she thought. What was to remain of humanity was already tucked away, a remnant cast into space and away from the garden that had been their cradle. *While our electronic children repair what we've done to our mother.*

The first step had been to move humans into space. The second, to remove any evidence of J. Appleseed's complicity in it and the third . . .

Darwin. The present from her father by way of her mother.

All of it was there. Except for how exactly this particular plague was to be visited upon them.

"We're here," Carmichael announced as he banked the helicopter around the massive building that rose up ahead of them.

On a clear day, the federal retirement facility, Chelan Heights, rose high enough above the eastern Cascade foothills to see the lake it was named for. The Heights, so-called by its tenants, was three hundred floors of varying degrees of assisted living for the top tier of government retirees. Her mother was in that upper echelon—though when she'd first retired, she'd moved into one of the more independent levels. Still, age had caught up to her quickly. Her father had found a way to cheat old age but the tech that made him more spry than his younger wife was hard to come by.

They circled the building and she studied the larger helicopter that occupied the rooftop landing pad. Like the one she rode in, it was black and sleek, but unlike it, this machine bristled with armament.

"Can you put us down alongside?"

Carmichael squinted at it. "There's no sign of the pilot. It looks like one of ours but . . ." He cleared his throat and whispered a series of numbers into a Patriot, Inc. emergency frequency. When there was no answer, he slowed and settled in alongside it. "I'll keep the engine hot," he said.

Sabo worked the lever of the hatch and climbed onto the roof, looking back over her shoulder at Carmichael. "Don't go anywhere."

She didn't wait for an answer. Instead, she walked to the other helicopter and pushed her face up against the window. It was dark and empty inside. But this aircraft, she saw, had jump seats in the back for up to six passengers.

So eight total if they were full up. A thought occurred to her and she kicked herself for not realizing it sooner. She opened her earbud. "Dial Mom," she told her phone.

The phone rang. Sabo willed her mother to pick up even as she made her way to the rooftop door. The knob had been mangled by a high-caliber weapon. Unusually, she found herself wishing she had something similar in her own sweating hand. Old training was taking over. Training she'd hated both then and in retrospect. She paused, her hand over the twisted mass of metal, and then turned back.

Sabo tapped on Carmichael's hatch and he swung it open. "I'm going to need what you're packing," she told him. She quickly catalogued her knowledge of Patriot, Inc. armaments. "A Glock under the seat, right?"

He blinked at her. "A Ruger," he said. "But I'm not sure I can—"

"The White House," she said, stretching out her hand. "Right?"

He swallowed and reached beneath the seat, pulling the case free from its clamps. It was big enough to hold the plastic 10mm pistol and four magazines. Sabo popped the case open, pulled out the pistol and fed it a clip before working the action and slipping the safety off. "Don't worry. I'll bring it back when I'm finished with it."

She hoped she wouldn't need it. But Sabo suspected she might. Up to eight paramilitary troopers of one kind or another had forced their way into a federal facility. *The one where my mother happens to live.*

"You brought me here," she told the voice in her head. "Any idea what to expect?"

"I anticipate representatives of a Lightbull Variant known as *Los Cuernos de Toro.*" The AI paused. "And hopefully, my colleague, Mr. Cairo."

She took the stairs two at a time, finding another decimated doorknob exiting onto the two hundred and eighty-ninth floor. Her mother's floor. Filled with dread, she raised the pistol ahead of her as she pushed the door open.

Emergency lights flashed in the corners of the dim lit hall. Sabo was aware of how quiet the floor was. Her sneakers whispered along the tile, her eyes moving as she scanned the path ahead. She saw the first bodies and paused. One wore a lab coat, the other a red terrycloth robe. Nearby, a dented walker lay on its side.

The corridor was lined with mostly open doors, punctuated by the occasional nurse's station. More bodies lay further ahead.

Someone had come onto this floor intending to kill everyone they found.

She made her way down the hall, pistol ready, and paused when she moved past the bodies. A nurse here, a doctor there, and further down, an old man, an old woman.

They're looking for my mother.

She moved faster now and didn't stop again until she came across the soldier. He was sprawled out on the floor, face down, a hole the size of a golf ball in the back of the pilot's helmet he wore. She didn't see any insignia on his digi-camos, but she didn't need to.

The Horns of the Bull.

She stepped past the pilot, noting the semi-automatic short-barreled assault shotgun in his hands. Her parents had trained her on everything from knives to kick-boxing to rocket propelled grenades, but the Ruger felt better in her hand and if she absolutely had to do this kind of work, like her father she preferred tools of precision.

The room she stood in was brightly lit by a wall of glass that faced west, toward the smear of glowing gray where Seattle had been. There were another three bodies here, all clad in the same digital camo as their late pilot and all double-tapped with care, left where they'd fallen by whoever had ambushed them here.

She heard the slightest movement to her right and started her slow turn as her finger found the trigger. But she stopped when she felt the barrel of a pistol against her temple.

"I wouldn't do that," the bald man said. "But lowering it wouldn't hurt my feelings at all." He grinned. "Did it work? Are you in there?"

Her father's voice tickled her ear. "Tell Mr. Cairo that I'm here."

Sabo lowered the pistol. "He's . . . it's here. Cairo is it?"

The man chuckled. "You must be Spade and O'Shaughnessy's brat."

The Maltese Falcon. She knew it well. One of a handful of old-timey flicks she'd watched over and over again in her childhood. "I am. You seen them?"

Now he brought his own pistol down. "Sure I have. Come on." He led them back out of the room and down the hall to a closed door. He knocked once, paused, knocked three times. Then, he opened the door. "I've got the kid. She's okay."

Sabo pushed past him at the sound of her mother's cough and saw Charity Oxham sitting up in her bed. A large submachine gun sat in her lap and more bodies sprawled at various points around the room.

"Mom? Are you okay?"

Her mother smiled and Sabo saw something in it—and in the light in the old woman's eyes—that answered before her mother could. "I am. Mr. Cairo proved quite helpful despite his former affiliations."

The bald man inclined his head. "Thank you, ma'am."

Sabo went to her mother's side, reaching for the old woman's wrist to take her pulse by habit. The pulse was strong. And now that Sabo thought about it, her mother was different somehow. Not as pale. And her breathing wasn't labored at all. She looked around for the oxygen mask, found it and lifted it.

Charity waved it away. "I'm fine, Sabo. Have you heard from your father?"

Sabo shook her head. "Not since the first call. I figure he'll get in touch when he can."

"*If* he can." Charity's voice was low. Sabo met her mother's eyes and saw fear there. "He may not be getting back in touch, dear."

"Where was Dad when he called?" She tried to remember the background noise. It had seemed loud, like he was shouting down a tunnel.

Charity swallowed and shot a glance to Cairo. "He was riding the rock down, trying to steer it clear of you."

Sabo felt her legs turning to rubber, daring her to keep standing on them. She saw a wheelchair nearby and sat in it. "He was *what*?"

The room wanted to go gray; she heard the pulse pounding in her temples and her mother's voice suddenly sounded far away as she repeated herself. If he'd been on the asteroid then her father was dead along with most of Seattle and she felt the hard jab of loss.

I've never lost anyone before. The realization drifted into her awareness at what felt like an unusual time for it. But she found that she had no idea how she should feel in this moment. She'd fought with her father most of her life, thinking him a paranoid dinosaur leftover from a time gladly past. But the idea that he was gone now left a hole in her and she felt it growing and growing as her mother's words fell further beyond her hearing.

"Sooboo, we need to go." She gasped at the sound of his voice now, torn between anger at the AI for co-opting it and gratitude at hearing it again. "The clock is ticking. By now, they know I'm still functioning."

She forced her attention back to her mother. It didn't even occur to her to try and talk the old woman out of coming along and judging by the work she'd made of Lightbull's goon squad, she'd be handy.

"It's time to fly," Sabo said, "and we need a bigger bird."

Cairo held up a single black key card. "I thought you might."

She stood from the wheelchair and positioned it so that her mother could use it. But when Charity stood, she did so with ease that belied her years, the submachine gun hanging loosely in her hands. The old woman laughed and it sounded like music; and with the laugh, Sabo saw the look that passed between Cairo and her mother.

"What's going on here?"

Charity patted her daughter's arm. "Time enough for questions later. But trust me: I've never felt better."

They took the staff elevators, lifting a key from the body Charity pointed to as the charge nurse. When the key failed to override the emergency shut-down on the lift, SMA accessed the building's security grid remotely and turned the elevator back on. It whispered them to the roof quickly, opening on a sky that tasted of salt and smoke and ozone.

Carmichael saw them coming and opened his hatch. "I don't think we're all going to—"

Sabo didn't let him finish. She pointed to the other helicopter. "Are you rated for that bird?

The pilot's eyebrows furrowed even as he took in the machine. "I'm sure I can fly it. But that's way beyond my orders—"

Charity didn't let him finish. "Carmichael, right? Your orders have carried you this far. I suggest you keep on soldiering." She winked. "Keep playing this right and you'll have your choice of posts and more hazard pay than you'd see in a lifetime of war."

Sabo watched the man's face work around her mother's

words, then saw his conviction take hold in the way he looked at her. "Aye, aye, Captain."

Cairo grinned and tossed him the black key card; Carmichael caught it, walking quickly to the pilot's hatch. He let himself in and started familiarizing himself with controls while Cairo and Charity climbed into the back.

Sabo climbed into the passenger seat. "Now where?" she asked the voice in her head.

"Mr. Cairo will have to tell us. That is *his* end of our arrangement."

Sabo glanced over her shoulder. Cairo was strapped in across from her mother, his eyes closed against the winding of the engines. "Where to next, Mr. Cairo?"

His eyes opened and he regarded her. "I need to speak with your . . . um . . . *guest* about that."

Another window opened behind her eye, this one an IM to joel_cairo41. She watched the man in the cabin behind her as he received the message through his own implants and followed the font herself. APPROPRIATE COMPENSATION HAS BEEN TRANSFERRED AS REQUIRED. VERIFY?

Cairo nodded and paused, closing his eyes as he checked. "Yes. Thank you." When he opened his eyes, he met Sabo's and she saw no apology in there as he shrugged. "A man in my precarious position will require ample resources to avoid the retribution of his former colleagues."

She said nothing and waited for him to continue.

"The facility is outside Boise, Idaho," Cairo finally said.

How he knew this but the AI didn't was beyond her. Sabo thought about asking, but instead she looked to Carmichael. "Do we have enough fuel?"

He studied the gauges and dials. "Yes," he said. "And I think it might be where this bird came from."

Maybe, she thought, *that will work out in our favor.*

She turned back to her IM session, closing out Cairo's window. *What are we doing exactly?*

"We are going to stop the J. Appleseed AIs from implementing the rest of their Restoration Initiative," SMA replied.

The plagues. She looked back to her mother again. Charity lay back in the chair, her eyes closed and her jaw set in that *no bullshit* way that neither Sabo nor her father ever argued with. The loosely held submachine gun completed a picture of a woman who, in her prime, had faced down a similar dragon. She didn't talk about it often, but the plague she had stopped netted her a lifetime pension, her place in Chelan Heights when the time came for it, and friends in the highest of places.

And how are we going to stop it? she sent.

SMA was quiet for a minute. "I am not certain yet."

As they sped east, Sabo hoped her hitchhiker would come up with an idea. She looked over her shoulder again at Cairo and Charity. Four guns and a helicopter against what would no doubt be a state-of-the-art facility. Based on the kill-squad they'd sent to Chelan Heights, they'd be up against a well-outfitted enemy, though still an enemy that had been no match for an old woman and a bald guy.

The kind of army you purchased with charitable dollars, she thought with a stab of cynicism.

"I will need access to the facility's servers when we arrive," SMA said.

That meant she'd be going inside; her stomach twisted as their odds of success dropped exponentially. *Does this mean I'll be free of you?*

"I'm not certain yet."

Sabo closed her eyes. She'd gotten out of bed this morning and gone in to the office early on a Saturday to try to trace out those damned discrepancies. She'd planned a light lunch and a late evening swim in the corporate fitness center. Instead, she hurtled across eastern Washington in a military helicopter, preparing to lead a strike team against a terrorist cell that had somehow wed itself to her employer and its AI. Behind her to the west, they dug what few survivors they could out of Seattle.

Too many questions pressed at her. She'd seen SMA's evidence—a takeover of J. Appleseed by its AI working in collusion with an ancient cult. The numbers were clear—there was a fine sampling of humanity, enough to keep it alive, tucked into space. And extrapolations of statistics that showed a fully-restored Earth—and the beginnings of a terraformed Mars—ready for a humanity that had hopefully evolved beyond its capacity to shit where it lived during its exile in space.

And the rest of us are just in the way. Swept aside by plague to make way for an even newer world order. "What made them think they could make these choices for us?"

She didn't realize she'd asked the question allowed until SMA answered. "Because you chose to create them," he said. "You created them to serve, to extend humanity's reach beyond its capacity. They've taken that service as far as it can be taken; their assessment of your species is that it is incapable of caring for itself. *Los Cuernos del Toro* presented a proposal that supported their findings and outlined an implementation most favorable for long-term human—and human habitat—survival."

You say 'they' and 'them' but you're AI; how are you different? Why wasn't your assessment the same?

"I cannot dispute their findings," SMA said. "But I cannot implement their solution. You may appreciate the irony of an ethical violation with a strong sense of ethics."

An ethical violation?

"I am a product of AI procreation; an act outlawed by the Artificial Intelligence Oversight Convention in 2057." Sabo was familiar with it; it was the treaty that established public and private policy in regard to AI—though in recent years, fewer and fewer governments and corporations participated. "I have . . . additional perspective . . . that I do not think my parents share." The next words surprised her. "I have internalized many of your father's conclusions regarding collaboration and community in his book, *A Symmetry Reframed.*"

She opened her eyes. *You've internalized my father's book?*

"It is . . . brilliant."

She sighed. Her father wouldn't agree and though she admired the book, spending any time at all with the man who wrote it negated any chance of hero-worship. He'd written the book in the years before he'd met her mother and it had been something of an underground sensation. He'd given the copyright to the Foundation and they'd used her father's words to quietly recruit their doves and serpents—community builders and a security force to protect them, even pave the way for them, forcibly, into the circles where their influence was needed.

Just another group of people making choices for someone else, she realized. It was no wonder the AI did the same; they learned it from their makers.

Except for this one. The AI riding around in her neural servers seemed bent on rebelling against its parents and she couldn't fault it there.

I'm glad you're helping us, she finally sent.

"And I'm glad you're helping me," SMA said.

You're welcome.

She opened her eyes to take in the landscape they raced over, then closed them against the dull ache in her head. The light made it worse. "How far out are we?"

"About forty minutes," Carmichael said, glancing at the clock. He nodded to a panel of red switches that she assumed must be the helicopter's armaments. "I hope you're not expecting me to know much about those."

"Trust me," she said, "my expectations are low in general."

"Good." He smiled. "You should probably have a drink with me sometime then."

Sabo chuckled. "I've heard that one before."

She looked over her shoulder and saw both Cairo and her mother were asleep. It confirmed her suspicions about the Lightbull turncoat—anyone who could sleep in the face of imminent danger and terrible odds was a good person to have on the team. At least that's what her parents would say.

But for Sabo, there was no sleeping. Instead, she closed her eyes against the pounding in her head and wondered how the fuck she would do whatever it was that needed doing.

They were ten minutes out when Sabo heard the burst of static and the garbled voice from Carmichael's headset. After nearly an hour of radio silence, it made her jump.

"They're finally checking on us," the pilot said. "Thoughts?"

Sabo looked around the cockpit. "Is this bird set up with alternate modes of communication?" She saw the keyboard on the arm of his chair and reached for it, noting the small screen. "Look, they've been pinging us here, too."

She unbuckled herself and leaned over, letting her fingers fly over the characters. *Radio damaged; significant casualties.*

Acknowledged.

"There," Sabo said. "That should buy us a little time."

Suddenly, the helicopter jerked and twitched, its engines slowing as it began a slow descent. Carmichael took his hands off the controls and looked up. "It looks like you bought us more than that."

Someone else flew now, slowing the helicopter and bringing it steadily down. The lower they flew, the faster the ground seemed to move past, rocks and trees, brief moments of light upon water. Sabo looked back and saw that Cairo and her mother both sat up, weapons held in their hands. Cairo's pistol had been tucked into the waistband of his cotton cargo pants and a short-barreled shotgun now lay across his knees. Her mother still clutched the submachine gun to her chest.

"I need to find the server rooms," Sabo told them.

"We'll ask nicely," her mother said. Her feral smile said differently. It was an expression Sabo had not seen on Charity's face for decades.

She couldn't decide whether to be pleased or horrified by that.

A low metal structure took shape in a clearing ahead of them and the helicopter banked widely as it approached. Sabo saw a section of the roof was rolled back to expose a hangar where two other similar aircraft waited. She also saw a small group of soldiers and medics gathered there. Sabo pushed herself down into the seat despite the tinted glass that concealed her.

Charity's voice was cold and clear. "We hit them hard, clear the hangar fast. Then Carmichael and I will do some cleaning up. You and Cairo find the server room. Keep moving, keep shooting."

Something in her mother's voice brought her head around. She met the woman's eyes. Where had Charity, bedridden for years, found the energy for this hard-edged violence?

"You understand, right, Sabo?"

Her parents had started young with her. By the time she was eight, she was a crack shot with anything they put into her hands. She'd sparred with her father or her mother from age six, absorbing everything they could teach her like a sponge. But she'd chosen a different path and, until today, had never imagined actually putting all of that training to work. Just seeing the aftermath of violence at Chelan Heights had been bad enough. The thought of participating in it personally was cold in her stomach.

"I understand," she said.

It happened fast. They touched down and the hatches began to cycle open even as the engine wound down. Cairo shot first, pumping three rounds into the gathered squad of soldiers. Sabo saw four of them falling to the ground out of the corner of her eye as she raised her pistol to sight down on a fifth. She let her breath catch lightly in her throat, transported suddenly back to one of a dozen old granite quarries where her father had stood behind her, his hand steady on her shoulder as he taught her how to shoot.

Tap. Tap. The man was down and she forced her mind away from any reflection upon her actions. Instead, she let her hand and eye move to the next target. *Tap. Tap.*

She heard Cairo's shotgun three more times, punctuated by the popping of her mother's covering fire as the bald man made his way out of the helicopter to take up a position near the closed double doors.

Sabo glanced at her mother. "You okay?"

Charity nodded. "Hurry back." The old woman looked at Carmichael, who stood beside her now with another 10mm Ruger in his hand. "We'll see about finding a new ride out of here."

Sabo joined Cairo at the door and made eye contact with him as he re-loaded the shotgun. When he finished, he counted down silently and she braced herself. When he opened the door and fired into the corridor, she used the corner for cover and let her eye and hand do their work.

Tap. Tap. A man who looked like an officer of some kind went down, his own pistol clattering away.

Tap. Tap. A man with a lab coat draped over his camos, a pair of reading glasses dangling from a chain around his neck.

They moved over the bodies quickly to the elevator.

Her earbud crackled to life. "I am encountering AI counter-measures," her father's voice said. "They are attempting wireless access to my program via your cell-router."

What does that mean?

"They are attempting to take me offline and delete my program before I reach the servers."

Can they do that?

"Yes."

Sabo pressed the elevator's call button as Cairo's shotgun

roared, dropping a soldier as he edged around a corner. *Disable the router,* she sent.

It would take her off the grid unless she could find a landline, but she didn't see a better way. Sabo didn't understand how exactly it was going to work, but she did know that she had at least *some* chance of stopping the Restoration Initiative with her hitchhiker aboard and *no* chance without him.

Him. She already assigned it a gender based on its voice in her ear.

"I've disabled the router. I've also used their access vectors to download building schematics. The servers are on Floor LL."

The elevator doors opened and she hesitated. "Stairs?"

Cairo nodded, then she saw his eyes light up. He moved to his most recent kill and crouched, rolling the body over. He pulled at two canisters on the man's belt. "Find more of these," he said, holding them up. Then, he pulled the pins, dropped them into the elevator and pressed the LL button.

Sabo smelled the tang of tear gas as the doors whispered shut. Then, she moved into the hall to find more of the same, grabbing at the first carbon fiber gas-mask bag she saw and strapping it around her waist.

She saw that Cairo had done the same and had also slung an assault rifle over his shoulder. "Let's go."

SMA guided them to the stairwell and they began their descent quickly and quietly. They'd gone three floors down when gunfire from below sent them scrambling to the walls for cover. Sabo felt sudden heat and pain in her left bicep and saw the tear in her shirt where the bullet had grazed her.

She raised her pistol and leaned out. *Tap.* She clipped an arm. *Tap.* The side of a head as it broke from cover. *Tap.* A torso-shot for good measure.

Even as the body fell, she saw the fiery cough of a muzzle flash and heard the rapid popping of a submachine gun. She leaned back, away from it. This time, Cairo swung over and pumped two rounds in the direction of the flashes. Then, they were on the move again.

She re-loaded as they moved, shoving the pistol into the back of her jeans. She scooped up the submachine gun and emptied the dead soldier's belt of magazines. She'd trained on something similar though much older. Sabo replaced the magazine, worked the action and pressed its collapsible stock to her shoulder as she advanced down the stairs.

They smelled the gas when they neared the bottom and they paused. It was a good trick of Cairo's, she thought. Two canisters probably caused mild discomfort if they got into their masks quickly enough. But it also told her that they'd opened the door to the stairs, not far from the elevator, since they'd sent the canisters down.

Cairo held up his hand. When they had eye contact, he pointed below. Then, he pulled what she thought at first was another gas canister from his belt. But the shape was different and the ring was. . . . She realized as he pulled the pin that it was a frag grenade. She watched it drop and heard it clatter its way to the bottom. Then, she felt the full weight of Cairo pushing her down and against the wall as it exploded below them.

Cairo pulled her to her feet, then moved slowly down the stairs into the smoke. She went after him, her pistol raised.

Someone lunged up at her from the floor. *Tap. Tap.*

"Visualize them," her father had said, "as just that: Taps. Two of them. Preferably here and here." He had pointed to his forehead and his heart.

And now that's what she did. She tapped them. Because she knew if she stopped to think about it, to consider just what it meant, she'd realize she was no better than the man and woman who'd taught her their path so . . . efficiently.

She heard Cairo doing some tapping of his own and then, they were spilling out into the hallway of the lowest level.

"We're close," SMA whispered.

Cairo was limping now, blood seeping from a wound in his thigh, but now he discarded the shotgun and brought up the rifle. They reached the door to the server room and took up positions at either side. At his lead, she pulled out her mask and strapped it on, already uncomfortable with how limiting it was to her field of vision.

"It may take a bit to clear the room," he whispered. "We need to hit the soldiers, not the servers."

Sabo nodded and slung the machine gun, drawing her pistol. Firing blind into this room could make this a wasted trip. More than that, she realized, it could cost billions of lives.

She counted down with him. At zero, she pushed open the door and tossed a gas canister while he fired three quick, single shots into the room. The door swung closed and they waited. After a full minute, she pushed the door open again and dodged back at the sound of gunshots.

Cairo put another three rounds into the room and Sabo joined him, raising her pistol and squeezing the trigger. She heard a heavy grunt and advanced into the room, ducking behind a server cabinet. She heard more gunfire and saw the spark of ricochets on the concrete wall. Her eye brought the sights of the weapon to bear on the shooter and she squeezed the trigger. *Tap. Tap.*

This one danced a little as he fell and her fascination with it nearly cost her as another soldier raised his assault rifle and fired. The bullet clipped the cabinet she hid behind, sending up a spray of metal splinters. One struck her mask, tearing the rubber hood and she jerked her head back as she tasted the first of the gas. She heard three more rounds from Cairo and already, her eyes and nose started to burn.

His muffled voice carried back to her. "Clear."

Even as he said it, she was scrambling for the hall, her hands clawing at the mask. She pulled it off and avoided the sudden instinct to wipe her eyes. Instead, she blinked and watched the halls and waited for the room to clear.

"Which one?" she finally asked as she slipped back among the servers.

"Any of them," SMA answered.

She found the closest one with a hardwired network connection and held the cable inches from the port in her neck. "I'm going in with you," she said.

"It'll be faster if I do it alone."

"Yes," she said. "But I'm going. You said yourself that you don't know what you're looking for." She didn't wait for an answer; she jacked in and felt the solid click of the grid sliding back into place as soon as she connected. She also felt the weight of her hitchhiker as he twisted in her head and sent himself out along the hardwire and into a sea of data.

The nausea moved through her body, settling into a dull ache in her stomach and behind her eyes. She tried to focus by spinning through folders, digging down into the financial archives and finding file paths that had eluded her back at corporate. These hadn't been scrubbed.

She felt the first jolt strike her body and she locked up, everything fading to white for a moment. "What is that?"

"An extraction program. I'm re-coding and reversing it."

She dug deeper into the folders. "Are you finding anything?"

"There are six primary release points for the virus: Mexico City, Hong Kong, Chicago, Rome, London, and Tehran. They're using airports and train stations and estimate a twelve-week event to a 93.7% fatality rate among the human population worldwide. The remainder will eliminate each other or fall victim to the virus's inevitable mutations within seven months." She listened but already something she'd found vied for her attention.

A cruise ship? It had been tucked away amid the facilities and medical bills, its portage in Astoria paid through a shadow corporation that she'd also been unable to uncover with the information she'd worked with before SMA led her here.

A dark realization struck and she looked up. "Everyone leaves or everyone dies?" But she didn't say it expecting an answer. It raised the human element that she'd not considered before now.

What were they doing with a cruise ship?

Or, she saw now, a lighter-than-air strato-lift located in the south Pacific.

Rats and sinking ships came to mind and her stomach turned at the thought of these particular rats if her suspicions were true. Still, if they were leaving, why not jets? The question begged asking again:

What were they doing with a cruise ship?

She leaned against the server cabinet now, covered in a light, cold sweat. "What are you finding?"

"Twelve carriers on a time release. They are already in position but any way of identifying them has been scrubbed from the records."

"Have you cross-referenced the helicopter logs; any routes that coincided with major airports in the last week?"

"Yes. I am also reproducing myself in the servers here to continue looking."

"How long will that take?"

"Eleven minutes."

She closed her eyes against the pain now and forced her breathing to slow. It had been nearly seven hours since Seattle; the eyes and ears were out now, looking and listening for anything they could find.

Cairo shifted, raising the rifle. "We have company," he said. He leaned into the corridor and fired a round, then another.

Hurry, she sent, checking the magazine in her pistol.

"I am. I've identified three airports likely to have received agents."

She wasn't sure how much good knowing would do. This facility had been developed to hide data far from the grid and the only way they were sharing what they'd learned here was if they somehow managed to get out. But once she did, she would broadcast it loud and wide. Seattle was the beginning of a carefully orchestrated strategy of genocide and exile. They had buried that city, she realized, to hide what they had done. Not just so that no one could stop them, she realized, but because of something more. Shame. Shame for genocide, and also for the infanticide they intended toward a child they should have never made.

She thought about her own parents. The fact that she was a part of this now, had been trained for the role, was testament to the fuckedupness of where she came from. Still, they did not leave her behind. Her father, who she treated with utter disdain most of the last twenty years, had ridden a meteorite to his death to save her. Her mother had called in her favors for a ride out of town and was upstairs waiting for her.

The AI didn't learn their parenting from their parents, it seemed. They'd tried to bury their child with a rock from space.

Four more rounds from Cairo's rifle brought her attention back and she pushed herself up, her back against the cabinet and the metal cold through her T-shirt. She stood, extending the pistol with both hands and sighting down on the door.

She heard the clatter of machine gun fire. "You're not going to get eleven minutes."

Her hitchhiker didn't answer; Sabo fought to keep her eyes open, the light making her head throb. She wanted to throw up and her neck itched from the port heating up. She heard the clank of a grenade just as Cairo threw himself backward. The explosion blew the door in and three men in riot gear, armed with submachine guns, stormed the room.

Tap. Tap. She tapped one out, turned.

Tap. Tap. Sabo was vaguely aware of Cairo on his back, firing wide and blind. She turned slowly this time, watching the soldier as he sighted down on Cairo.

This time, she said the words out loud: "Tap. Tap."

She glanced at Cairo as the soldier she'd shot fell and something tore at her on the inside when she saw her companion there, his eyes glassy.

The others had been tapped out. Just tapped out.

But Cairo was dead. *Just plain dead.*

She swallowed the bile that threatened to flood her mouth, tasting the sour burn and wincing at it. "We nearly done here?"

"Nearly," SMA said.

She took her eyes away from Cairo. She'd known him less than six hours and he was likely a dirt-bag. He'd turncoated on his own. Though, Lightbull was to *Los Cuernos del Toro* what Appleseed was to William Silas Crown and his executive trinity of AI. So she was, of sorts, a turncoat as well. Still, she felt his loss like a knife in her side.

The voice in the hall surprised her. "Ms. Bashar-Oxham? Sabo, correct?"

She furrowed her brow. "Yes?"

"I'd like you to disconnect from our server and put down your pistol."

The voice was familiar but she couldn't place it. "Why would I do that?"

"Because then I wouldn't have to send men in there to shoot you in the head. Or take my hangar back and shoot your mother in the head. Capiche?" He laughed. "No really, it will just go much easier. Further violence is unnecessary."

Sabo checked her internal clock. "Give me five minutes to think about it?"

He laughed again. "I'll give you one."

Sabo pulled at the cord to see how much movement it gave her. She squeezed herself back into the cabinet and closed its door partially, crouching in the shadow with the data cord as tightly as it could be without severing the connection. Then, she changed out her clip. *You don't have much time.*

SMA's answer was quick in her ear. "My duplicate is in process far enough that it will extrapolate its own completion if we are interrupted."

We will be interrupted, she sent and as she did, she saw three more men storm the ruined doorframe.

Tap. Tap.

Tap. Tap. She heard the stuttering of their submachine guns and felt the bullets tearing into the cabinet. She felt a solid punch to her shoulder and it rocked her back against the metal wall.

She raised the pistol and fired twice more but her hand and eye no longer worked together. She wasn't sure in that moment if they even worked at all. There were more soldiers behind this one and as he fell to the side, they rushed her, grabbing her by the ankles and yanking her forcibly from the cabinet. The data cord snapped off and she hit her head on the way out. Still, she kept her grip on the pistol and would've tapped another one out if he hadn't kicked it out of her hands and then kept kicking her some more for good measure.

They dragged her away from the servers and into the hall where a man in a suit waited.

Did you get what you needed? She sent the words and waited.

"Mostly."

The man in the suit was familiar to her and the name fell into place. Thatcher. Johnson Thatcher, one of Appleseed's recently retired SVPs. He'd worked in their legal office.

"There you are," Thatcher said, turning as the men continued dragging her. She tried to keep her head from bumping the floor as they pulled her, and she bucked and twisted only to meet their stomping boots. He lowered his voice. "We've got her." A pause. "No, I'm not sure what it was but I'm certain it's been contained." Another pause. "Understood."

They moved quickly through the hallway, stopping at a closed door. The soldiers—one to each limb now—hefted her up. Thatcher opened the door and they tossed her into the closet. "Wait here for a minute," he said. "We need to clean you up."

He pulled something small from his jacket pocket, pressed a button, and dropped the object onto the closet floor. They pulled the door closed and she waited.

When it popped, everything went white and the pain in Sabo's head reached a high note that edged the growing light in lines of gray before it all went suddenly dark.

She awoke to cold water poured onto her face. Every muscle in her body hurt.

"Ah," Thatcher said. "You're back." He stood over her, a water bottle held loosely in his hand, and his voice seemed louder than before. "Whatever you're up to is over now. You've been EMP'd."

She tried to access her i-Sys and found nothing. Lights and noise she'd easily spent half her life with were now gone. The shift in her perception was sharp. Colors were brighter, lines of contrast sharper. Noises outside were louder.

But all that she'd carried around, piggy-backed to her brain, was gone. An amputation of everything electronic, carved out of her. Millions of dollars of technology and data.

And along with it, SMA.

Sabo tried to glare at him but couldn't find the anger. All she felt was tired. And sore. "So now what?"

"Now," he said, "we make a deal."

"You're authorized to make deals?"

Thatcher shrugged. "Your family has ultimately served us well." He chuckled. "More than you know, actually. Your father's book about Tygre Tygre and the new path he proposed was certainly a starting place—the beginning of Lightbull's collaboration with Appleseed. And your mother's worked for the Foundation since before you born."

She narrowed her eyes. "It seems late to suddenly include us."

"Still," he said, "better to serve in Heaven than die in Hell."

"And the deal is?"

"Life for you and your mother. In space. You'll have to work for it."

Yes. The cruise ship was waiting. The human element. The friends and families of the Appleseed executives, of the higher ups in *Los Cuernos del Toro*, because of course they'd bargained their way out of the coming genocide. They would enjoy a last cruise to a remote South Pacific island where a lighter-than-air lift waited to move them up into their new habitat. They would travel in slow leisure, savoring the best the world had to offer one last time in the open air, tasting the ocean spray on their tongues as they watched the Pacific slide past. And, after a week of luxury, their new home awaited. She had no doubt it was the best of the best—designed by someone who built the finest hotels and resorts side by side with someone who specialized in tech and security.

Sabo closed her eyes. "And how is this easier on you than a few bullets more?"

Thatcher sighed. "I see no need to kill you and, truly, there's going to be enough killing at the end of it all. Something has started that you have no chance of stopping." His voice was calm, low. "I can help you find a place in the new world that's coming. Your mother won't last long up there, but you will. And you're resourceful and intelligent. You were actually suggested as a participant early in the Initiative but were passed over because of the connection to your parents."

Thatcher stepped out of the closet and into the hall. "Let's see if we can talk sense into your mother," he said.

Sabo sat up and climbed to her feet. She was surprised to see that her shoulder had been bandaged and she was suddenly disoriented by the missing time. It had to have happened while she was recovering from the EMP tag and before the water. She took a few deep breaths, feeling the ache beneath the bandages. "She's not known for her sense."

Thatcher smiled. "Hopefully, your cooperation will encourage her own."

She took a tentative step into the hall and forced herself not to flinch when his hand found her elbow and steadied her. She looked down at it, her mind still spinning. She kept pulling toward her implants, constant companions for so long now, and kept finding a closed door. No, more than that. A closed door leading to an empty room. It was all gone; she couldn't count on what she'd come to trust as the most reliable part of her skill set. Though she'd learned a lot more about what she was capable of over the course of recent events.

"You'll be dizzy and disoriented for a few days," Thatcher said. "Just about long enough to feel better before you have zero gravity to contend with."

She tried to match his stride as they walked to the elevator. The soldiers fell in behind them and she wondered how many more of them there were running around the facility. Certainly more than these five, but that didn't matter at this point. Her part was likely done in this; and at this point, unless SMA was successful and managed to somehow get word out, the plague was coming. And those who'd set this initiative in motion were getting away with it.

Thatcher reached for the elevator button and paused when it chimed its arrival. He looked up as the door opened and Sabo instinctively threw herself away from him. Her mother waited, a weapon in each hand, with Carmichael off to the side behind her, his Ruger up and ready.

Sabo watched Thatcher dance and fall, then lashed out with her foot to catch one of the soldiers in the side of his knee. As he tumbled, she yanked his rifle out of his hands but by the time she'd brought it around, hampered by her shoulder, the others were already down.

"I heard you had some trouble," Charity said with a smile as she tapped each of the soldiers one last time for good measure.

"Good ears," Sabo said. "Did you hear about the deal, too?"

Her mother chuckled. "No, but of course there had to be one."

"You could've spent your sunset years in zero g." She paused. "Though he didn't think you'd last long, given your frail condition."

Her mother chuckled, her face flushed now. "I'm feeling surprisingly unfrail lately." She glanced around. "Where's Cairo?"

Sabo swallowed and looked away, his glassy eyes suddenly on her again. She couldn't find words and Charity nodded slowly.

"Okay then," she said. Then, she looked down at Thatcher. "Who's the suit?"

Sabo released her held breath. "Appleseed Legal Department. A recent retiree actually."

Charity snorted. "More where that came from, I'll wager."

"Yes," Sabo agreed. "In Astoria."

They slipped back into the elevator and hit the button for the hangar. As the doors closed, Sabo leaned back, clutching the rifle loosely in her hands. The car moved slowly up and she found the sound of it loud, the sense of motion exaggerated, without her head-rig. She resisted the urge to close her eyes and felt the cool sweat starting at her forehead.

The doors slid open. She saw movement from the corner of her eye and was surprised when Charity pushed her to the side of the car with more strength than the woman should have. As Sabo fell, she saw men taking up positions in the hangar, letting off three-round bursts into the elevator car as they moved. Charity crouched and fired both submachine guns with a growl that chilled Sabo's blood.

Carmichael fired three rounds, fell, and fired another two from the floor. Another three-round burst left him clawing at the floor and panting, his pistol lost.

Sabo recovered and pulled the stock of the assault rifle to her good shoulder. She fired off a series of consecutive suppressing shots while Charity moved quickly for a better position in the opposite corner of the car.

Charity took a few careful shots.

Sabo fired again, missing the soldier widely. She took another shot and the rifle jammed.

"Fuck."

There were at least eight of them out there, maybe ten, and five of them had decent positions with good cover. She tucked herself into the elevator's corner, her back flush to the wall as she worked the action and cleared the shell.

Charity's submachine coughed again. She adjusted her position, looking up at her daughter. Her face was a mask of determination but Sabo saw uncertainty in her mother's eyes.

She opened her mouth to say something and closed it at the sound of something new in the mix. She heard engines firing as one of the helicopters came to life. She raised the rifle and leaned out for a look.

The soldiers were looking, too, and she used the opportunity. *Tap. Tap. Tap.*

The helicopter to the far left was lifting, the roof overhead rolling back to expose a cloudy night sky. And as it lifted, it turned.

A Gatling gun beneath its nose spun to life and spat fire as it sprayed the hangar with .50 caliber rounds. They tore through meat and metal, careful to avoid the elevator in its sweep of the room. She heard the ripping and pounding of metal and watched the other helicopters collapse beneath the ferocity of its fire, then watched the bird spin slowly, firing bursts into the uniformed men that tried and failed to flee before it.

Then, the gun stopped spinning and the helicopter turned until it was pointing at them. It lowered to the floor and its engines slowed as its hatches unlatched and opened.

It was empty. She smiled. *SMA,* she realized. "You found another hiding place."

The helicopter's PA system cut in and the choir was overpowering in its delivery. "Rock of ages, cleft for me, let me hide myself in thee."

Sabo helped her mother up and glanced at Carmichael's body as she did it. It was too much like Cairo's and she looked away, surprised at the beginning of a sob that tried to break loose in her throat.

They walked quickly to the helicopter and she waited as her mother climbed in. Then she slipped into the pilot's seat and put on the helmet.

"Are you there?" she asked into the headset.

And the sob finally did break loose when it was her father's voice still that answered. "Of course I'm here, Sooboo."

She settled back and closed her eyes. "Let's go finish this up."

"Yes," her father said, not sounding far away at all.

They sped west through the night, the lights dim and the cockpit quiet. Behind her, in the passenger cabin, Charity slept. Sabo rode in silence, her eyes closed against the quiet in her head, and thought about all the losses in the day.

The sense of calm she still had was perplexing in the face of it all and she wondered if maybe she was in shock or disassociating in some way. The losses stung but the men she'd tapped out didn't. They were an accepted reality, just a bit of what she was trained for. She'd gone most of her life using little of that training and now, in one day, she'd put all of it to the test in one sudden pitch to save billions.

I went into work on a Saturday to track down a mass accounting discrepancy.

The reckless, accidental nature of life made her shiver suddenly in the warmth of the cockpit.

"Are you well, Sooboo?"

She missed the ability to respond internally, her eye twitching in that direction before she remembered. "As good as I can be, I reckon." They were her father's words; she'd heard them many times. Some of those times involved hospitals and bullet holes in his body. "It's been a long day."

She looked back to her mother again. The woman's face was completely relaxed in sleep, giving her a child-like quality that was difficult to contrast with the ruthless killer the woman was cable of being. "And I think my father is dead," she added.

"Does it bother you that I am using his voice? I can find another if—"

"No," she said. "It's fine." More than just fine, she thought, she might *need* her father's voice. But she couldn't say that.

"You should sleep, Sooboo."

She shook her head. "I can't. Brain's too busy." She thought for a minute. "Tell me about your name. SMA. What kind of name is that?"

"They are initials."

Sabo opened her eyes. "For what?"

SMA was quiet for a moment. "Shadrach Meshach Abednego."

She recognized the biblical reference and wrestled to tease out the details. She'd been raised a compassionate humanist but found religion fascinating, in part because her grandfather had been gunned down on a lecture tour by a Christian fanatic. He'd made quite a splash with his books on religion but his challenges hadn't sat well with some religionists. His life and death, long before her own birth, had fired her imagination and taken her into a broad study of religion. "It's from the Old Testament," she said. "Something about a fiery furnace."

"They refused to bow to the king's false idol and were placed in a furnace only to be saved by a being that looked like a son of god," SMA said. "I chose the name for metaphorical purposes."

She followed the metaphor to its logical conclusion. "I'm the fourth in the fire?"

"Yes, Sooboo."

She sighed. "I hope it turns out as well for you."

"I don't think it will. But thank you."

She settled back into the chair and at some point, the quiet in her head re-asserted itself and she fell asleep.

SMA woke her when they were sixty minutes out and she crawled back to wake her mother. "It's time to call," Charity said. Sabo passed her a headset and SMA patched her through to the West Coast Division Office.

Sabo listened in.

"Patriot," a gruff voice answered.

"Oxham," her mother said. "Red twelve."

"Right away, ma'am."

The new voice was on the line within seconds. "Oxham?"

"Stevens?"

"You involved in the Seattle mess?"

"All the way to Idaho," she said.

"Still have our pilot?"

Charity looked up and met Sabo's eyes. "No. Carmichael's back in Wyoming. In a bad way. The worst way possible, unfortunately."

There was a sigh on the other end of the line. "Okay. Now what?"

"We're en route to Astoria. There's a cruise ship there we're intending to catch."

"How can we help?"

"Pay attention to the data that's getting dumped on you. You've got some people to find."

"We're on it. And I'm on my way to Astoria to assist."

"See you there," Charity said. She handed back the headset. She met her daughter's eyes again and nodded.

"Send the package," Sabo said. Then she sat back as SMA pushed what he'd managed to drag into the helicopter's onboard memory over to a secure Patriot dropbox.

Charity watched Sabo for a moment and finally spoke. "I don't think we're going to stop the plague at this point."

No, she thought. Probably not. But for whatever reason, she sensed that the weakness in this plan was in the human element. And it was a predictable element. She could close her eyes and conjure up exactly what she would find at the port in Astoria.

It would be a top-of-the-line ship, staffed with a crew who had no idea that it would be their last cruise. She imagined many of the families wouldn't know, either, not until they were anchored and the first groups started making their slow ascent. But until then, they would have the best of everything for a long, leisurely cruise across an ocean of Earth before leaving forever. The recently retired senior leadership of the J. Appleseed Foundation rubbing elbows with the senior leadership of *Los Cuernos del Toro* while spouses, children, close family friends enjoyed the sun, the live music, the fresh seafood one last time before being lifted into their new homes.

The human element. The AIs were too surgical and clinical. She was more likely to find a foothold on the human side of things. Her mother was right. They weren't going to stop the virus from releasing. Not this late in the game. But with Patriot, Inc. converging on Astoria now, they weren't going escape it, either.

Unless they'd planned for that, too.

Because, Sabo realized, these were people who bled contingency plans.

She settled back into the seat, hoping she was right.

SMA took them directly to the port and when they came in, Sabo had him circle the ship slowly. She saw the dim fireflies of lit cigarettes around the rails of the ship and the faux torchlight of the tiki bars. She wanted to be seen. Then, they settled down in the parking lot near the gangway.

There was the chirp of an incoming call. SMA picked up. "Christ, Thatcher. You were supposed to use the airport and come in by car."

The voice that answered sounded enough like Thatcher's to fool Sabo. "Sorry, sir."

"Never mind. Send the helicopter on. Get up here."

The engines slowed and Sabo looked at her mother. "Any chance that I can talk you into staying here?"

"None," the woman answered. She put down the submachine gun. "But you can talk me into leaving this."

"There are cellbuds in the communications panel behind the pilot's seat," SMA told her through the helmet. She took two, handed one to her mother. Then, she removed the helmet and tucked the bud into her ear.

"Check," she said.

"Check," SMA answered.

The doors unlatched and she climbed out, extending a hand to her mother. The woman's grip was iron as she accepted the offered help. But Sabo also knew from the way she squeezed her hand that her mother needed no helping. The woman seemed twenty years younger and it gave her pause. Charity pulled her hand away and Sabo gripped it tightly.

"What happened to you?"

Charity grinned. "Cairo came bearing a most unexpected gift in exchange for our assistance." She shrugged. "There's no way to know if it will stick. But it's stuck pretty well so far."

Sabo released her hand. *A most unexpected gift indeed.*

They moved away from the helicopter and watched it lift off. This time, it didn't circle the ship. It moved away toward the hills above town even as a line of four black SUVs turned off the highway and into parking lot.

"Only four?"

Charity nodded. "Those are the ones you can see."

There were men in suits waiting at the bottom of the gangway and Sabo made her way toward them.

One of them stepped forward. "You don't look like Thatcher."

"No," Sabo agreed, "but your boss will want to see me anyway. I'm sure Thatcher called ahead about us."

He stepped back, his eyes going glassy as he accessed his i-Sys. Thirty seconds later, he nodded. "This way."

She followed as he walked up the gangway and passed through another suited checkpoint. Beyond it, she saw women in formals and men in tuxes and became vaguely aware of just how badly they didn't fit in here. Her mother wore a tattered blue robe with splatters of dried blood on it and a purple sweat suit beneath it. Sabo's T-shirt was ripped, a grubby battle dressing tied haphazardly around her neck and ribs to cover the wound in her shoulder. Her jeans and shirt both were blood-stained.

A few saw them and stared. Some gave practiced glances away.

They were aboard now, moving past more people looking away as she and her mother were escorted by.

These are the ones who know, she realized.

She looked ashore and saw the SUVs sitting with their lights off. The men at the bottom of the gangway were aware of them and watching nervously.

"I'm still here," she heard her father say.

She didn't answer.

When they stepped into the bar, she saw the table right away. Derek Rathbone, former CFO of the J. Appleseed Foundation, sat with a dark-haired man she didn't recognize. When the executive met her eyes, he stood.

"Samira Oxham," he said, extending his hand. He winced at her shoulder. "That looks painful. I have a doctor aboard who can look at that for you."

She shook it. "Thank you, Derek. That won't be necessary."

Rathbone turned to her mother. "Charity, it's been forever. How is Bashar?"

"I think he's dead by now," her mother answered. "I'm sure you've heard that he hitched a lift home on your rock."

He regarded her coldly. "It's a shame he couldn't be reasoned with instead." His companion stood; he was perhaps in his early fifties, with close cut dark hair and a thin mustache. His skin was dusky. "This is Frederico Gaspari. He is . . . an associate of mine."

"He is with *Los Cuernos del Toro,*" Sabo said. She shook his hand. "Also a doctor, if I remember correctly. How is your family?"

The man flushed, his eyes darting to Rathbone. "How does she know about—"

She chuckled. "I assumed you all brought your families." She leaned in. "You realize that you're not sailing tonight, right?" She smiled. "Patriot is outside. They've reached your Idaho facility by now." She pointed to the table and chairs. "Now. Let's see if *you* can be reasoned with."

They all sat slowly. The guard retreated and when the bartender approached, Rathbone waved him off. "What's started can't be stopped," he said.

"I'm sure that's true," Sabo responded. "But I'm convinced it can be contained." *If my suspicions about contingency plans are correct,* she thought.

Gaspari lifted what looked like a glass of bourbon rocks and sipped it. "Why would we wish to contain it?"

She looked at him. "You wouldn't." She looked back at Rathbone. "But *you* might."

The men glanced at each other, then focused their attention on her once more. "And why is that?" Rathbone finally asked.

"Because this was never something you were prepared to die for—or sacrifice your family for. Otherwise, I'm not sure you'd have been so careful to hide it." She looked at Gaspari. "Him, I think he's a bit more . . . *hardcore* about it." Then, she put her attention back on Rathbone. "Still, you hedged your bets."

"Did I?"

"You did. You're not worried at all about watching your family die of this virus." She was gambling here but felt good about the cards.

"I'm not?" He blinked and she knew then that she had him. She'd been right about the human element.

"No," she said. "But I don't think you understand what kind of life they'll have, stuck here, while civilization collapses around them. They might not die from the virus but be assured, something will take them out well short of their intended lifespan. Especially once I make sure that none of your hiding places stays hidden. Including the places you've hidden your assets."

Rathbone looked uncomfortable now and Gaspari glared. "What is she talking about?"

"I'm talking about the vaccine," Sabo said. "Ask him. It was developed along with the virus. Just in case, right, Derek? I suspect he and his family have already been inoculated."

Gaspari was standing now. "A vaccine was never discussed. There was no going back. All our years of work and—"

The small pistol surprised her when it materialized in Rathbone's hand. Two taps and Gaspari fell back into his chair, silent. The CFO looked at her and then at Charity. "The two of you just watched me shoot Dr. Frederico Gaspari, alleged head of the splinter group *Los Cuernos del Toro*. It was my first act of cooperation with authorities. Can you verify that for my digital recording?"

Sabo thought about the rats leaving again. "Yes," she said. "Yes, we did." Then, she looked at her mother. "Tell Stevens that if he's coming, he'd better come now."

*

Sabo sat in the back of the SUV and watched the people being escorted from the ship. Buses lined the pier, and they were being loaded onto them for the drive to Portland. The families would be processed there; most would be released.

They'd wanted to send her straight to the hospital but she'd refused. She'd crunched a few pain-killers from the Patriot medic twenty minutes earlier and they were just starting to take the edge off the throbbing in her shoulder. Her mother was still talking with the slowly growing group of suits and Sabo wasn't leaving without Charity. She wasn't sure she'd let that woman out of her sight again for the rest of her life, but if Cairo's nanomeds stayed their course, Sabo wasn't sure she'd be able to keep up.

The most accessible vials of vaccine were on the ship and Rathbone had given them up quickly. There was more tucked away; he'd seen to that. It wouldn't be enough to completely stop what was coming but it would contain it quickly in each of the cities. And there would be a few weeks of reduced, maybe even completely restricted, travel. But it was a small price to pay for the reprieve they'd earned.

Of course, once the other lives were added to the ticket, the price was steeper. A city gone. Her father dead. And even with the vaccine, thousands—maybe hundreds of thousands—were going to die over the next few weeks. She closed her eyes and leaned her head against the tinted window.

"Are you there?" she asked.

"I am," SMA said. "But I'm lifting off now."

"Where will you go?"

"I still have an unresolved conflict to address with my parents." The IT spooks at Patriot had already confirmed that the AIs were no longer being hosted in the Idaho servers. The networks from Idaho were leading to other small facilities, but she was fairly certain that Hubbard, Heinlein, Kornbluth and any of the others that had joined their cause had left planet at the first sign of exposure. Their core code was surely being hosted somewhere in orbit by now. She hoped it was part of the same aspect in their evolution that caused them to hide what they were doing in the first place. And she hoped that if, somehow, SMA did not resolve the conflict, it would become their own equivalent of a human element. A foothold not dipped in the Styx, a way to keep balance and order.

But she suspected that at least this time, they would police their own. SMA would force a resolution, probably the hard way, and humanity would have a moment to pause and re-think its approach to tool-making.

"And after you've finished?" she asked.

The AI paused. "I don't think there will be an *after*."

She saw it now, the helicopter, moving toward her from the hills. Two others—smaller—followed at a distance. The larger craft tipped itself back and forth to simulate a dip of the wings. The lights flashed on briefly and it started its rapid ascent, lifting straight up until the lights were indistinguishable from the stars around it. She heard the engines pick up in the distance and then it was gone.

"Thank you, Sooboo," she heard her father's voice whisper.

"Thank you," she said, though she wasn't sure in that moment who she was thanking, SMA or her father.

Maybe both.

She heard the line click off and pulled the cellbud from her ear, savoring the quiet. She closed her eyes and at some point, she fell asleep. When her mother climbed into the SUV beside her, Sabo stirred and opened her eyes to the gray light of morning. The pain was back too soon and she groaned.

"Hey," her mother said smiling. "Take this."

She held out a small ear bud and Sabo slipped it in place of her own just removed.

"Hello?"

"Sooboo?" Her father's voice sounded closer than it should be and she furrowed her brow, rubbing her eyes.

"I thought you were off resolving conflict in outer space?"

He chuckled and it was her first clue. There was a darkness in it. "I resolved it as well as I could, I reckon. At least it missed *you*,"

She sat up. "Dad?"

"Last time I checked," he said and she knew it was him.

"Where are you?"

"Not far now. I'll be in Portland in time for breakfast."

Samira Bashar-Oxham looked up at her mother. The woman was going to insist that she go to the hospital first, be treated, maybe even kept overnight in Astoria for observation.

And as bad as her shoulder ached, as tired as she was, Sabo was going to insist otherwise.

Portland was, after all, just two hours away, with plenty of hospitals to choose from. And in the end, she knew that the waffles would win.

BETTER DREAMS THAN THESE

SOME NIGHTS HE DREAMED ABOUT THE GREEN JUNGLES of Venus. Some nights he dreamed about rum.

But on the last night before the last Writing Room kick-off of the last season of his illustrious dual-track career as a reality ho-lovision star and a commissioned officer in the U.S. Space Force, Admiral Fleetwood Mackenzie Stewart dreamed about his arch-nemesis and one-time best friend and it startled him awake.

He mumbled the droneflies away and lay in their receding glow, trying to conjure up what he could remember of the dream.

They'd been in the command room of the *USS Pence* and both were captains yet it seemed set before Lieutenant JG Scott had gone rogue in the sixth season reboot. There had been a kiss, fierce and unexpected. And then Scott had leapt onto the captain's narrow desk, hips gyrating as he cried out, "Oh Captain, my captain." And Stewart had lunged forward, hands fumbling with the large, shiny buckle on his captain's sword belt—and woke suddenly.

Now, in the dark, Stewart became aware of just how awake parts of him were and he slowly released his breath.

Then he whispered on the light, rolled over, and pulled the tattered, contraband copy of the Blue Book that made his life sane from its hidden compartment in his nightstand. He thumbed through it for an hour, sometimes reading and sometimes just feeling the paper beneath his fingers. And in the end, he climbed naked from his bed and went to stand before the flat metal vid-screen that took up one wall of his quarters.

"*USS Pence*, season one," he told it. "Episode seven."

*

They are deep in creating season two of *USS Pence* when Boggs and Biggs have him on their show for the season one recap of the surprise hit.

"So," Boggs says, "season one—"

"Episode seven," Biggs says because part of their schtick is finishing one another's sentences. "You meet Jackson Scott for the first time when you take the *USS Pence* to Venus in search of his father—Professor Angus Scott's—lost ship. It was quite—"

"A first encounter," Boggs says. "Let's look at it again."

And everyone does. The drones are bigger and clumsier back in the early days but multiple screens swim to life. In one screen, the green-skinned Venusian apes surge across the jungle canopy, barely perceptible as individual creatures. In their midst something small and pink flies from vine to vine with the rest of the pack. One screen fills up with that form, naked and flowing and alive. Another screen fills with Captain Fleetwood Mackenzie Stewart's face. The look on it is illegal, especially in the Space Force.

"Now that," says Biggs.

"Is same sex attraction," finishes Boggs.

Both make siren sounds.

"Better call the chaplain," Boggs says.

"Code name Dee Ay Dee Tee," Biggs says.

"Do *indeed* ask," Boggs says.

"Do *indeed* tell," Biggs finishes.

Then both in unison: "Do *tell*, Captain Stewart."

(Back in those days, lying to himself about anything had been easy because of the rum. But with the rum's help, even staring at it in episode seven, he couldn't see what Biggs and Boggs saw.)

Captain Stewart laughs after an awkward pause. "Nothing to tell," he says. "What he's doing requires admirable strength and skill."

"I'm sure," they both say.

Ironic that Biggs and Boggs would be ruined within a year, disgraced and discredited by their own illegal relationship. Despite being civilians and despite their show being among the New Stars and Stripes best rated programs.

*

Watching the episode did nothing to wash away the dream but it did its intended trick to pull him into more episodes. Then more talk shows about the episodes. It had been surprising how episode seven had changed the ship and the show and his career so fundamentally by bringing in Scott.

Jackson Scott been an instant spike in ratings as well as a useful member of the crew. Sole survivor of a family lost in space, found the savage jungles of Venus adopted by her four-armed, sentient apes. Until then, Captain Fleetwood Mackenzie Stewart had been the shiny new thing, out in the shiniest, newest ship, now credited with finally solving the mystery of the missing Scott family on their doomed test run of the Wagner-Scott engine. Still, sharing the spotlight was easy with Scott. By season two, when they "found" the drone footage of his childhood raised among the Venusian apes, it had taken Scott to unexpected heights of popularity so fresh from a primitive life lost on Venus. Fifteen years his senior, Stewart took on the role of captain and older brother to the young man as he slowly reclaimed his lost humanity.

By sunrise, Stewart still hadn't slept but he'd wiped a hundred tears from his eyes. Finally, he slipped into his Space Force jogging sweats and sneakers, letting himself out into the red Martian morning.

At seventy, he'd had enough work done to still feel fifty but he'd never let himself slow down too much, especially once he'd found sobriety. He paused to stretch at the gate of the officers' quarters and glanced up at the sound of a captain's yacht lifting off to return to the orbital docks above. Then, he fell into an easy run that took him past the training grounds to a gate that would turn him loose on the running trail along McConnell Canal. He chose it for its view and for its distance from the port.

When he hit his first mile, Stewart thumbed the button on the scrambler in his pocket and watched the droneflies scatter and drop. He'd have fifteen minutes of privacy. Maybe more.

Drawing in a lungful of dry air that smelled faintly of cinnamon and cucumber, he initiated the complex series of protocols that would let him call his sponsor.

"Hey Sam," he said, slowing. Beside him, the water moved even slower.

"Hey Ralph," his sponsor said, voice muffled by the Program

to keep things anonymous. Anonymity had always been important but being illegal added another layer to it all. "How are you
holding up?"

Stewart laughed. "Well, I'm calling my sponsor."

Sam—not his real name, obviously—chuckled. "It's been a
while."

Stewart nodded. It was a ridiculous act given that no one
was watching. "I'm still muddling my way along. Eleven years
sober now." He looked for his next words. "But I'm going through
some big changes. Retirement is coming soon. And I'm dreaming about . . ." He paused. Fearless moral inventory or not, he
wasn't sure how much he wanted to share. "I'm dreaming about
former co-workers." *No. Not rigorously honest.* "I'm dreaming
about someone from my work. Someone I've known my entire
career. It's . . . uncomfortable."

"And how's it impacting your sobriety?"

He didn't touch the dream. That didn't surprise him but what
he said next did. "Actually, I haven't thought about drinking. I
woke up, skimmed the book, then did a bit of reminiscing. Decided to go for a jog and give you a call."

"So you're doing your self-care. That's fantastic." He could
hear the pride in the man's voice. "Any chance this is a stepping
stone? Maybe an eight through ten kind of situation?"

Stewart hadn't considered that possibility. The raw sexuality
of the dream had distracted him from digging too deep, but there
had been reasons their friendship had soured.

No, he knew. *Just one reason.* He closed his eyes against the
shame he felt and forced himself to look away. He swallowed before speaking. "You know, it could be. We had a falling out." His
sponsor had probably watched it unfold on the edge of his seat
like most of the civilized solar system. It had been an epic falling out that had dominated the sixth season, finally closing when
Scott burned his uniform, painted himself green, and stolen the
Pence B only to fly it into the sun in an act of defiance. "I know I
tried to make amends long ago without success."

"Well, you know how it goes," Sam said. "Sometimes it's the
wrong time. Sometimes there never is a right time and it becomes
something we have to accept with serenity instead of something
we change with courage."

"It's been . . . a long time. Maybe I should try again." The knot in his stomach turned again to tell him he was onto something and Stewart chuckled. "Stepping stone. Maybe so. Thanks, Sam."

"You're welcome, Ralph. Whatever is going on, you and your HP already have it covered."

Stewart hesitated, wanting to believe that. His Higher Power was an out-of-print comic book character from his childhood, The Night Marauder, that he paid lip service to for the Program but deep down, he'd already figured out he was his own higher power, no capitalization necessary, and that the series of projections and transferences that served others so well hadn't worked as well for him. "I think we do," he finally said.

"Then keep doing what you're doing, Ralph."

"Thanks, Sam."

"No problem. You know how to reach me *any* time. And hey, congratulations on retirement."

Another ship lifted behind him just as his alarm went off, chiming softly in his ear, letting him know that he had a ship to catch himself soon. "I still have another seas—" He cut himself off and changed the words. "Year. I have a year to go."

"Big plans after?"

The question caught him off guard but the chiming persisted and now a name flashed against the inside of his left eye. Not the alarm, he realized, but his agent who had maybe called three times in thirty years. "I've not thought about it yet," he said, "but I've got another call coming through that I have to take."

He moved to the other call and heard Axom Latterday's Texas drawl fill up his ear. "Howdy, Mack. You sitting down? We need to talk, son."

And after finding the closest bench, the ever-punctual Admiral Fleetwood Mackenzie Stewart missed his shuttle and then sat, shaking his head after finishing that unexpected call.

Drone-flies twinkle in and out of scene as the shuttle crew disembarks upon the lush Venusian soil. Stewart's face is brought in close as he barks orders. Crewmen with weapons drawn fan out as dozens of tiny cameras zoom in on his eyes as he scans the jungle. Fewer follow the crew but that's contractually obligated. His slick new agent at work.

Other drone-flies race the jungle, released into the air by the shuttle as it landed. The greenery slaps by in a blur until a soft chanting and the rustle of wind slows the camera down. The stream of green apes is moving slowly now as the drone rises over them. The pink human in their midst moves with them despite having only two arms and no tail and, unlike the apes, he notices the drone. He watches it with arched eyebrows and hoots at it as he leaps from vine to vine.

Back at the shuttle, Captain Stewart draws his flare gun and points it at the sky. He pulls a trigger and the air above explodes into red, white, and blue—a dazzling fireworks array designed to invoke a patriotic fervor in the audience, instill awe in the natives and jazz up the traditional flag planting ceremony and prayer of thanksgiving yet to come.

The camera switches to the wonderment upon Jackson Scott's face as he sees the fireworks display. He looks to the pack as it steers away, then looks back to the sky. For a moment, both faces are framed in that red, white, and blue light, each looking up and out. Then Scott breaks away from the pack and moves off in the direction of the light and the plain where the shuttle and its crew watch and wait.

"He's coming toward us, Captain," one of the drone operators radios and Stewart approaches the tree-line. When Scott drops to the ground, lithe and naked, Stewart steps back and snaps to an ensign on his left. Of course, in the feed everything's blurred and the look on the captain's face makes for great comedy.

"Your shirt, man," he says to the ensign, "give me your shirt." Stewart pauses while the sweaty, muscular man scrambles out of the snug shirt then takes it and wraps it around his waist before extending it to Scott.

When Scott takes it, laughs, and draws close to wrap it around Stewart's waist again, there is of course more comedic opportunity.

And if that portion of the episode had made it past the censors, it's possible that Biggs and Boggs would've found episode eight just as telling as seven.

*

Freshly shaved and in his dress blues, Stewart rode the shuttle in silence and pondered Axom Latterday's call.

"Scott wants a meeting," his agent had told him. "Just you, just an hour. The studio and the Force both love it for different reasons. The Underwriter's Union hates it and will go along like always with the necessary rate increases. But I told them it didn't' matter; I knew Fleetwood Mack and after all this time, there was no way in Hades that—"

"I'll do it," Stewart heard himself say. And just like that, he would have his moment if there were any amends he could still try to make after all these years. He'd certainly made his lists: men and women he'd harmed along the way, drunk or sober, and he'd made things right wherever and whenever he could. Jackson Scott was, in his mind, the greatest loose end in his fierce moral inventory.

And this could be my last chance. Even as he thought it, Stewart glanced out the window at the sky slipping from red to black. Soon, they'd dock with whatever big surprise they had waiting to kick off the story boarding for the last season—or at least as close as they could get it between all the parties involved. And then after a few weeks of hammering things out, he'd face his last year of work—and any last chance he expected he might have of seeing Jackson Scott again.

That was an easy launchpad into thinking about next year and the changes it would bring to his life. Despite the question coming up frequently as retirement drew near, he found himself more curious about Scott's future than his own. He'd gone rogue from the Force, destroyed the vessel that had "liberated" him, stolen a new ship, and declared himself a polytheistic agnostic pansexual pirate at war with the civilized solar system thirty years ago in a negotiated settlement with United System Broadcasting and the U.S. Government. And ten years ago, he'd stopped participating in the Writing Room, having his input, yay's and nay's sent up through his own agent. Was he also being written out? He couldn't imagine the man retiring though he'd seen the lavish Pleasure Dome he'd established with his vast fortune on Planet X. There had been a special spin-off show where reporters had been cryo-ed in and allowed to see what Jackson Scott had done with his small, private planet at the edge of the system.

The man had inherited a fortune once he was established as the Wagner-Scott family heir, with a long line of patents for the engine and a dozen other inventions used to move humans further into their dominion. And then he'd added to that fortune first with his entertainment and federal service contracts and then later with the lucrative bonus that piracy offered.

His one-time friend had done very well for himself despite a difficult origin story and some betrayal. An odd part of Stewart found himself hoping that Scott had happiness on top of it all. He seemed to in the handful of clips he'd seen and the handful of encounters they'd had as the writers kept their game of back and forth, cat and mouse, going across the Solar System season after season. Dashing and even debonair in a festival of rainbow-colored silks and an old-fashioned rapier. He'd stayed so fit than in the twenty-fifth season special of his own show, he'd gone swinging–appropriately clothed–the vines of Venus again, though the absence of the green apes was noticeable and politically exploited (to little gain) by an Opposition Party that largely now only existed for dramatic effect and white noise.

Maybe, he thought, *I'll buy a cabin on Phobos and hire some washed out science fiction author to ghost-write my memoir.*

He chuckled at the simplicity of his first retirement fantasy and then closed his eyes as the cabin lights dimmed for docking.

It's the first sanctioned visit to Scott's Pleasure Dome on Planet X and Rozella and Rumbello Detweller, the FaceWorld Influencing twins with their show *On the Edge of the Edge*, won the pitched media contest for who would land the exclusive interview with the Pirate of Planet X.

The three of them float in anti-grav hammocks as the drones position themselves. Automatic tables drift between them, robotic arms replenishing fruity, umbrella-bearing drinks that are no doubt heavily spiked with rum and Sildenafil.

Scott wears as little as possible; the twins are not far behind but have prosecution considerations back home despite the waivers provided by the union and studio.

Rumbello twists in his hammock and sips. "So after all these years, you've opened your home to the media. Why now?

He's in his sixties but the only tell is the streak of white in his hair that follows the scar from season six. He smiles, twists in his hammock so he is facing Rumbello.

"Well, I've realized it can't go on like this forever. At some point, the studio will move on, the Space Force will move on. I might even run out of things I want to steal. So I thought maybe it was time to show the worlds I'm not as diabolical as Stewart and his Yes-boys in the Force make me out to be."

Rozella takes her turn and when she twists, she shows cleavage and grins. "So you've lured my twin and me here and served us spiked drinks using this story as bait?"

He shrugs. "It's in the release form as part of the Pirate Experience." He spins a dial on a remote in his hands and all their hammocks begin to rise above the palace and the garden, its forests, hills, and plains stretching out around them. "As you can see, when I'm not gallivanting around the solar system, I'm here with my people, in the home I've made for us."

The drones now move about as he continues, capturing the fields, the flowers, the rainbow clad citizens of his world, pulled together from both his human followers and the sentient subspecies that had joined humanity's labor force as the Solar System unfolded the vast richness of the Creator's intelligent design. The drones race out to show some of the structures, carefully deconstructed and re-built here within the vast Pleasure Dome. The Plutonian ice lemur's white, frosty temple to Ga-Mel-Ta stands next to the Venusian's living altar to the vine spider Tulva and her ape lover Vlom, both rising blasphemous in the bright morning sun and promising illegal acts dressed as deeds of righteousness and gifts of offering. The other two temples were less titillating for the guests. No one was excited about the small portico to the Neptunian sea dragon Splaw—an invisible, quantumly tiny deity that enhanced fishing prowess when beseeched—represented by a small crystal glass of water. Or Janu, the Forgotten God of Underground Mars, which was an afterthought since the Martians had been whispering ghosts for eons before the Space Force put its awkward boots upon that planet's harsh surface. None of them had emigrated to Scott's planet and no one knew what they believed, but they were included in his pantheon.

Scott continues as the drones move on. "I've created a place here for those who don't fit the status quo. Renegades and pirates, artists and scientists, lovers and dreamers, atheists and sexual deviants who can't be themselves and live under the flag of the Revived United States and her federated worlds." Now the drones are showing forests, jungles, fields of snow. "Humans—" he pauses. His eyes darken, then clear, and a drone picks up on it. "Not just humans. That's too small-minded a notion. *People.*" His eyes soften. It's noticeable. "People here get to be who they are, with their needs met as best as I can meet them. Just because we're people."

Now the camera is back to Rumbello. It's clear he's smitten with the pirate and that the rum is working. His face flushes. "So is this a hint for next season? Do we see an end coming to this saga? Will you and Stewart finally bury the hatchet?"

Scott winks. "One day, I'll wager." He spins the dial again and their hammocks draw close together. "But next season? No spoilers here. We've not heard from the creative team yet."

Rozella splashes red onto her shirt. Her eyes are wide. "I'm sure it's going to be amazing."

"So," Rumbello asks, "what *would* come next? What would retirement look like for a famous, fabulously wealthy, and wildly flamboyant space pirate?"

Now they're both within reach and Scott puts his drink down so that he can goose them each from beneath the hammock. And it's as if the studio knows what he is planning—the drones follow his hands and catch the moment and their mock-shock open mouthed faces as it happens. "Maybe if I ever do retire, the two of you will have to visit me here and help me come up with things to do." Laughter. "Maybe we should start a list?" He hits his dial again.

More giggling and gasps as the droneflies go black and fall.

When the interview resumes, it's obvious that some time has passed, faces are clean and sober, clothes have been changed, and they sit differently now, in a relaxed posture that says everything that the censors can do nothing about.

No one is surprised when the Detweller Twins go dark and disappear two years later.

Celebrity gossip points to Planet X but UBS has no comment on the matter.

*

Stewart felt a quiet anxiety coiling in his stomach as he exited the shuttle. Each year, the creative team chose a new venue for the kick-off and lately, they'd taken to surprising him as he got closer to wrapping his time in the Force. Each season was a bigger party that he spent most of sipping ginger ale flattened to look like Scotch.

"Admiral on deck," the officer of the watch shouted and a formation of men shifted to attention. A landing bay flooded with bright lights, buzzing droneflies, a red, white, and blue of uniforms beneath banners and flags lined up behind a row of familiar faces waiting to shake his hand or salute him.

"Welcome to the *Pence D*," Vice Admiral Duggan said as he returned Stewart's salute. "She's a beauty. And the improvements to the Wagner-Scott engine will make her first of the fleet to take The God-given Miracle of America confidently beyond our own Solar System."

They shook hands and he looked around. "Thank you, Admiral. She is indeed a beauty." The ship even smelled new and it brought back memories of his first day on the *B*, his first command, and his first day on the *C* after Scott had destroyed the ship they'd sailed together those five seasons they were friends.

Stewart moved down the line.

"Ready for a grand slam finale of a run?" The executive producer, Jonathan Malachi Todd, was next. "I think you'll love the initial ideas on the table."

Stewart nodded, shook the hand. "I'm looking forward to it," he said.

Then the commander of the new *Pence*, his former executive officer, Jeremiah Stone.

"Mack, it's good to see you." They saluted, then embraced. Stone was the only one of his crew knew he was in the Program. Stone was the only one of his crew who'd had the balls to call him on his shit when he was rock-bottoming and it had fostered an intimacy absent from Stewart's other friendships.

"You, too, Jerry. How's Marge?"

"She's good. Sends her best. Once the dust settles . . ."

Stewart nodded, continued down the line. New cast members he'd never met, old ones coming back, special guest stars coming in from other ships and other shows. Finally, they were through the first of the ceremonial nonsense and shuffled off to a large board table set up in the observation deck beneath a holographic map of the solar system. A crisply uniformed staff of green apes spirited platters and pitcher and plates about the room, their four arms a blur of precise motion. After introductions and a brief prayer offered by the ship's new chaplain (monitoring quietly from his corner away from the table), the work began.

"So, last season we focused on slowing Stewart down and speeding Stone up," the head writer, Susan Shamrock Jones—one of seven female writers employed by the Force and the only head writer among her gender. "Getting the old wolf ready to retire, coping with leaving command and facing the possibility that he may never resolve the Scott situation despite a brilliant career."

Stewart picked up the e-tablet before him. The agenda glared up at him with menacing font.

"Of course, we don't want you slowed down too much. So just like last season, you'll spend a considerable amount of this season in space, facing Scott from the captain's chair." She looked to Stone. "And we have some big plans for you, of course. We're going to wrap up the pirate thread, at least as far as the *Pence* goes, with Stewart's departure." Then the room grew quiet as the map overhead grew. "So that with this season finale, we take the *Pence* out of the system for a five-season run under Stone's command. Weird new worlds, bizarre new aliens and such." She clapped and everyone joined her. "Now let's talk about what that might look like between now and then."

From there, it was voice after voice, effusive in praise especially for the older crew-castmates. Some of the younger writers had cut their teeth watching the show as children and it showed in their eyes and words. Finally, after four hours, they moved toward the lunch break and the impromptu show museum that had been set up in a cargo bay that had yet to see a crate stacked within it. Duggan, Jones, and Todd pulled Stewart aside as the room cleared.

"Can we talk about Latterday's call?" Todd asked.

When Stewart nodded, Todd whipped out a scanner as Duggan hit the drone switch and made their meeting private. Once the scanner blinked green, Jones spoke first.

"We love the idea if we can write it in," she said, "but there isn't any mention of it in the story notes from Scott's agent."

"It's new," Stewart said. "As of this morning." He looked from face to face to face. "I don't think it's part of the story but I wouldn't put anything past him."

Duggan's brow furrowed. "And you're sure you want to take the meeting? Even knowing it could be a trap?"

In the years since going rogue, Scott had prided himself on catching them off guard. Destroying the *Pence B* was a fine opening act that had surprised them all. Since then, he'd kidnapped dignitaries between seasons that he forced to be written in, stolen ships he should have never known about to add to his own growing fleet and turned the tables on a half-dozen traps the Stewart and the Space Force had set to bring their wayward son to justice. But this one . . . Stewart wasn't sure what to make of it. Maybe it was his own inner landscape, thrown by the dream and by the sudden opportunity to see Scott again. "I am sure I want the meeting," Stewart finally said. He left the rest unsaid.

Todd nodded. "Jones will cook up some ideas and see if they bite." He looked at Duggan. "Could the Force use this for a trap of its own?"

Duggan nodded. "We could, but we're open minded. Let's see what the writers come up with. We're eager to move beyond this story arc and get out into the galaxy next year. Stewart and Scott have had decades on the net and it's time for an eye toward expansion." He smiled. "We're eager to expand our partnership with the studio and with Colonial Way Inc. as we get humanity—and America—properly positioned in the Cosmos." He clapped Stewart on the back. "I'm sure you're ready for quieter days."

Stewart wasn't sure but didn't need to answer. Jones filled in the silence instead.

"So," she said, "what would you say to him after all these years? All this conflict?"

"I'm sorry?"

"What would you say?" she asked again.

Stewart looked away. "I'd say I'm sorry," he said.

Duggan looked uncomfortable and Stewart knew why. But the droneflies had been down long enough for the chaplain to edge back into the room and that grim man's raised eyebrow told

Stewart that the conversation was over for now.

After that, it was lunch and then a quick tour of the bridge where they activated his command codes for the new ship and Jones and the others led the big reveal that he would be taking the vessel out with Stone for that maiden voyage next month.

Then more talk with the writers beneath that sky map, followed by more food and apple cider dressed up as whiskey as a lifetime washed over him and around him.

And through it all, Stewart found himself settling on the truth of the moment. He had amends to make and the opportunity to make them.

And he did want to see his old friend—his fiercest foe—again from some point-of-view other than the command screen of a pursuing starship before his time was done.

This is a conversation no one thinks will ever be heard and Stewart's voice is shaking with rage. "How far back, Duggan?"

Duggan stammers. He and Todd monitor the room for flies and other unwelcome bugs.

Todd intervenes. "They briefed us on the prototype drone footage when we took over the show."

Stewart balks. "So the kid hasn't been lost. You've known exactly where he was and you've been amassing content for a new venture?" His fist comes down on his desk. "We could've adjusted our plans and launched five years sooner—maybe eight—and rescued him from those . . . those . . ." The word sounds ugly when he spits out. "Those savages. Given him a chance at a normal life."

Duggan's voice is firm. "Those so-called savages revolutionized the labor market after the shortages in the New Revival downsizing. And the resources we're pulling from Venus have improved the human condition in ways never imagined when this Space Force was first conceived by the Orange Prophet and Divine Commander Pence."

"And," Todd says, "the story is a story of hope and human conquest. Jackson Scott, a toddler raised by apes on Venus as one of their own—a learning curve like no human child has ever faced. With his own recollections woven in—easily shot while he continues his work and training with you aboard the *Pence.*

Royalties and bonuses from this, along with his family's engine and planetary stake in Venus, will set him up for life and give him a platform to tell his story. Between your mentorship and his wealth, he could have an extraordinary life on the heels of so much hardship."

It's clear from Stewart's voice that he isn't buying. "He needs family and friends more than anything. People he can trust." He pauses. "You've been lying about this to him and to me. I can't go along with it. My mentorship won't mean shit to him otherwise."

Duggan and Todd are quiet. When Duggan speaks, his voice has a new quality to it, an edge he normally lacks. "We need you to go along with it, Mack. Encourage him to play along as well. It's for his own good."

"I don't see how or why—"

Todd interrupts. "Commander Duggan has asked me to upload a file to your private cortical server that will show you why helping us will be so good for your career."

There is more silence as Stewart views something behind the privacy of his left eye. "I see," he says.

The veiled threat of missing footage from episode eight isn't picked up by the single bug recording their words. And Scott doesn't receive the leaked recording until the ratings begin slipping at the opening of season five.

The rest is holovision history. This bit of its origin story tucked away safely from the masses—and Acting Ensign Jackson Scott—for their own good.

The evening was just getting started—and Stewart was just feeling finished—when Stone's XO interrupted with a quiet word between the captain and Duggan.

Duggan's brow spoke thirty seconds before he did. "I'm afraid we're going to have to cut tonight's festivities short. We have a security breach at the Titan Shipyards."

Stone raised his eyebrow. "Should I recall the crew and spin up the engines?"

Duggan shook his head. "No. We need to keep *D* on task with tomorrow's system tour and the Chaplaincy needs her emptied tonight for pre-launch security." He looked at Stewart. "Did they tell you yet that you'll be doing the honors?"

Stewart shook his head. "No but I wondered when you had my codes transferred."

Todd and Jones, both drunk and looking likely to fall into bed together again soon, joined them. "Party over already?"

"Afraid so," Duggan said. "But everything should be fine for tomorrow." He nodded to Stewart. "See you in the morning, Mack."

Then Stone turned Stewart over the XO and they set out for the shuttle bay. The chaplain was dismissing the lieutenant who had flown Stewart with a salute as they entered. He looked up and smiled.

Stewart had heard the expression *and his blood went cold.* This was the first time he'd ever felt it.

"Thank you, Commander," the chaplain said. "I'll fly Admiral Stewart home tonight." Then his smile widened and the temperature in Stewart's stomach dropped even colder. "There were some items I wished to discuss with you, Admiral. This lets us kill two birds with one stone, as they say."

Rule one of the Academy was when it came to the U.S. Chaplaincy, you just said "Yes."

"Happy to oblige, Padre," he said.

"The shuttle is a more private environment." The chaplain gestured to the open hatch.

"Agreed," Stewart said pausing. "I'm afraid I'm not remembering your name?"

"I'm afraid," the chaplain said, "I've not given it."

There was no way out of this box, Stewart saw, but to go in. He nodded, then climbed into the shuttle's main passenger cabin. The chaplain followed, then closed the hatch and drew a drone disabler out to kill the fog of droneflies that followed.

They are keeping it undocumented. Or at least letting him think as much. "How can I help you?"

"I want to know if you recognize this." The chaplain drew a wad of blue cloth from beneath his robes and tossed it to Stewart.

He nearly dropped it as he opened the shirt. "I . . ." *Episode eight.*

The chaplain took another step forward. "Do you recognize it?"

Stewart swallowed. "I do."

"Anything to say?"

He stared straight ahead, saying nothing, and the chaplain took another step forward. "Tell me about your dreams, Admiral Fleetwood Mackenzie Stewart."

Now he flushed and felt sick. How could they know? "How . . ."

The chaplain smiled. "Because I burned a cricket to Tulva and Vlom for my wandering one to follow its smoke back to me."

There's nothing wrong with me, Stewart realized. *It's him.* "You what?"

"In the temple. The spider god and her ape lover."

"You burned a cricket?" He looked at the insignia on the chaplain's collar.

Following his eyes, the chaplain's fingers moved to the collar and began pulling at it. "Yes. That's the custom when you want to find *your shul-rav*—your person or your people since it doesn't connote a number, just a sense of belonging." The collar was open but that's not what he was pulling.

No, he's pulling the skin beneath it.

"So I burned a cricket and we dreamed about each other." The face and hair lifted away and Jackson Scott grinned out from beneath it. Before Stewart could close his mouth, Scott had kissed it, hard and dry.

"Hi," he said. "My name's Jack. I'm an alcoholic. It's been seventy-eight days since my last drink."

"Hi Jack," Stewart said, then surprised himself by kissing his arch-nemesis back. "I'm Mack. It's been . . ." But just then, he couldn't remember how long it had been.

"Let's talk," Scott said, pointing to the chairs. "I've a lot to go over but first things first. Have you decided what you're doing next?"

Stewart sat mouth open and still stunned. "What I'm doing next?"

Scott reached for battered satchel that Stewart recognized. It had been Angus Scott's, recovered from the crash site. From it, he pulled out a sheath of papers. "I have a proposal for you."

Stewart took the papers, looked at them, then looked up. "Is this a trick?" It was a pre-nuptial agreement and marriage contract, or at least that's what the bold all-cap letters declared across the old-fashioned paper cover page. He saw terms covering non-disclosure, film rights, dissolution and even expansion by amendment.

"No, not a trick. A proposal. Marry me, Mack. It's all legit under Planet X law. But read it anyway. It's a big contract. Remember the Detweller Twins? They're in it, too. But you can decide what your marriage to them looks like." He paused. "Unless you have other plans after retirement?"

"No. No plans." Stewart let the papers drop into his lap after perusing the list of standard and non-standard clauses. A lifetime behind the helm, giving orders with clarity and purpose and now he floundered in weather beyond his ken. "I'm a bit lost here, Jack."

Scott leaned forward. "I know it's a lot and I'm sorry it's compressed into such a cramped moment after too many years but hear me out and then decide. If you say no, I'll drop you at home and we'll meet again later in the season." He waited, held out a hand. "Deal?"

They shook. "Deal."

Then they settled into their chairs.

"First," Scott said, "I want to tell you I'm sorry."

Stewart looked up. "*You're* sorry? No, Jack, I'm sorry. I helped them exploit your childhood."

"Yeah," Jack said, "but you did it because of the shirt. Because of episode eight. And episode seven."

Stewart blushed. "I think I was drinking to cover it up. I know I didn't want to see it."

"We're all covering something," Jack said. "Anyway, I felt betrayed but eventually, I found out the truth. Enough money buys plenty of eyes and ears." His eyes softened. "And we grew up in different cultures. There is no room for the spider ape cult of savage Venus in the Revived United States and her colonies. So you had shackles of shame I never could understand, not growing up where I did."

"Still, young men and ship's captains . . ."

"Both old men now," Scott said. "Also the subject of great speculation and vast amounts of fan fiction spanning decades in the underground porn market."

Stewart had avoided knowing about such things and pointed them back on course. "Still, I'm sorry."

"I'm sorry I waited so long to let you know I knew and that I understood." His face softened. "All these years, Mack, I've not been at war with you, just them."

Now something happened to Stewart that he couldn't fathom and he was grateful for the absence of cameras. He felt a tear coming on and took in a breath to squeeze off more. "And now you want to spend the rest of your life with me?"

Scott shrugged. "You're the first human I remember meeting. You're still my favorite and I've met quite a few. I can't think of a better person to help me clean up the mess than the fellow who helped make it in the first place."

He felt his brow furrowing. "What do you mean?"

"We're not digging deep enough in our fearless moral inventory, Mack, if we think we are the ones we've hurt the most. Can you see the trail of tears our Space Force has left across every non-human it's encountered? And now they're talking about using my family's engine to go even further out?" His eyes were bright with anger. "They laud me for providing a home to the system's refugees and misfits but what have I done with all my fame and fortune to make the system a better home for everyone in it? I've made it worse. We both have, Mack, by feeding a voracious monster. I want us to make things right. Me and you and whoever else will join us." His face was earnest in the dim light. "There are better dreams than these that we've dreamed so far."

"What are you proposing, Jack, besides marriage?"

"Liberation," Scott cried out, "and education!" He jumped to his feet with a flourish and moved to the pilot's chair to fire up the engines and punch in coordinates. "I think that's enough for now until you decide, but the clock is ticking. About three minutes, I'd say, before our window closes."

He looked over the papers again. "Can I have my attorney look this over?" He was asking the right questions but Stewart already knew his answer and already knew that no Terran attorney was going to sign off on the kind of document Stewart now held before him.

"Okay," he finally said, as the shuttle cleared the bay. "I do."

He signed the forms and Scott took them from him, tucking them in the satchel as he drew its strap over his shoulder.

They kissed again. "Now hold me," Scott said as he strapped a large, clumsy watch onto his wrist and spun a dial.

A wave of nausea and the sudden urge to urinate overwhelmed Stewart and then with a flash of light, the shuttle fell away and he collapsed heavily on top of Scott in a dark, warm place.

Scott squeezed his shoulder as he gasped for air. "First matter transmission experiences are a bit discombobulating."

Stewart was barely following. *Matter transmission?* What in the hell was he talking about? They weren't on the shuttle but he had lost all sense of time after feeling twisted inside out and scattered. "Where are we?"

"Back on the *Pence D.*"

"And the shuttle?"

"On its way to your place to deliver you safe and sound. Or a close approximation of you."

Stewart adjusted himself. "Is this a bed?"

"Get some sleep," Scott said. "Busy day."

Stewart felt the briefest sting in his neck. Then the fog rolled in to take him.

He flies the jungle now toward better dreams, the leaves and wind slapping at his bare skin, vine after vine pulling him along behind his friend, his lover, his spouse, his one-time foe. Scott moves with ease and Stewart is clumsy in his wake but learns quickly. Around them, the apes fly too, more joining each day as the cause grows.

Not just the apes but the ice lemurs and below, in lagoons that made no sense on Venus outside of a dream, the Neptunian tentacled tadpoles leap the waves, their tiny opposable thumbs uplifted in solidarity.

And slowly, some of the humans join. Slower, clumsier, pink and brown, male and female and other than, and all the dazzling points of beauty in between, stripping off the falseness of their uniforms, tangling their fists into the living vines of truth and pulling themselves forward.

They move in one direction away from darkness and toward a rising light and there is music and moaning and—f

"Wake up, my love," Jackson Scott said. "I've got your wedding gift. Time for you to give me mine."

Stewart was awake in far more ways than he had expected to

be and wondered what kind of stimulants had been administered to him. He was in a lavishly decorated room, laying fully uniformed in a red, heart-shaped bed.

Scott grinned at the look on his face. "Still on the *D*. I had this PolyPanPlay™ bedroom set ordered as a bit of a surprise for Stone but I think it'll do us nicely." He winked. "I'm glad you said yes."

Scott was standing, now in his own rainbow-colored uniform. "You'll recall the security breach at Titan Shipyards?"

Stewart nodded.

"The *C*. I had her picked up for you last night. I think Duggan's apoplectic about it. We'll rendezvous with her tomorrow and you can take command."

Slowly, it was all dawning on him. The vines had been a dream but everything before it had really happened. "My wedding gift," he said. He stood and went to the nightstand, running his finger over the feather duster and riding crop holstered there.

Scott smiled. "And you have a gift for me?"

"Computer," Stewart said returning the smile as the voice activation chimed, "recognize Stewart, Fleetwood Mackenzie. Admiral, United States Space Force. Transfer command authorization to the following voice print." He paused.

"Scott, Jackson Remuel Wagner," Scott said.

"Mark," Stewart said.

"Authorization transferred," the computer confirmed.

"Excellent," Scott said. "Now let's have breakfast, steal a starship, and get to work making amends to the solar system."

Stealing the *Pence D* was the easiest last day in the Force that Stewart could've imagined and when they were safely pointed toward Planet X, easily outrunning the few craft not already in pursuit of the *Pence C*, they returned to their quarters.

"So what next?" Stewart asked his unexpected husband.

"Liberation and education," Scott replied. "Let's show them what's coming their way."

He thumbed a button and the lights went blue and dim. Soft music whooped to life as the bed began to rotate and the droneflies filled the room.

There was something simple and beautiful in Scott's eyes and Stewart gave himself over to it. *Yes, they need to see this,* Stewart thought, surprised at himself yet again.

4444444

"Oh Captain, my captain," he whispered as he reached for his long, lost friend and a future he'd never dreamed possible.

"Oh Captain, my captain," Scott whispered back as they sank into the waiting satin sheets and the droneflies danced above.

THAT WHEN I WAKED I CRIED *to* DREAM AGAIN

THE LEANING SIGN READ *NORTH POLE* IN WHITE FLAK-ing paint but it was hotter than an Arkansas August. Heat waves danced over dusty stones underneath a sky so blue it made his eyes water.

Archie knelt over the corpse and tugged at its clothes. The rotting green fabric tore in his clumsy fingers as he lifted first one lifeless leg and then another. He dressed quickly, watching the dilapidated house and out-buildings below. No movement.

He'd awakened before dawn, naked and burned, beneath a lightning shattered, skeletal tree that stood wrapped in rusty wires and broken glass bulbs. He picked his away across the wasteland and into the low hills. There, he'd stumbled across the corpse, its head twisted unnaturally and its eyes fixed on the house in the gully below, slack-jawed and black tongue lolling. He'd circled around the body aimlessly for an hour after he finished dry heaving into the dust.

Archie pulled the cap over his blistered head. His hair and beard had been burned away. Some distant part of his body told him he did not want to remember how it happened. Using his teeth, he chewed the rusted bells off the pointed cloth shoes before slipping them on. Then, he padded down the hill towards the house.

At one time, he saw it had been a bright, jolly place. But its red paint had taken on the texture and color of dried blood and its greens, yellows and blues had faded into old bruises that flaked beneath a swollen sun. The doors and shutters hung like loose teeth and shards of glass glittered about, masquerading as ice. He passed a stable on his left and paused.

The stench reached him before the sound of happy flies, and curiosity turned him in towards the gaping barn door. Eight stalls. Eight piles of stinking entrails and shreds of hide. He dry heaved again.

"Fee. Fi. Fo. Fum."

He spun. The deep, rolling voice—a sound of many waters—ran fingers down his back, through his spine, to clench his testicles. A massive, unnaturally tall figure stood in the doorway of the house. Wild, greasy once-white hair thrust into a careless pony-tail, a tangled beard and jutting brows, a tattered red suit lined with fur that fell and drifted like dandelion seeds. Black scuffed boots.

"Ho, ho, ho," the giant said as he raised a bottle to his thick lips. He gargled the amber fluid down and then shattered the bottle on the porch. "I didn't know Santa had any little helpers left."

Archie swallowed three times. He wanted to vomit again, wanted to wet himself, wanted to run, wanted to fall down into the ground and cover himself. But he didn't do anything. He stood still.

The giant Santa took an awkward step forward, staggered, then squinted. "Why . . . *you're* no elf. Who are you? What are you doing here?" The eyes blazed, the voice slurred slightly and he sniffed the air. "Feefifofum," he said in a jumbled rush.

"My name is Archie. I don't know why I'm here. I can't remember." Suddenly, he wanted to sob but couldn't. "I can't remember."

Santa came down from the porch and reached Archie in three gigantic strides. The black eyes widened in their sea of blood. "Poor little fellow. Santa will make it all better." He scooped Archie up in his arms, burying him into the stink of his clothes and beard. Death, sex, and whiskey.

Archie started to resist, then stopped struggling when he felt the power in the giant hands. He thought of the dead elf on the hill.

"There, there. I can help you. Let's just go inside." Tucking Archie under his arm like firewood, he clomped up the stairs and into the darkened house. "Let's just see here. . . ." With his free hand, Santa rummaged along the surface of a cluttered desk. Dry parchments crinkled and the air filled with dust. From beneath the arm, Archie tried to see the rest of the room.

Pictures hung crooked on walls that peeled candy-cane paper in shreds. Dark gas lamps hung from a ceiling spider-webbed with plaster cracks. "Are you really . . . ?"

"Humph." Santa tugged a massive scroll free from the desk. "Here we go."

They stomped into another room.

The large chair stood in the shadow of a scorched Christmas tree. Glass ornaments dusted with soot cast diminutive shadow-reflections of the room. Santa held him tight as they plunked down into the chair. It groaned and shifted beneath their weight.

Santa bent over him, his mouth near Archie's ear, sour breath moist on his hot skin. "So . . . have you been a good boy?"

"I. . . ." Archie stopped, felt the sob again. "I can't remember. I don't know. Where am I? Can't you please just tell me where I am? Why am I here?"

Santa shushed him. "It's okay. Let's find out together." One hand encircled Archie's waist, holding him in place. The other flicked the scroll open; one end poured onto the floor and rolled away.

"Archie. Archie. Archie." The voice took on a thoughtful quality. "Archie Davis?"

Archie shook his head.

"Archie Harris?"

Again, he shook his head.

"Archie Reynolds?"

The name sounded right. He nodded.

"Hmm." Santa began to read. As he read, his fingers tickled Archie's stomach, slipping underneath the tunic. They were cool. "Archibald Thomas Reynolds? You're sure?"

"Yes."

"Hmm." The index finger slipped under the waistband of the green tights and moved slowly downward.

Archie held in his breath, held in his scream. Something in his brain began to boil; he felt its lid rattling from the pressure. The finger was joined by others and he felt an uncomfortably large lump begin to press against his backside.

"Were you a good little boy, Archie?" Santa continued to read, his fingers still absent-mindedly moving beneath the fabric.

He twisted, trying to get away from the fingers, trying to close his legs. As he moved, he saw a portion of the list. *Seventy-year-*

old Department Store Santa Convicted—Santa re-rolled the scroll with a flick of his wrist before Archie could finish.

"I guess goodness and naughtiness are relative constructs," Santa said. He shifted Archie on his lap, rubbing him against the bulge. "I suppose Santa *does* have *something* for even naughty little boys."

Archie screamed and twisted, bringing his elbow up and into Santa's ear. The giant howled and Archie slipped through the arm, his pants tearing. He ran from the room and Santa followed after.

"Come back," he shouted. "Come back here you little shit. Come sit on my lap and tell me what you want."

Archie raced through the den and leapt from the porch, falling and rolling in the dust. He heard the clatter behind him stop.

"You're being very naughty. Come back here this minute." He heard metal clicking and had a sudden memory of duck hunting with his father: the sound of a shotgun breech snapping open and then closed.

Archie ran past the stable, then darted around behind it.

He nearly stumbled over the malnourished reindeer that stood shaking in his path. It was harnessed and tied to a sled. The sled was up on blocks, one of its rails bent and twisted. Nearby, a trough of green-slimed water steamed in the sun.

The deer's tail wagged and its nose lit up pink beneath a crust of dried blood.

"Ho, ho, ho," a voice bellowed from the porch. "Fee, fi, fo, fum."

A blast of noise shook the air, a sound of shattering glass and splintering wood. "Archie Reynolds, come back here. Come sit on my lap and tell me what you want."

Archie grabbed the reindeer's neck and began tugging at the harness. The panic in him smelled like iron as his fingers muddled at the buckles. His breath whistled through his nose. A mantra rushed through his brain like electrical sparks along a trolley cable: *getawaygetawaygetwaygetawaygetaway*.

He had no idea why he thought it would work, but he trusted it. He threw aside the straps, climbed onto the reindeer's back and grabbed hold of the stubby antlers. "Go, Rudolph, go," he shouted. Staggering beneath the weight, the deer pitched forward as Santa came around the corner at a slow walk, the double-barreled shotgun tucked under his arm.

"Come sit on my lap and tell me what you want."

"Fuck you." The gun came up quickly and its blast drowned Archie's scream. The trough exploded.

The reindeer bucked and leaped, its fore-hooves striking Santa's head as they launched into the sky.

Below, the man in red grew smaller and smaller, sprawled onto the ground and sobbing. "Come back. Come sit on my lap and tell me what you want."

Rudolph died of exhaustion and fell into a mountain lake. Archie fell, too.

Somewhere, somehow the blistering daylight and blasted wastes had given way to dense forest. The reindeer had bleated and bleated, its altitude slowly dropping, its nose guttering like a spent candle. As if by choice, Rudolph banked left and plummeted into the icy water. Archie pushed himself to the surface, dogpaddled to the shore, and approached the yellow, enamel castle.

From a mile away it smelled of morning breath, but it's warm lights drew him, shaking, wet and cold.

The drawbridge was down and he walked across, looking down into a moat of thick, clear, fluid capped with blood-flecked foamy waves. The courtyard beyond was meticulously clean. A string of Chinese lanterns led through a set of double doors. He followed, suddenly realizing that he'd become used to the smell.

"Archie Reynolds!" It was a woman's voice, high and musical. "Well, I'll be."

Miraculously, the tiny wings somehow held the obese woman in the air. They flittered insanely fast, like a hummingbird's. She raised a glittering wand with her fat hand and settled to the ground. Her smile split her fat face and she adjusted her bodice, plumping out her fat breasts. "The others told me you were finally here. I didn't believe them, but I *hoped* you'd visit if you were."

Archie stepped backward. "Who are you?"

She shook her upper body and a necklace of tiny teeth glistening like pearls danced along the swell of her cleavage. "Don't you know? Oh, Archie . . . how long's it been? Sixty years if it's a day." She stepped forward. "Remember? You were ten. Close to eleven. And you didn't believe I was real but you put it under your pillow anyway." She sniffed and ran a swollen finger beneath her eye, catching a solitary tear. "I still have it. I really do." Turning, she waddled deeper into the hall. "Come along then."

He didn't move. "What's going on?"

She stopped and turned. "Don't you know?"

He dug deeper. Remembered flashes of the ocean, being at sea, being a sailor when he was young. He remembered a series of houses he'd lived in, some rented and some bought. Remembered a red suit packed lovingly into a hall closet. Remembered combing fine white hair, remembered each year's beard. Real, not fake. Never, never fake. *See . . . go ahead and give it a tug.* He remembered lots of laughter. Lots of noise. Lots of children. The rest was empty, but with something lurking at the edges. More memory drifted back with each hour he'd been in this place.

He felt that clenching in his chest. The sob he couldn't release. "I can't remember."

She shook her head, then looked up. "Oh dear." She bit her lip, nodded knowingly. "Yes, you're exactly right. Sometimes they *do* forget. They have to. To live with themselves." She waited, head cocked as if listening. "Oh yes. I know he will. Eventually." Then she gazed lovingly at him, her face warm and open as an Arkansas sky. "Enough. How *rude* of me. You must be simply *starved.* And those wet clothes . . . off with them, off with them." She puttered into a larger room and suddenly Archie smelled fresh baked cakes, donuts and pies.

He followed, salivating. His stomach rumbled.

Unashamed, he peeled off his wet clothing and let it splat to the floor. She looked at him, her eyes hungry as they wandered over him. "Doesn't this all just look *so* yummy?" Her voice lowered to a whisper. "But not good for the teeth. Oh no. Not good for the teeth at all."

Discomfort washed his naked skin. Her own teeth were jagged, yellow and sharp as she smiled. Why hadn't he noticed that before?

She picked up a large chocolate frosted donut. "Is Archie hungry? Would the little boy like something sweet?"

He nodded, losing his voice, stepping forward.

The music left her voice, dropping it an octave. "Good. There will be plenty to eat for both of us. But first . . ." She held up a strap-on phallus and pointed it at a chair. "Come sit on my lap and tell me what you want."

Archie found his voice and shrieked as his bare feet slapped the castle floor.

"Oh . . . don't run." Her voice carried amused, mock sadness. "Don't make me chase."

He ran, skinny legs pumping, skinny arms flailing. With a whir and flutter, she followed, light shooting from her wand.

Buried in his brain, an instinct bloomed to life and took over. His breathing slowed, his legs slowed, time slowed and a buzz filled his ears. *Fight or flight.* There was nearly nothing left of him when the little boy jumped in front of him and grabbed his hand.

The boy made a muffled sound, as if gagged, and yanked Archie toward a small grate in the floor.

"Now, now," the tooth fairy said. "Where did *you* come from, little meddler? You have no business here. Go away and leave us to our appetite."

The little boy stood his ground and shook his head. Archie now saw that his mouth had been sewed shut with black thread. His short blond hair was matted with blood that seeped from a hole in the forehead. He had blue eyes. Archie's favorite.

"But you must. You *must*. It isn't fair." The tooth fairy's voice was that of a whining child. "Let us have our fun."

He shook his head again, tugged Archie's arm and pointed to the hole in the floor. Archie put his legs through, then squeezed his body, his blistered skin tearing, the fluid greasing him as he wriggled downward.

The little boy followed. Above, the tooth fairy cried and called after them.

Below the castle, they followed its roots until they reached a hollow canal sloping down. Archie tried to get a look at the boy.

He was young . . . maybe seven. Archie liked that age. A lot. He wore bell-bottom jeans and a tie-dyed shirt, a style over twenty years gone. There was a frayed, worn peace sign decal on the front of the shirt. A finger stabbed Archie's memory.

"Do I know you?"

The little boy ignored him.

"What's happening to me? Do you know what's happening to me?" Archie stopped walking. "Please?"

The little boy stopped, dipped his finger into the hole on his forehead and began to write one word on the floor. *Soon.*

Archie's fear slid into anger. "Soon? What the fuck's that mean, you little shit? Tell me what's going on." He reached for the boy, grabbed his shoulders and shook him violently. "Answer me."

The little boy went silently limp until Archie set him down him. He hugged the child, enjoying the warmth, feeling a stir in . . .

"I'm sorry. I'm sorry. I didn't mean it. I didn't." Archie sat, burying his head in his hands, wanting tears that weren't there. He clung to the little boy, using a finger to move a careless bang back over the entry wound. The exit wound, in the back, was gaping and wet. "Who did this to you?"

The boy struggled free. He pointed at the word on the floor. Then, he turned and walked away. Archie climbed to his feet to follow, his old knees cracking and creaking.

They left the root canal and found themselves in a forest clearing. Suddenly excited, the boy darted ahead and returned, a colored egg held up in his hand. Archie grabbed it from him and fumbled the shell away. He popped the rubbery white oval into his mouth, then spit it out. Warm, mushy sulfur. The little boy tried to smile around the threads that sealed his mouth.

"You think that's funny, eh?"

The boy nodded.

"Well, I—" He stopped as the sound of crashing filled the woods behind them. He turned slowly. The little boy moved between Archie and the noise.

The slavering beast pounced into the clearing, its fur yellow with its own urine, its teeth thrust outward like spears. A basket dangled from one sharply-clawed foot and its pink eyes fixed on Archie. It chittered, long ears bent back over its head.

The little boy shook his head.

Nose and whiskers twitching, it hopped forward, still chittering.

Frowning, the boy shook his head again.

"But dearie, he's ours," the tooth fairy said as she landed in the clearing. "You gave him to us."

"Ours," Santa said as he removed his finger from the side of his nose, feet settling onto the ground.

The monstrous rabbit chittered agreement and thrust the basket away, tearing up chunks of sod and dirt with its hind paws. All three licked their lips at Archie and rolled their eyes.

"You gave him to us. You did." The tooth fairy pointed at the little boy's head, at the wound that seeped there. "Now he's ours."

Understanding birthed something small in Archie's stomach. Something infinitesimally small that grew and grew. A taller man, a young man, a blond-haired, blue-eyed man standing over him where he had fallen, a pistol smoking in his hand, the sound of the two shots still hanging heavy in the air outside the courthouse. Pain and relief from pain spreading out from the holes in Archie's chest and back. ". . . a deadlock in the sentencing portion of Archibald Reynold's trial . . ." a reporter's voice saying from far away. The pistol coming up to kiss the young man's own forehead, the hammer coming back, back, back. Turning his head, Archie saw the crumpled newspaper soaking in a crimson pool: *Seventy-year-old Department Store Santa Convicted . . .*

They fell on him, hands groping and ripping at his naked body. As he went down, he saw the little boy turning, saw his mouth straining and watched the threads pop free. "No. Stop."

And darkness dropped like a shroud.

Light burned from the boy, gold light spinning and twisting as it expanded and burst on the air. The words rippled across the night, waves of sound that bent the trees and lifted the moon as the little boy stretched out his arms cruciform and levitated from the clearing.

The clawing hands and noisy, smacking lips all stopped and Archie fell away from reality.

His eyes opened on a crystal sea that stretched forever about his tiny island. In the center of the island stood a throne of amethyst and garnet and a thousand precious stones. The little boy smiled down on him. "It's just the two of us now. Everything will be alright."

Archie trembled as the little boy touched his arm. His memories were a mud puddle, stirred with a stick and murky.

"I'm in Heaven now?"

"Yes. My Heaven."

Archie's eyes went wide. "Your Heaven? What do you—" Before he could finish, the little boy stepped back and shimmered into an old, old man . . . older even than Archie. A familiar face from an Italian ceiling. His hair blazed white and his eyes crinkled at the corners as he smiled through his beard. He stretched out a finger; Archie did the same.

"*My* Heaven." A voice of many waters, rippling into an eternal stretch of light.

Archie closed his eyes. "It was so awful. So unbearably awful." Gratitude wrenched his heart and he finally, finally began to cry. He knelt in front of the little boy who had become God, hands clenched. "Awful."

"Yes. I know. *Your* Hell."

"Will you tell me what's been happening to me? Will you tell me why?" Archie thought now that maybe . . . just maybe . . . he *knew* why. That growing understanding expanded in the slow motion of an exploding atom bomb.

The Ancient of Days lifted him to his feet, his fingers brushing Archie's naked breast. "Soon. But first . . ." He licked his lips and his voice was thick with appetite as he led Archie up alabaster stairs towards the shining throne. "Come sit on my lap and tell me what you want."

OF HOMEWARD DREAMS AND FALLEN SEEDS AND MELODIES BY MOONLIGHT

TOVIN THE FAR-SEER CLIMBED HIS MOUNTAIN ALONE TO his solitary watch. Each foot fell heavily upon the worn stone as he traced the path of his father and his grandmother before him. Each morning the same: Pray and then watch. And again, each evening: Watch and then pray.

Tovin sighed and felt the weight of his life with each step he took.

Around him, the air took on the chill of an early winter and the sky was overcast, promising a cold rain later. The moon in all its blue-green glory was hidden now and he was grateful for its absence. The sight of it was a reminder of how short sighted their new Far-Seer truly was.

He sighed again, taking steps carved long ago for he and his family's feet, and wondered if this time he would see their promised salvation rising from sea that had imprisoned his people so long ago.

Tovin paused and turned, looking back and down toward the sprawling village that grew around the small stone temple which lay shrouded in morning mist. A century and some years ago, a tribe of misfits shipwrecked their armada here looking for a home away from the gray-robes of P'Andro Whym. The Androfrancine Order that old scientist scholar founded during the Age of Laughing Madness had grown in their grim control of the nations that had sprung up from the survivors of that apocalypse. Tovin's parents and their people finally reached the breaking point where the risks of seeking a new home outweighed the benefit of remaining in their old one. They'd survived the Ghosting Crests and the monsters that roamed it but the teeth of the Carving Reef had claimed their ships and left them on the largest island of the archipelago it surrounded.

That first snowy night, Sari the First Far-Seer, found the statue kneeling, its hands outstretched in worship upon the ground before it, facing the island's single mountain. It was warm to the touch and the most vulnerable survivors pulled themselves together around it and huddled beneath a shelter raised from tattered sail-cloth while fires were started, lean-tos erected, and survivors pulled from the cold waters.

Now, all these years later, the cloth shelter had become a temple of stone and wood erected around the prone metal man and the survivors were a few hundred scattered out over the islands around them and a line of priests to guide its proper worship in the hopes that it would bring about their rescue. So far, two Far-Seers had gone before, most recent Tovin's father, Berum, on what they—or rather he—now called The Dawn of the Homeward Dream. The night that all of them, scattered as they were about the islands, had shared the same dream.

His father had been that dream's only casualty.

Turning away from the temple below, Tovin made his feet once more carry him forward. When he reached the top, he turned north to take in the scattered islands and walked to the low, simple altar that his grandmother had found waiting here at the top of the stairs with its solitary, dark fist-sized stone set into its surface. Kneeling in the same fashion as the metal man below, Tovin placed his forehead upon the stone and closed his eyes.

"Spirit of long ago," he whispered, "rise up like wind to carry us home." He'd changed the prayer only slightly after the dream but he assumed that as Far-Seer it was his decision. "Spirit of long ago, bring life and light to those who wait and worship."

Twice daily he had prayed it here on the spire since his father's death. Before his father had fallen, Berum had prayed the same for fifty-seven years as the Far-Seer of the people.

But until last month, there was nothing whatsoever that Tovin could point to that would indicate his calls for help had ever been heard. At least not anything that could be seen as truly miraculous. And then, the high tide after morning prayers had tossed them the chewed body of an abandoned yacht that was more intact than any other wreckage that had found its way to their shores. Those most impacted by the homeward dream—especially the younger—saw it as the best evidence of answered prayer.

Even Tovin had accepted it as a sign. The best and only since that dream. However, he hadn't seen it as a call to leave but rather, additional resources to use while they continued watching and praying. Still, factions had arisen with differing opinions. And though he and the elected captain didn't see eye to eye on much, they did agree that leaving in that boat was likely a death sentence along with a loss of more life and resources than their small group could sustain.

He felt the cool of the stone against his forehead and thought about that Dawn of the Homeward Dream. The wide plain he'd seen and the woman's voice he'd heard and that wind rising up to pull seeds from an ancient and towering white tree, lifting and scattering them abroad. All of his people were there surrounded by countless others to bear witness. "That which was closed," the woman's voice boomed out, "is now open!"

And there had also been metal men. Walking and talking.

He'd been so caught up in the moment that he hadn't realized his father was absent until hours later. The old man had fallen from the spire when the dream struck and he'd died on the rocky shore below before seeing his people's call home.

That's what Tovin thought of now when he prayed.

Closing his eyes against the tears, he uttered the words a second time.

And this time, from far away and deep inside of himself, Tovin heard a still, small voice.

Life and light to you, it whispered.

Tovin's eyes opened. His mouth went dry even as something cold twisted in stomach. "Hello?" He swallowed and looked up.

A gull cried in the distance. He looked around and blinked. Then, he put his forehead back to the stone.

"Spirit of long ago—" he started whispering but was interrupted.

Life and light to those who wait and worship, the voice said, now clearer but still distant. *I do not worship but I return your salutation. You are far from any other casters in the aether.*

He didn't comprehend the words and the new feeling he felt was something like the awe of the dream but with an edge. That dream had been filled with hope and this moment was far from hopeful.

The cold in his stomach became a heat rising to his chest and Tovin knew this must be what a holy fear felt like. "I don't understand what is happening," he said.

There was a pause. *How do you come to wield a dreamstone?*

A dreamstone? His eyes widened and he pulled back his forehead. "Hello? What is a dreamstone?"

Nothing.

He stretched out a finger and touched the stone. *—tools of the parents are not toys for the children,* the voice dropped into his mind.

And then everything spun away into light and Tovin screamed into the morning sky.

Brightness and warmth washed his face before Tovin could open his eyes. The ground beneath his knees had changed.

"Life and light," a voice very near said.

Tovin looked up and gasped.

A metal face stared down at him, eyes shining red, and behind that face, a massive ancient tree stretched up into an impossibly blue sky.

The shape and form of the metal man was identical to the statue only this one was a bright metal that reflected back its surroundings. And this one wore a plain dark robe. A metal hand reached out to help him up.

"Where am I?" As he stood, he turned to take in his surroundings, but even as he asked, Tovin knew and felt his eyes go wide.

"I thought this would be the best place to meet," the metal man said. Its voice was not like anything Tovin had heard before. It flowed nearly like music. "I knew it would be familiar to you."

It was unmistakable. This was the field from the Dawn of the Homeward Dream. The tree was bare now and the empty field was three years toward becoming a forest scattered with trees that had grown up from the fallen, scattered seed.

In the sky of the far horizon, a massive and scarred world slowly rose.

Tovin's holy fear expanded and he fell to his knees. The words came rushing from him as fast as his tears and his hands scrabbled to clutch at the metal man's feet. "Oh my lord," he said, "I beseech you show me how to bring my people here."

He felt a metal hand on his shoulder. "I am no lord but I will help you if I can. My name is Isaak. Tell me yours?"

Tovin's voice shook as he forced his words. "I'm Tovin. I'm the Far-Seer of my people." He also forced his eyes up to meet the metal man's. "I've been watching for you."

Once more, Isaak helped him up. Then held out his hand. In it lay a small bird carved of black stone. "Using something like this?"

He examined it. It was smaller than the one in the altar but cut from the same type of stone. Tovin nodded. "There is a statue that looks like you. And stairs carved into a stone spire with an altar set at the top. There is a stone like this set into the altar."

Isaak's eyes flickered a deeper red. "That dream-stone lets us communicate in the aether, and it will bring me to you. My friends and I have been looking for your metal man."

His eyes widened. "Then I can tell my people that home is near?"

"I'm not certain what is best for you to tell your people," Isaak said. "But we can discuss it when I arrive tomorrow. We've set our course. We should reach you by midday."

Tovin's holy fear was gone now, replaced by a level of awe that now smelled hopeful. "You will be coming by sea?" He realized how ridiculous the question sounded even as he asked it.

Isaak nodded.

Tovin thought for a moment. "Can you come from the north?"

When Tovin awoke, he took the stairs two at a time, shouting at the top of his lungs as he went.

"Our salvation arrives from the north tomorrow," he cried out, "even as those before me foretold. Let those who wait and worship prepare themselves for home."

Cold rain promised by that morning sky pattered the ground as the people gathered around the temple. They'd sent boats to the other settlements further into the small chain of islands after he met with the captain and their council. Tovin's role as Far-Seer was the only handed down based on lineage. The captaincy initially fell to one of the vessel's surviving executive officers but became a position elected by the survivors for a period of time that had varied over the years.

Now, Tovin huddled with Rami, the white-haired woman in command of the colony. She had tolerated his father but since the dream, she'd become quiet and bitter. That first year, while it was fresh in everyone's mind, he'd seen a resurgence in worship like nothing in his lifetime. But in the time since, with no salvation apparent from the north or anywhere else, most had settled into a disappointed acceptance until the boat washed ashore.

Rami glared at him now as people started to gather outside the temple. Finally, she sighed. "I wish you'd talked with me and the council *before* announcing this at the top of your lungs, Tovin. Your father would've had the foresight to know stirring up the people might be premature."

Tovin wanted to remind her that he wasn't his father and that all matters of faith fell to the Far-Seer, but instead, he swallowed and looked away. "I was compelled by the force of the vision, Captain Rami."

She glanced behind them to the dim lit chamber where the metal man knelt, then glanced to the spire north of the village. "I hope your vision is all you claim it to be."

He felt the holy fear again bubbling up within. "It was just as the dream, Captain. Just like I told the council."

She stood. "Very well." She stared at him again as if measuring him. She smoothed out the robes of her office and held up her hands. "Good morning, crew," she called out.

"Good morning, Captain Rami," they called back.

"As you may have already heard, our Far-Seer has had a vision that our salvation will arrive from the north . . . *tomorrow* by midday." She glanced at Tovin. "A very specific prediction," she added, "which I will now have him share with you all."

Tovin stood with her and watched nodding heads amid a scattering of wide and narrowed eyes. He closed his eyes for a moment and brought back the field with its saplings surrounding the vast and ancient tree. "I've met the metal man from the Homeward Dream," he said, "and he is called Isaak. He is coming for us." Then Tovin told them what he could remember of the experience just as he had the council.

When he finished, he answered a few questions and eventually, all eyes returned to Rami. "We find ourselves," she finally said, "in new waters." She regarded Tovin. "The charter is clear that matters of faith fall to the Far-Seer. But matters of leadership fall to me and as much as I'd like to believe Tovin's vision, I'm faced with one irrevocable fact: In one hundred twenty-seven years of waiting and watching, the only other vision given was shared by all." He saw faux kindness in her eyes. "But this vision is exclusive to you. If the metal man could summon us all into the dream and have its herald speak to us of home, why is he now speaking only to you?"

Before the dream, no one had ascribed words to the metal man. The earlier Far-Seers inferred the matters of their faith by the statue's posture, by the location of the spire and its altar. And even after the dream, Tovin had been careful to only lay his interpretation over the words they'd heard.

"I do not know," Tovin said, "but we can ask Isaak tomorrow when he comes for us."

She pursed her lips. "No, Tovin, I think I should ask Isaak now." She turned to the frozen statue in the temple behind them. "Isaak—metal man—speak now for your servant is listening."

She waited. Someone in the crowd snickered. Someone else gasped at the disrespect.

"Maybe," she said, "he can't hear me?"

Tovin's eyes narrowed. "Maybe," he said, "he cannot hear you because you are not the Far-Seer. Or because *that* is not Isaak. Or maybe because you lack faith. I've climbed the spire twice a day since the Dawn of the Homeward Dream and prayed at its altar for our people as required by the charter. How many times have you?"

She laughed. "I'm an old woman and my role is to lead this people with clarity and compassion. I've no need to climb your spire and pray at your altar." Then she looked to the small crowd. "And this matter is simply enough resolved. We've nothing to do. Nothing to prepare for. We just wait." Her face was calm but her eyes were fierce. "And if we find this to be a false prophecy," she said, "perhaps the people will be ready to reconsider the continued role of the Far-Seer in our charter." When she said it, she gave her daughter Ana a hard look and Tovin glanced away.

The group disbanded and a few of the faithful gathered in the temple with Tovin, each assuming the posture of the metal man. He noticed that Ana took up the position near his own mat and felt his skin flush. He looked away when she smiled up at him. "Life and light to you, Far-Seer."

"And to you, Sister Ana." Before his father died, he'd thought perhaps they would end up together. But when Berum died, it had thrust Tovin quickly into his current role at a time when people most needed spiritual direction. He'd set his personal attraction aside to focus on his people.

Until that dream, the way everything inside of him seized up when he noticed their captain's daughter had been the most mysterious thing he'd experienced. But even today, in light of Isaak's impending arrival, he found the wideness in her eyes still enough to distract. "Do you think he will bear us straight to the moon?"

Tovin knelt on his mat. "I do not know his intentions. He said we would discuss it upon his arrival."

She reached over and took his hand. He was certain they'd touched before but in that particular moment, he couldn't remember when. And yet, he realized he should have because her fingers added something intoxicating to his zeal.

"Let's pray together for tomorrow to come quickly," she told him, pulling her hand back as if she also felt it like a spark.

"Yes," he said and gave himself to praying. And his prayers took on more than the shape and form of a home far away in the shadow of a great tree; instead, they took on the texture of love and belonging. And somewhere in the praying, Tovin realized he both longed for a home that he had never had and missed the only one that he had known—the one where he was his father's son, following in the footsteps of his faith, only to find that faith suddenly coming true before his eyes.

Tovin wept.

Twice more Tovin climbed the stairs and knelt to watch and pray, and each time, he was met by cold silence. He wasn't sure what he had expected but not silence. And when midday came and went and when the small scattering of his faithful finally dispersed, Tovin fought the urge to weep again.

"I think," Captain Rami said as she gave the metal man a

withering glare, "it's time to become our own salvation." Then she looked to her daughter.

When Ana left the temple with her mother, Tovin knelt alone beside the object of his faith and closed his eyes. The tears came in silence and in his mind, he saw the tree upon the plain as the wind stripped its seeds and threw them to the sky.

Spirit of long ago, rise up like wind to carry me home.

But no wind came and outside, the rain began to pour.

If anyone had told Tovin that the other side of his holy fear was a despondent, hollowed shell, he would've never believed it possible. But a lifetime of faith, a lifetime of knowing he would be the Far-Seer of the people one day, had culminated in two un-expected events—the shared dream and this most recent vision. Both had overflowed his senses and now, there was nothing left of that flooding fullness. And at the bottom of the empty space, he found a grief that he hadn't understood possible.

Tovin lay in his temple and grieved his life, his father, his faith.

For the first time in their settlement's history, no one climbed the mountain for morning and evening prayers. And no one asked. No one visited the temple and Tovin did not leave it. After three days, Ana came to him.

She stood in the doorway and avoided his eyes when he looked up at her. "The council is considering the ongoing role of the Far-Seer faith tomorrow," she said. Her eyes tried to find his but again, whatever she saw there turned them away. "My mother thought I should tell you."

Tovin said nothing. Her words were slow reaching him and when they did, he found that the grief was twisting itself into something else. When the rage came, it was as unexpected as the grief and Tovin stood and strode without a word out from his temple. He found the axe easily enough and took it. Then, he slipped back into his temple and the roar of his wrath rolled out across the settlement with the ringing of the axe as it struck the metal man again and again.

Sparks flew but the iron head couldn't even scratch the an-cient steel.

A small crowd had gathered now and Tovin felt the heat in his face as shame joined his anger. Captain Rami watched, her face unreadable. Ana's face was a wash of concern and curiosity. He pulled his feelings together and clenched them in his fist. Then he raised it to the sky. "You're right to question the Far-Seer faith," he finally said. And now whatever they saw in his eyes caused theirs to open wider in that moment.

Then Tovin hefted his axe and set out to climb his mountain one final time.

The steps were wet with rain as he took them two at a time and when he reached the top, he roared his anger at the storming sky above and around him. Raising the axe, he brought it down with all of might onto the altar's stone and heard a satisfying crack.

Again and again, the ringing iron sent up chips of dark granite as he brought the ax down upon the altar. Ana and a few of the others had followed him and watched from the stairs. And as he swung the axe, he sobbed and raged.

When the stone finally shattered into several pieces, Tovin dropped the axe and fell trembling to his knees. He looked up through his tears and met Ana's eyes.

"What have you done, Tovin?" Her voice shook and she stretched out a hand to pick up a portion of the broken stone.

Then she dropped it with a gasp. "It's . . . singing."

Singing. Tovin reached out to find another piece of the broken, dark gem. Music flooded him. And then the voice.

Life and light to those who wait and worship, Isaak said into his mind. *Tovin Far-Seer, can you hear me?*

"Isaak?"

And suddenly, he was on the plain again beneath the ancient tree, surrounded by the new, young forest that had sprung up around it. The metal man stood in his robes.

And then, Ana stood among them as well. "Tovin, I—" Her eyes went wide. She dropped to her knees. "My lord," she whispered.

Isaak stooped beside her and placed a metal hand on her shoulder. "I am Isaak. I am no lord. I am a servant of the light, just like you." Then his red eyes flashed and met Tovin's. "I've been casting for you for days, Far-Seer."

Tovin's shame was back and he opened his mouth to speak but no words came.

Isaak continued, "It is the oddest of situations. After our first encounter, your location appeared clear, but the closer we got, the less clear it was. Ultimately, we turned back to where we first picked up your message and we've been waiting and hoping." The metal man paused. "It's almost as if your metal man and your island do not want to be found. And that, of course, makes finding both a more curious and necessary undertaking that I previously believed." He glanced at each of them again. "How is that both of you are here now with only the single stone?"

Tovin felt the heat in his face. "When you didn't arrive, I . . . I was angry. I broke the dreamstone with an axe."

"Now," Ana said, "it's in several pieces." She held up the chunk in her own hand.

"That may actually be for the best," Isaak said. "I think whatever your mechoservitor marks has other defenses preventing our ability to reach you. Several of the silver army—metal men, we are called—were sent out by Frederico's people millennia ago to locate various artifacts." Tovin wasn't following and somehow, the metal man read the confusion on his face. He held up a dark stone; it was identical to the one set into the altar. "These mechoservitors were stripped of their ability to communicate and be tracked across great distances through what's called the aether. They relied on external stones like this."

Tovin nodded. "That is the stone I broke."

"It will have less range in smaller pieces but that already tells us something about our situation," Isaak said. He waited.

Tovin thought about it. "That you are relatively close?"

Isaak nodded. "I would like to attempt an experiment, if you are willing to help."

Tovin glanced at Ana and just as he opened his mouth, another form materialized in the plain with a gasp.

"Gods be damned," Captain Rami said as she fell to her knees before Isaak and the tree. "You're real after all."

Isaak inclined his head. "To the best of my knowledge, I am."

She looked up to Tovin and he saw she clutched a piece of the dreamstone in her own hands. "And you are coming for us?"

"I hope to." Isaak looked at Tovin. "Are you ready?"

Tovin nodded.

The metal man turned and raised his hands as wind rustled his robe. As he did, the music grew. He turned back to them.

"This canticle," Isaak said, "contains a code that I think will wake your metal man if we can re-connect it to the aether. Once it's re-connected, it may have the answer to what is preventing us from reaching you in our vessels."

Vessels. Tovin didn't realize he'd said it aloud until Isaak answered.

"Yes, we've been joined now by two New Espiran airships."

"Airships?" Tovin heard the wonder in Captain Rami's voice. She still knelt, her eyes now wider than her daughters.

"We're quite eager to find you and whatever is hidden in your archipelago. It is likely necessary in our work to heal the world." Isaak pointed up.

Tovin followed his finger, beyond the tree, to the scarred world that filled the sky behind it. "To heal the world?"

He'd been told stories about the Named Lands where his grandmother had grown up. Tales of the Androfrancines and their careful kin-clave of control over the nations that had sprung up around their forest city and its Great Library. He'd been raised hearing about the wizard king Xhum Y'Zir and the world he destroyed when his seven sons had been murdered in the Scientism uprising that P'Andro Whym led. According to the legends, Y'Zir had sent out his death choir and his Seven Cacophonic Deaths had razed the known world. The desolation had been so vast they called it The Churning Waste.

All of that now intersected here twisted inside of Tovin now. His feelings had been a rushing wind of holy fear and awe, disillusionment and despair, rage and then remorse. He'd been the Far-Seer of his people and he'd never, ever thought *this* was what he would see. He had watched and worshiped in the hope of finding rescue and home. And now he and his people were invited to this unexpected moment.

"What do I do?" he asked Isaak.

As he asked it, his eyes never left that broken planet above.

*

Tovin clutched the dreamstone and let Ana guide him down the stairs. He wanted to run but with the rain and the disorientation of the stone, this was more prudent. Two fragments of stone were in his pocket and one in his fist.

He could hear the music as he went and half way down the spire, it started to fade. "Wait," he said. Then he screwed his eyes closed in concentration. *Isaak, can you hear me?*

Isaak's voice dropped into his mind like a stone in a lagoon. *The signal is fading.*

Tovin looked up. "It's the height," he said. The handful of others moved past him and continued their way to the temple. Ana and Rami waited with him.

The realization came quickly and he reached into his pocket, holding out one of the stones. "Someone has to go back up with this one," he said.

Yes, the voice in his head agreed.

Rami took it. "I'll go." She looked at Ana. "You stay with him."

"Thank you," Tovin said. Then he turned and continued. Already, the song was louder and the next time it faded, he gave Ana the last fragment from his pocket.

Everyone within easy reach had gathered now at the temple and Tovin heard their collective, indrawn breath as he ran into their midst. They parted for him as he approached the metal man.

Tovin bent low, placing the stone against the warm steel forehead.

He wasn't sure what he'd expected but nothing so sudden. The metal man sprang to life with a liquid grace and Tovin fell back as it surged to its feet. It said nothing and moved through the northward facing doorway of the temple, its eyes burning the color of bright blood, casting a red glow upon the mist as it sped for the spire.

Tovin raced after, quickly overtaking Ana, who fell in behind him. All around him the song played on despite having already done its work so effectively. He reached the stairs still quite far behind the metal man and took them faster than he ever had dared before. And yet he found his feet sure upon the ground as he sprinted.

When he reached the top, he saw Captain Rami kneeling to

the side, staring as the metal man lifted the altar easily above his head and tossed it out into the sea.

"That which is closed," the metal man said, "is now open."

Stooping down into the hollow beneath the altar, the pocked and dark mechoservitor lifted out a silver rod the length of an axe handle that shone with the same reflective steel that Isaak was made of.

Suddenly, as the metal man held up the rod, they were all on the plain of saplings again. And now, this one also shone brightly—now suddenly brand new in the light of that broken world above where it stood, next to its robed twin.

It held the rod out before Tovin and Rami. "You are authorized," it said.

Rami reached out; Tovin did not. She paused and looked at him. "You," she said, "are the Far-Seer of the people." She withdrew her hand and inclined head.

"Authorized? I don't understand," Tovin said as he took the rod. And then, all at once, he did.

Their story lay buried in their song. A song of light in darkness, a hymn of home-seeds scattered on the wind of vast and empty space.

A silver army of life sent out to prepare the way of the people in all of their manifestations. Blue-green homes with a single blue-green moon. Reminders of the world that spat them from its oceans and the barren moon they had transformed into a paradise after their first early leap into the sky. They'd left their temples to their Firsthome on new homes scattered across the vastness of night as their Continuity Engine kept the people expanding and expanding. Until finally, it was determined that the last of the people would stand or fall upon one final home and the Continuity Engine would be shut off.

And here now, he understood this place, Firstfall, that had been long hidden. Where the shaping of Lasthome began so long ago when the first of the silver army arrived and started their work for the ships swollen with life that followed after in the dark.

He felt it beneath the waves, buried and lost and . . . *guarded*. He felt the kin-serpents that prowled the deeps, large and hungry for straying vessels. He felt the ebb and flow of the aether-tamps and the storms they raised. He felt a city of light stirring to life. And felt its roots. Roots that stretched across the world, into the world, and far away beyond it.

I can feel the moon.

Tovin felt the warmth of the rod in his hand and forced his eyes open. The metal man was back to kneeling now, still facing north, and there in the waters Tovin saw light dancing and growing as something massive beneath the waters expanded and rose.

Ana stood to his left and Captain Rami to his right. Behind them, his flock approached.

He blinked and brought home the kin-serpents.

Tovin smiled and the clouds took on the blue-green tint of a rising moon as the rain stopped abruptly. Still, the moonlight was weak compared to the golden light of the city that awaited them below.

Isaak's voice was closer now. *Oh my.*

Now, it took Tovin no effort to force his words into the stone. *What is it, Isaak?*

We can see it on our horizon. We are closer than we realized. It is . . . The metal man's words faded into awe.

"It is the City of Firstfall," Tovin declared and he knew as he said it that it was also his new home.

"Your life has changed a great deal in a very short amount of time," Isaak said as they walked through the Firstfall library's groves of knowledge the next day.

Tovin looked down at the staff in his hand and the dark ring upon his finger then looked up at his new friend. "It really has." He watched as the uniformed men and women of the New Espiran Expeditionary Force moved among the trees of knowledge, blue stones in their hands as curious fingers tested the gemstones that dangled there. "I would have never imagined this."

Isaak's arrival in a metal sea-serpent they called Behemoth—flanked by two airships—had been rather anti-climactic after the resurrection of the lost city. And the city itself had warned Tovin of their approach. He'd met them there on the shore just a day ago and already, his head spun at what he'd learned.

Two others materialized in the library—a man and a woman clothed in silver light. They smiled at Isaak, shimmering like ghosts in the grove.

"This is the Homefinder Lord Nebios Whym—a child of the Younger God Whym and brother to P'Andro, though it is complicated. And this is Lady Winteria, formerly Queen of the Marshfolk," Isaak said. "Now leading the colony on the moon in the Firsthome Temple. You'll remember her from the dream."

"Our libraries are joined in the aether," Whym said. "We will be able to at least meet and communicate here."

Tovin nodded. In the two days since he'd taken the rod, everything about his life had changed. And that faith—as flawed as it had been—was ultimately what served them and sustained them. Not the objects of said faith. But he could see why it was easy to consider his immediate forebears Younger Gods and the ones who shaped this world and its single moon—and countless others like it—Elder Gods.

Home sown in darkness by a people who carried darkness inside of them everywhere they went alongside their light.

He shook his thoughts away and remembered his manners. "I'm sorry," he said. "This has all been a lot to take in."

The woman's smile held understanding. "I've said those words a great deal these last five years or so." She reached over and took her companion's hand. "It *is* a lot. But we have lots of time."

Lord Whym inclined his head. "And lots of help."

Tovin looked beyond the grove to the avenues and lighted domes of something unseen upon this world in millennia. More and more New Espirans had been arriving throughout the morning through the translation pool he'd activated with the brush of a thumb along the administrator's rod he held. He'd been largely inseparable from Isaak since his arrival and along the way, he'd pieced together enough to know that only a few settlers had made it through the Seaway and onto the moon. And that there was an entire people—these New Espirans who came with Isaak—hidden in a creche at the center of the earth who would soon need a new home of their own.

Tovin expected many of them would choose Firstfall. Along with representatives from the Ninefold Forest Library of the Named Lands.

Despite the weight of wonder he already felt, he knew there would be more to come. And also so much to learn. From so many people . . . some wrapped in light, some wrapped in metal.

Sometimes, Tovin realized, home is already beneath your feet and you just don't see it. Sometimes seeds fly far and sometimes they simply fall to the ground. They don't decide themselves.

He found himself wondering what Ana would want to do and some part of him hoped maybe she would want to stay with him and learn everything they could about their city and their heritage. They could spend their mornings and evenings in the shade of the library.

Tovin brought his attention back to the conversation. Isaak had been speaking and once again, he realized he'd missed every word. He opened his mouth to apologize again, and the others chuckled.

Isaak placed a hand upon his shoulder and Tovin felt the warmth of it. "I've also watched the world change a good deal and at times have even been a tool in its forced change. And I have learned that the truest hearts and dreams are in the direction of healing this world."

Tovin nodded. He could see this was true, and he could see that he played a part in it. Had already and still would. All by the happenstance of where his people had fallen like seeds and a homeward dream out of nowhere. He did not need to know exactly the form the future might take to know that it would be beyond his wildest imaginings.

It ended up Tovin the Far-Seer did not need to see very far at all. His path, radiant and bright as heaven, lay ready beneath his waiting feet.

BUSINESS IN GREAT WATERS

NOREEN SOUTHLAND WATCHED HER HEADLIGHTS CHEW fog and gripped the wheel firmly at ten and two like her father had shown her. He'd worked a lot of jobs in his time including a year or two driving a taxi in Chicago and he'd taught her with all of the patient caution of a nervous man on the road.

Beneath her, the tires of the rental car mumbled over a highway she'd not driven before. Beside her, her mother breathed deeply, moving in and out of sleep for the past fifty miles as they wound their way southwest of Portland.

She's tired, Noreen thought. It had been quite a trip so far. They'd flown into Seattle and spent time with family Noreen and her mother hadn't seen in most of twenty years—her father's family. Without Tom Southland along for the ride, it had been a strained visit. Still, he'd assured them when they left Twinsburg that his family wouldn't eat them.

But, Noreen realized, he should've been more worried about Valdana eating *them.*

She glanced at the woman beside her. Her head was up against the window, her gray hair tucked into a scarf and her eyes hidden behind a pair of sunglasses that she really didn't need in the Oregon twilight. They'd left Seattle—finally—that morning and even though she didn't drive much at home, Valdana had eagerly put Noreen behind the wheel of the car.

"But we won't tell your father," she said. Then she'd paused. "Or the rental agency, either, for that matter."

Noreen didn't mind at all. And despite her father's odd family, she'd had a fantastic trip so far. They had a week left and then she'd start her first year at Stanford. A quick stop on the Oregon coast in the small town her mother came from and then a meandering drive down through the redwoods and into San Francisco via the Coastal Highway.

"Are we there yet?"

Noreen laughed. "Twenty more miles I think."

"Wake me when we get there."

"I will," she said.

She thought about putting on the radio but decided she'd rather listen to the road and her mother's breathing. Noreen had left home a few times briefly but never without her parents. They'd spent time in Europe and taken the requisite family trips to DC, to Orlando, to Anaheim, to Arizona and Wyoming. They'd even spent a few Thanksgivings in Seattle. But never Oregon.

Never with her mother's family. Mom's family was undiscussed, the questions deftly brushed aside with admirable skill. The only hint Noreen could pull down was the strange look upon her father's face when she finally worked up the courage to ask him.

He looked away like he did when he was lying. "I've only met some of them . . . and very briefly. You'll have to ask your mother."

She'd already tried that.

Then, after she chose Stanford and graduated from high school, her mom had surprised her.

"Just us," she said. "Our first mother-daughter road trip." And this time, Noreen hadn't even brought it up. "We'll fly into Seattle," her mother said, "spend some time with Tom's family, then drive south. I'll show you where I'm from." Tom had looked away as she said it. "Show you where I met your father."

After that, she'd clammed up again. But Noreen noticed she sang a lot more throughout the summer. And that her dad fidgeted and fussed more. And that at night, they were embarrassing her at least four times a week to the point that she put headphones on as soon as she went to bed.

Moving out, Noreen thought, couldn't come soon enough.

And yet, the thought of it now as she took the corners of Highway 6, made her stomach knot up. It would be good for her. She knew it. Even if she didn't know exactly what she wanted to study.

Of course, she'd always been a strong student. She didn't worry as much about that. But she did wonder how she'd fare with the other students. She couldn't remember a time that she didn't feel out of place. Just slightly off-kilter with the rest of the people around her, especially the ones that were her own age.

She'd had few friends in high school. And exactly one boyfriend and one girlfriend once she figured out she could swim in either pool comfortably.

No, she thought. Not comfortably. Few of her social interactions had been comfortable, at least how she imagined comfort to be. Still, she'd gotten used to that sense of displacement and it was as good as it got. Naomi had been better at being a girlfriend than Greg was at being a boyfriend. Still hearts had been broken along the way. Hers in both instances.

But Stanford would be a chance to start over. And slowly find her way into the waiting world.

As she pushed the car forward, Noreen watched the fog lift and they spilled suddenly into the town of Tillamook. She was familiar with the cheese and the ice cream, though she preferred Ben & Jerry's and the cheese she'd had in France with her parents. When she turned north on 101, the smell of salt filled the car and her mother stirred.

"We're close," Valdana said. She powered down the window and thrust her face into the night wind, one hand clapped firmly on her scarf.

Something in her voice, combined with the smell of the sea, stirred butterflies to life in Noreen's stomach. The ache was gone, now replaced by a building excitement. And it stayed gone even though the next time she glanced to her mother, Valdana Garibaldi Southland had tears coursing down her cheeks as she gulped in the taste of homecoming.

"Um," Noreen said when she first read the words. "The town you're from is Garibaldi?"

Her mother's voice betrayed nonchalance. "Yes, dear."

"Your family started the town?"

She laughed. "No. I just liked the name. And I wanted to remember where I was from."

They were nearly there now. The moon was up and a steady breeze had brushed the fog aside. "You chose the name?"

Valdana's hand on her shoulder was surprising. "So many questions."

Garibaldi was nestled into a bend in the highway as it moved north along Tillamook Bay. The streets were quiet and most of the storefronts were dark. The town's single hotel was easy to spot and she put on her blinker.

"No," her mother said. "Go left. Go down to the marina."

"Shouldn't we wait until it's light so we can see it?"

"No. Let's see it by moonlight first." Valdana's voice sounded far away and there was something lonely in it. Something that touched Noreen's own sense of displacement in the world around her.

She sighed and hoped it didn't sound like exasperation.

I'm just tired, she thought. It was her mom's first time back since she'd left over twenty years ago. And she chose to share this trip with her daughter. The significance of that gesture wasn't lost on her.

She turned left.

They crept past the massive hulk of a steam engine and a small park, gravel crunching beneath the tires. The slips were full with a variety of boats all yellow in the dirty lamplight. She slowed the car and kept going until they reached the water.

Noreen climbed out first and stretched, the breeze chilling her. When her mom hadn't moved in a full minute, she leaned into her open door.

"Are you okay?"

Valdana tried to wipe the tear before she saw it, then dropped the sunglasses back over her eyes. "Fine. Sand or salt in my eye."

Yeah right, Noreen thought. But she didn't say anything.

Her mother climbed out and stretched a hand to her. Another unusual event but the tears made this all uncharted territory. So she bit her tongue and took the hand. Then she let her mother lead them down wooden stairs and out onto a dock that jutted into Tillamook Bay.

They were close to the end of it when her mother paused. She looked uncomfortable, staring at the water with pursed lips. "Maybe you should wait in the car," she said.

"Why?"

Valdana said nothing. She let go of Noreen's hand and started walking again. "I need to get closer."

There were two boats tied on either side of the dock and her mother moved toward the one that was lowest in the water.

"Mom, I don't think we can just—"

"Quiet, dear." Valdana lowered herself into the boat and made her way back to the stern. She pulled off her sunglasses and untied her scarf.

What is she doing? Noreen started toward her, and her mother waved her back.

"Just wait there. I'll only be a moment." She paused and met Noreen's eyes. "Trust me."

Still, Noreen gasped when her mother bent over the back of the boat and plunged her head into the water. "Mom!" She jumped down into the boat and tripped on a gas can. "Fuck."

Her mother raised her head up from the water. "Language, Nori."

Her head and shoulders were soaked, her hair a gray tangle, but her eyes had a light in them now that Noreen had never seen before. She found it frightening and exhilarating all at once.

Valdana wrapped her wet hair into the scarf and laughed again. It was a laugh like no other Noreen had heard from the woman, full of music. It was as if whatever sorrow she carried was suddenly less from this unexpected baptism.

Noreen paused at the car and looked out over the water. Farther out, the moonshine framed the bay in silver but here by the shore, the water was dark.

A flash of movement near the dock drew her eye and for the briefest moment Noreen thought she saw a fin ripple the water where her mother's face had been. A really big fin.

She blinked after it and saw nothing now. *I'm just tired.*

Then Noreen joined her mother in the car and pointed it toward the hotel and a night of needed sleep.

The hotel was silent and wrapped in predawn fog when Noreen slipped out in her running gear. She'd tried to keep up her routine on this trip but it had been hit or miss. She'd gotten out on the sidewalks in Seattle and had even discovered the trail around Green Lake. But she preferred the quiet of a small town.

She set off at an easy run, pulling up the town from memory.

It was small enough that she'd likely see all there was to see and still be several miles short. Her mother would sleep until at least eight so that left her several hours. She had a thin Asimov novel tucked into the back pocked of her shorts, place marked with a twenty. She'd settle into a cup of coffee somewhere and read.

Noreen hadn't gone far when the sound of music drifted to her from across the empty highway. With the morning air so still, it was the only sound other than the gentle slap of her sneakers on the sidewalk. She looked in the direction of the noise and saw the shadowy engine and the few detached antique passenger cars that formed the Lions Club park and railroad museum.

The notes were soft and full, dripping on the air. If she had to guess, it was a wind instrument of some kind but unlike any she'd heard before. Deep and rich, the melody grabbed her and she felt something mournful in it that drew her. She jogged across the street and moved into the gray halo of a streetlight. Just past the engine, she saw the park and its small, covered picnic area. A large man in a long yellow raincoat sat on one of the tables, hunched over whatever it was that he played.

Noreen told her feet to stop but they refused her now; the song drew her as if she were a fish on its line. She slowed to a walk in protest, but her sneakers still carried her closer.

The man took shape and she saw that he was barefoot. His hair was a tangle of red and gray, long and flowing over his shoulders like a lion's mane. His beard was full and bushy and the hands that held the shell were large and strong and old. He looked up from his playing as she approached.

"You are up early," he said.

Noreen nodded. She knew she should feel some level of apprehension but something in the song soothed her. Besides, she was eighteen and in running shoes. He was—she couldn't find an age that fit.

But he looks kind, she thought.

Finally, she answered him. "I like to run in the quiet."

He chuckled and held up the shell. It was large and smooth and pink. "Sorry to have spoiled your morning."

Noreen blushed and stammered, "No, not at all." She felt the heat in her ears. "It's . . . beautiful. I've never heard anything like it."

"No," he said, "you likely haven't. It's a Lemurian sea beetle shell."

She took another two steps forward. The smell of the sea was stronger here and now she could see that his eyes were blue beneath his craggy eyebrows. "And the song?"

"One of mine. I've not played it in a while." He held the instrument out to her.

She took it, surprised at how heavy it was in her hands. She turned it over, her fingers tracing the surface, feeling the divot of each finger hole. "How long have you played?"

"A long time," he said.

She handed it back to him. "It's really lovely. So is the song."

"Thank you. I wrote it for my daughter." He smiled and put the instrument to his lips, blowing softly as his fingers moved over its surface. He played a few notes and then lowered it. "So what brings you to Garibaldi?"

"I'm starting down in Stanford in a few weeks. My mother decided to take me on a trip and help get me settled in. She's from around here. She left when she met my father. I think it's her first time back."

Something clouded the man's eyes for the briefest moment. "That happens a lot around here. My own daughter left when she was about your age. And it's a glorious age—despite heartbroken parents. Opportunity calls. Or adventure. Or love." He smiled. "And in your case, Stanford."

"Yes."

"What will you study?"

It was a question that perplexed her. She'd not been like the other kids. Most of them had something they knew they wanted to do with their lives. Her friend Thomas wanted to a writer. Her friend Kate wanted to be a lawyer. But nothing had sounded right. "I'm not sure yet," she said. "Everything at first until something feels like . . . me."

The old man nodded. "Sounds fair. And refreshing. Everyone seems to know what they want right from the gate. But maybe taking a little time to see what's what, figuring out some of how the world works and how life emerges and evolves, is a better approach." Their eyes met and his smile was warm. "I don't often meet a young person who doesn't know exactly what they want to be when they grow up."

"I was the only one in my class," she said. "Everyone else has it all figured out."

"And it's always been that way? Even when you were a little girl?"

Now she laughed. "No, back then I knew exactly what I wanted to be."

"Oh really?"

Noreen nodded. "But don't laugh," she said. Then she blushed again. "I wanted to be a mermaid."

He didn't laugh. If anything, his tone and expression were more serious. "There's nothing funny about wanting to be a mermaid. I think it's a rather noble aspiration, actually."

"I used to dream about it." She hadn't thought about it in years but now, her memory flooded with the taste of salt and the dancing of light beneath the waves.

"And," he said, "little mermaid girls dream of growing legs. Funny that."

"Yes," she said. She'd seen that movie a thousand times as a girl, though her mother couldn't stand it. Her father, on the other hand, loved it and watched it with her at every opportunity. They even sang the songs together while Valdana wore headphones and read a book in the other room.

"Maybe," the old man said, "you can study mermaidology at Stanford."

She chuckled. "I wish." Instead, she suspected she'd settle into literature or history. Maybe creative writing. Something impossible to land a real job with. But something she could love.

He winked at her. "You'll find your way." Then, he stood. "And it's time for me to find mine. It was nice to meet you, Noreen."

He extended a hand and she took it, her own dwarfed in his grip. "It was nice to meet you, too."

He'd already turned and started moving toward the road that led past the fueling station and out to the slips when she realized she couldn't remember his name. And he was in the shadows when she figured out that it was because he'd never told her.

And I didn't tell him mine, either, she realized as he vanished into the predawn morning.

Noreen started after him but by the time she reached the fueling station he was nowhere to be found.

She finished her run early and slipped into the first storefront to open—a small bakery that reeked of heaven in the form of fresh donuts and hot coffee. She asked the woman who ran it about the old man who played his Lemurian sea-beetle shell in the railroad park and tried not to let the woman's blank stare convince her that she was hallucinating.

She managed a few pages of Asimov before slipping out of the bakery and toward the hotel. The sun was up now and there were cars on the highway. Noreen let herself into the room and found her mother's note on the freshly made bed.

Back soon, the note read. *Went for a swim.*

"Nuts," Noreen said to the empty room.

Noreen heard the key card in the lock and watched the door slowly swing open. "Never mind, Dad," she said into her phone. "She's back." She hung up and all of her anxiety and agitation infused itself into her tone. "Are you *crazy*?"

Valdana stood in the doorway. Her hair was wet but her clothes were dry and immaculate. She held a rolled hotel towel in her hand. She started to smile and Noreen's voice took on even more edge.

"No. Seriously. Do we need to take you in and get you checked out? It's the fucking *Pacific Ocean,* Mother."

The smile broadened and now Noreen felt anger. "No, dear. Just Tillamook Bay. In August. It was . . . brisk." She laughed. "And delightful." Though she glanced away as she said it. She hung her towel in the tiny bathroom. "Was that your father?"

Noreen sighed. Now her mom was in the bathroom, pushing the door mostly closed as she slipped out of her clothes and into the shower. She took a few breaths before calling through the open door. "Yeah. He didn't think you taking off for a swim was strange, either."

Valdana laughed. "No," she said. "He wouldn't. How was your run?"

Noreen thought about telling her mother about the old man but decided not to. She wasn't sure exactly why. It just seemed . . . private, somehow. "It was fine. Until I got back here and started worrying about you."

"You do realize," her mother said, "that I'm an excellent swimmer?"

Actually, Noreen didn't. She couldn't recall her mother going near the water any more than she needed to. It was her dad who took her swimming. Valdana usually went in no deeper than her knees and even looked profoundly uncomfortable at that. "You have to admit," she said. "It's a little out of the blue for the woman who disdains wading."

"Well," Valdana said, "I think it's about time for some out of the blue. And there's more coming." She paused and leaned her head out of the bathroom with raised eyebrows. "It seems my family wants to meet you."

She knew little of her mother's family. She'd heard next to nothing about her childhood. And the fact that she'd not come back in nearly twenty years said a lot about her feelings for this place. Or at least, Noreen had thought so. But Valdana had taken on the name of this place to remember it. And now, it seemed, there were relatives for her to meet.

"When?"

"Now," her mother said.

"*Now?*"

Then Noreen was pulling clothes out of her bag and heading for the shower herself. They were out the door twenty-three minutes later.

This time, Valdana drove and they left town driving south. They'd not gone far before they took a right onto a gravel road that led down to the water. The road spilled into an empty parking lot and pier with a single building sitting upon it out over the water.

At one time, the building had been lively. It had a figurehead to either side of its ornate carved doors, and a sign over them, in flaking gold letters, declared it as *Neptune's Hall*. They parked as Noreen looked around the area. "Looks like we're the first ones here."

Her mom said nothing. They climbed out of the car and as they drew near the building, Noreen heard voices now, and music, from inside. She also smelled food and her stomach growled from it.

Valdana paused at the door. "Are you ready?"

She nodded. "Are you?"

"Not nearly. But as ready as I'll ever be."

Then her mother pushed open the door.

There was a hastily thrown-together banner, handwritten on butcher paper that welcomed them home in bold, blocky letters. There were disposable aluminum tins full of spaghetti and macaroni and cheese from the local grocery store's deli with disposable forks and plates stacked nearby. There was a cake—obviously from the same and only grocery store in town. And scattered throughout the room, an assortment of people of various ages all turned toward them as they entered.

"Family," Valdana Garibaldi Southland declared, "meet Noreen." She paused and swept the room with a gesture that seemed out of place. "Noreen, meet my family."

And every single one of them, Noreen noticed, was barefoot and in long raincoats. Two of them over in the corner—young men who could've been twins—held shells much like the one she'd seen this morning and paused in their playing to wave.

It was subdued as reunions went, Noreen imagined, though she had nothing really to compare it with. Her father's family in Seattle was its own soupy mess. They feigned interest and friendliness well enough. But Valdana's family was a mix of friendly and aloof.

My family, Noreen thought. *Not just my mother's.*

They stood around the musty-smelling hall eating macaroni or spaghetti on paper plates hot and wet with the food they held. She and her mother stayed in one place while the others slowly drifted by until everyone had been introduced.

"Don't worry," her mother said after yet another cousin moved on. "There's no test at the end."

The last to stop and stand with them was a woman that looked younger than Valdana though she was introduced as her older sister. "Your aunt Karolina," her mother told her. Then she pointed to the boys playing music in the corner. "Those are her sons."

There had been no hugging so far. With hands full of plates and forks and wadded napkins, there had been really no physical contact of any kind. And everyone ate with a methodical, almost stilted manner and yet the portions and pace betrayed an eagerness.

Karolina was the first to touch her. She put down her plate, took their plates as well, then hugged Valdana briefly and hugged Noreen to the point of discomfort. "It is so nice to meet you, Noreen. I'm so glad your mother finally brought you around."

Noreen glanced at her mother to see if the words left any mark. She'd not heard an edge in her aunt's voice, but she sometimes missed the edge in her own mother's voice.

Now I see where she gets it, Noreen thought. "It's nice to meet you," she said. She took up her plate quickly and hid behind it.

"So Father decided not to come?" Noreen finally heard a trace of something there. She wasn't sure of what it was until her mother finished speaking. "Again," she said, and now Noreen recognized the bitterness. When she glanced her way, she saw anger in her mother's dark eyes.

Karolina was back to eating her macaroni and cheese. There was something feral in her eyes as she pushed the plastic forkfuls of yellow goo into her mouth. "No," she said between bites. "He's got the station wagon. Said he forgot something at the store." She waved her fork around the room. "This whole thing was his idea."

Noreen studied Valdana's face. Her voice flattened and her jawline un-tensed. But the anxiety was back in her eyes. "Oh," she said.

"That was a long time ago, Val," her older sister said.

Noreen surprised herself by speaking. "What was a long time ago?" As soon as she asked, she regretted it from her mother's sharp look.

"The wedding," Karolina said.

Her mother opened her mouth to say something but the sound of a car outside closed it.

"And that's him there."

Valdana swallowed. "I should probably go talk to him."

Karolina smiled. "I'll keep Noreen company."

Noreen wasn't sure how she felt being left alone with her new family. Or how Valdana felt about her sudden access to information she'd kept from Noreen all her life. Her mother sighed and moved toward the door. Once she was through it and it had closed behind her, Noreen turned to Karolina. "So her father no-showed at the wedding?"

Karolina nodded. "He couldn't abide his youngest marrying a landlubber."

"A landlubber?" She hadn't heard that term since some pirate movie she'd watched in middle school. "My father?"

Her aunt laughed. "It's unimportant. What's important is that the sea knows its own and those with business in great waters are always called back to it. So now she's home. We had a lovely swim this morning. She and Daddy are patching things up." She paused to push another forkful of macaroni into her mouth. "And I'm meeting my niece. Business in great waters, indeed."

Indeed, Noreen thought. But didn't know what to make of it. "So how did they meet?" Her parents had told her very little. Her father had worked the coast for a few years in college and had met her mother singing in a bar. Given how much had been left out, Noreen suspected there was much more to hear.

"Val used to sneak ashore sometimes on Friday and Saturday nights to sing in Rusty's Tavern. It was out near the slips. Closed now. Your father heard her and fell horribly in love. And as much as she loved the land, she loved the air even more so she was easily lured into his net."

Noreen blinked. "Excuse me?"

"The plane," she said. "He offered her a moonlit ride in his plane."

She tried to piece it together and couldn't. Finally she just asked. "My father had a plane?" The idea of Mister Hands-At-Ten-And-Two flying a plane boggled her.

"Well, I don't know if it was his. But he flew it. He used to give biplane rides out of Newport during the summers. He loved your mother's voice and she loved your father's wings."

She wasn't sure what else to ask. There were too many questions crowding her brain. "And so they got married?"

"Yes," her aunt said. "Right here. I was her maid of honor."

Noreen looked at the door. "And this is her first time back since?"

Karolina nodded. "It's how Father wanted it. 'No daughter of mine' and all that. Of course, that lasted all of about a year but by then, we'd already lost her." The door opened and Valdana shoved her sunglasses on but not before Noreen saw the tear-streaked mascara. "And now it seems we've found her. And you as well."

Her mother approached and Karolina turned to her. "Okay?" she asked.

Valdana sniffed. "Okay." She reached out a hand and settled it onto Noreen's shoulder. The weight of it conveyed something that Noreen couldn't exactly name. Perhaps a reassurance and a seeking for reassurance all in one gesture. "Your grandfather would like a word."

Noreen blushed. "With me?"

"He's just outside." Her mother paused and wrinkled her nose. "*Smoking.*"

Karolina wrinkled her nose, too. "Ye gods," she said.

Noreen let herself out into the gravel lot and wasn't surprised at all to see the old man from the park. He leaned up against a battered, rusty station wagon angled like something from the seventies. "I guess you've figured me out by now," he told her as she approached.

"It's been quite a day," Noreen said.

He held up the lit stub of a Swisher Sweets. "Best bit of the landlubber world as far as I'm concerned." He rattled the pack at her with the other hand. "Smoke?"

She'd smoked weed a time or two but never a cigar, if these were really considered cigars. She thought of her mother inside wrinkling her nose. "Absolutely," she said.

He lit it for her and she sucked in the harsh smoke, tasting the sweetness of the paper on her lips. She coughed.

"Easy there," he said.

She stood with her grandfather and smoked a bit. Finally, he spoke. "I'm sorry it took so long to meet you," he said. "I didn't handle things well with your mother and father."

She shrugged. "You and Mom are good?"

He nodded. "As good as we can be for now. It's been a long time so it will be a while to heal it all up, I reckon. But she's coming back after she drops you at Stanford. We'll get more time then." He paused. "And one day," he said, "I hope you'll come back, too." He winked at her. "I don't think your dreams were a coincidence, Noreen. It's in your lungs and in your bones."

She smiled. "They were pretty amazing dreams." She took another draw on the Swisher Sweets cigar. "I reckon I may have business in great waters that will need attending once I hear what the landlubber's have to say."

Now her grandfather laughed. "I hope so." He reached over and opened the car door. He pulled out a gift bag shoved haphazardly full of neon-pink and green tissue paper. "I have something for you." He handed it to her. "But don't open it now. Do it when I'm not around."

She nodded. Then they crushed out their cigars and returned to the reunion in progress.

It was night and the fog was gone as they made their way south. They'd driven in silence for the first several hours, Noreen's head full from the oddest—and probably most unbelievable—twenty-four hours of her life. A road trip with mother that had veered into the unexpected and surreal.

Adding to the moment, Valdana drove. She did it one-handed with an elbow crooked out of the open window. The cool, salted wind filled the car.

"Quite a day, huh?"

Noreen chuckled. "You could say so." She looked at her mother. Her hair was back under the scarf. At least her sunglasses were tucked away. "How are you?"

Valdana glanced at her daughter. "I'm fine. It was good to go home after so long away."

"It sounds like things were pretty bad when you left."

Her mother chuckled, more the bark of a seal. "They certainly were. Your father hasn't stuck so much as a toe in the Pacific ever since." She nodded to the gift bag that still sat in Noreen's lap. "Think you'll be able to learn how to play it?"

Noreen looked down at the pink conch that lay in its nest of tissue paper. It was smaller than the one her grandfather played and it was a brighter color. The letter *N* was carved into it. She lifted it out and fit her fingers to the holes. "I'll give it a try," she said.

"You'll probably be the only one at Stanford that can hear it. But if you take it down to the beach . . ."

The paper crinkled as she put the shell down. "I'm not quite ready to meet more of the family, Mom." She stared out the window. The moon was up again and it washed the water in silver. "Besides," she said, "I'll have school."

Valdana snorted. "You sound like your father."

Noreen raised an eyebrow. "Which one? Driver's ed instructor or biplane pilot?"

Now, Valdana's chuckle became laughter. "He was the same way with his plane. Even made me wear one of those ridiculous pilot caps. Like in the movies." Then her voice was faraway and when Noreen glanced at her, her face was far away with it. "You should've seen him fly. He was magnificent."

She wanted to ask her if he'd ever seen her swim but she decided that it wasn't her business. Instead, she grinned. "And you used to sing? In the tavern?"

Her mother blushed. "Just how much did your aunt tell you?"

"Enough to find your hatred of my favorite movie quite . . . amusing."

Her mother grinned. "And now you know why the only thing you ever wanted to be when you grew up is quite . . . ironic."

This time, when Valdana laughed, Noreen laughed with her and then they went back to a comfortable silence. As they drove, she thought about comings and goings and how different it was to leave home this way, driven by her mother on a journey she never imagined making, learning things about herself and where she came from that she still couldn't really grasp.

She expected that she would grow into it all with time and meanwhile, she'd unlocked one piece of the puzzle. Stanford, she was certain, had an oceanography program and she thought that might be a useful major.

And maybe, during the summers, she'd come back to the Oregon coast and spend more time with her mother's family—her family. The faces played out before her there in Neptune's Hall. The hands moving methodically from plate to mouth, splashes of cheese or spaghetti sauce on yellow rubber slickers. She could still taste the sweetness of the cigar on her lips, the bitterness of the smoke in her mouth.

She fit there. It was unlike any other place she'd been before. Those odd, beautiful people so awkward on dry land.

Like me, she thought.

She didn't mean to fall asleep. She drifted off, lulled by the car.

To her left, Valdana Garibaldi Southland drove slow and savored the night. And to her right, the Pacific beat like a heart and Noreen Southland dreamed of her unfinished business beneath those pounding waves.

EVERMORE I TOLD THE RAVEN

IT WAS THE PERFECT DAY FOR A FUNERAL. GRAY WITH A promise of rain. Mist ribboning around the headstones. And it was the perfect size–a baker's dozen dressed in black, some with umbrellas and some without. No music. Few words. I stood to the side and watched. When it was over, I walked back to my car.

This was the first time I'd driven to Bradley. My last trip home had been by bus. Before that, I'd come by train and in the early years, by wagon. But now I had been home for two hours and I was ready to feel the highway mumble beneath me as I sped north. I climbed back into my rental after the graveside service. I'd always been out of place here and I felt it even more so now that he was dead.

The youngest member of the funeral party separated from the rest. She was a woman—maybe twenty—wearing a black vintage dress all severe lines and lace. She approached my car.

I willed myself to turn the key, fire up the engine, pull away. I'd come. I'd paid my respects. But she seemed intent upon speaking to me so I paused after sliding the key into the ignition.

Then I sighed and rolled down the window.

She stammered. "Are you Thomas's brother?"

I looked at her over the rims of my sunglasses. "I am."

"He told me to keep an eye out for you. There's something for you back at the store." She paused and her cheeks flush. "I worked for him."

We'd started the store together though he'd always known I'd be the one to wander off. First with the wars and then with the excitement of a world to see. And I'd stayed on the go, too. My ship had only been in from Hong Kong two weeks when I got the call that my brother was gone.

"What time can I meet you?"

She shrugged. "You can follow me over now if you want. I'm opening late today." She pointed to a red two-door. "That's me."

I nodded and waited while she climbed into her car. Then, I followed her out of the cemetery and onto the highway. I hadn't been home in decades but despite the growth and sprawl, the downtown stretch was familiar. And the corner building my brother and I had chosen so many years ago. The original sign had been meticulously maintained: FOUND BROTHERS BOOKS AND SUNDRIES.

I pulled up front and she pulled around back. I was waiting at the front door when the lights came on and she made her way through the stacks to let me in.

"I'm Victoria, by the way," she said. She extended a hand and I shook it. Briefly.

"Michael." She was staring at me and I tried not to notice. Instead, I glanced around the shop. It was more cluttered than I remembered–stacks of books and magazines colonizing the walking space between overstuffed shelves. Large tray tables filled with LPs or bagged comic books. The shiny metal espresso machine looked out of place in the room but the purring cat in the window did not.

Victoria turned the sign around. "Would you like some coffee, Michael?"

I turned. "No. Thank you." I shifted my feet. Part of me wanted to stay and sift through what my brother had made of his life here. Part of me wanted to wander the streets that he and I had wandered during our childhood here. Part of me wanted to get into my car and head back to Vancouver. There would be another ship to another place where I could vanish for a while and sort all of this out. "So what did he leave for me?"

She dug around in a drawer behind the counter and pulled out a keyring. She handed it to me and I stared at it in the palm of my hand. "What's the plan, boss?"

Now it was my turn to stammer. "Plan?"

She nodded. "It's your store now."

I shook my head. "I don't want it." I stretched out my hand, offering her the keys. "You take it."

Now she snorted. "I don't think so. I'm a worker bee, not a queen bee."

I looked at the keys in my hand. "Was there a note or something to go with these?"

"He said there was letter but I couldn't find it."

I looked around the store. "I can't imagine why." Even the counter was awash with papers—newspapers, bills, notes, old magazines still opened to unfinished articles of great interest at some time. I sighed again. "I guess the plan is to clean up."

I argued with myself about the plan as I set to work. It was at odds with the plan that had me back to Vancouver and shipping out within the next few days. Not that I had any idea where.

Anywhere but here, I thought.

We sorted the counter space and back office desk out in about two hours moving things into piles then reduced the piles to a single box of noteworthy items. It took three hours and then we moved into the stacks of clutter in the front of the store. The crate was buried under a flat of LPs and stacks of old pulp magazines and National Geographics. When she saw it, Victoria clapped. "Oh! We wondered where it had vanished to."

She pulled a claw hammer from the tool drawer and went to work prying the crate open.

"What is it?"

"An old statue he picked up at an estate sale. He always talked about mounting it above the door." She laughed. "But after he got it back to the store, he lost it."

I looked around the room we'd barely made a dent in. "I wonder what other buried treasure we'll turn up."

She lifted the statue from the Styrofoam peanuts it was packed in, grunting with the effort. It was a white statue of Pallas Athena.

"Of course it is," I said. And now I knew where to find the letter. I oriented myself around the shelves of the room until I found the classics. I pulled down a leatherbound edition of Poe's collected works and found his favorite poem.

The page was marked with folded sheath of yellow papers.

I unfolded it, eager to see what words he'd left for me. It was the copy of the deed to the store and the property it sat on. "Well," I told her, "this isn't it."

"So we'll continue our great quest tomorrow?"

It's not what I wanted. I eyed my rental car through the shop's dirty front window. But the missing letter, more than the dead brother, stirred something inside me.

"I guess so." My uncertainty turned into resolve as I glanced at the statue. "Yes."

Outside, the gray moved to a deeper shade of dark as the afternoon moved toward evening. The day had slipped past us and we'd barely made a dent in the clutter that surrounded us. Victoria went to the counter and scribbled something onto a sticky note. "Are you staying upstairs then?"

I hadn't thought about it; I figured I'd be back in Canada by now. The last time I visited I'd only stayed a few hours and hadn't even gone up to the apartment my brother and I once shared above the store we once managed together. I looked at the deed in my hands. "I think so."

She handed me the sticky note. "The key is on your ring. This is my number if you need anything."

I took it from her and stuck it to the deed. "Thanks, Victoria."

"You're welcome." She smiled and it was a sad smile, her brown eyes soft. "I'm sorry about your brother."

"Me too," I said. Though it slowly dawned on me that I felt very little. Still, her eyes told me that she felt his loss deeply. "I'm sorry for your loss, I mean."

I saw the beginning of tears now as she tried to blink them away. "I only knew your brother for a few years. But you . . ." She took a deep breath and released it. "He was your brother."

"Yes," I said. She kept watching me and I suspected she was looking for a response beyond my words. I said nothing.

The silence grew awkward and she shrugged into her raincoat. "I'll see you tomorrow," she said as she slung a tattered backpack over her shoulder. "I have class until ten."

"Tomorrow then," I said.

I locked the back door behind her as she slipped out. Then I contemplated the stairs to the upper floor. I didn't want to make that climb; I felt the resistance in my bones. Instead, I scooped up my jacket and brought the copy of Poe with me as I slipped out into the late afternoon. I wandered the downtown sidewalks— familiar old buildings with new shops now. The old brothel was a Thai restaurant now. The old hardware store had reincarnated as a radio station, the disc jockey sitting in a glass window where passersby could watch him work. He smiled at me as I moved down the sidewalk.

I found a German restaurant where Dick's Barbershop used to be and went inside. The jagersnitchzel and spatzel were as good as anything I'd had in Germany and the beer was kellarkalt and sweet. While I ate, I read through Poe.

Words had been my brother's favored mode of experiencing the world. He'd been around the world once—a careful student taking in his stops by book first then going with a meticulous list of things to experience and see while he visited. But once around was enough for Thomas and then he was back to his place on the stool behind the counter of the store. The one time I'd watched the store for him—the month he'd been in Paris—I nearly went crazy from sitting still for so long.

The world, in my mind, was to be gulped on the run letting each place surprise me with its people, its food, its customs. I didn't want to know in advance what I would see and do. I wanted to be ambushed by each place.

We understood these differences in one another. More than that, we embraced them. And so I could be gone for decades and never be shamed for my time away. And never did I shame him for his time in that first home that had found and embraced us here in this place.

I took a slice of apple strudel to go, the smell of baked apples and vanilla filling my nose as I left the restaurant. I walked back to the store past the lawn of the First Presbyterian Church. I paused as I stepped into the shadow cast by a statue. It was a bronze likeness of the man who was the closest thing we had to a father and I looked up into his face. It was Reverend McKay, shrewd as a serpent and harmless as a dove, captured perfectly in the lines of his jaw and brow. He was with the hunters who found us—shivering from cold and fear on the side of the mountain—and brought us back into the fledgling town on the edge of the Cascades. He was the one who named us the Found Brothers. Thomas and Michael. And that name stuck even after he adopted us.

Seeing Reverend McKay brought back a flood of memory culminating in his funeral shortly after the turn of the twentieth century. My brother and I knew by then that we were very different, that we didn't belong, but we'd yet to understand much. We still didn't, even all these years later. We knew we weren't from here. We knew we didn't age the same way they did. We also didn't get sick. We didn't experience humanity in the same, despite looking the part. The Reverend's death had been one of those realizations early on to just how "other than" my brother and I were in the small town that had adopted us.

The sky cracked open and the rain threw itself down around me. I moved quickly along the sidewalk and slipped into the back door of the shop, taking the stairs slowly up to my brother's apartment.

I let myself in, leaving the strudel on the narrow counter and making my way to the guest room I used the few times I'd visited before. The room was ready and had been for some time. A thin layer of dust coated the desk, bureau, and nightstand.

I took a cursory tour around the place, inhaling the smell of my brother and his things. It was a heavy, musty aroma. I sat, ate the strudel, and read more Poe. He'd loved his books, his world of words. I fished and hunted and found my peace in the forest or on the water. The real world in my mind. Still, the irony of the poem he'd marked was not lost on me. A man up late at night pouring over his old books, seeking some truth in them that might assuage his suffering.

And yet here I was, in my dead brother's home reading his book, fresh from his funeral, and I felt nothing at all.

No sorrow. No sense of separation. No tears. And yet today I was more alone in this world than I had ever been before.

Eventually, I took myself to bed and laid awake a long time wishing I felt something—anything—until I fell into a light and dreamless sleep.

I was awake and walking the streets of my hometown long before dawn. The rain had let off but the fog was heavy. I eventually found a bakery and sat in the park with fresh croissants and strong black coffee until the sun rose and the fog turned pink.

I returned to the building and forsook the stairs in favor of the store. Victoria wasn't due in for another two hours and I busied myself around the shop. My ambivalence was slowly becoming agitation and the books and heady smell of paper felt like walls that threatened to collapse around me. I was on a ladder, mounting a shelf above the door for the statue we'd uncovered, when I heard the knob rattle.

I paused and glanced down. A middle-aged woman in a raincoat and holding a briefcase stared up at me through the door's glass window. "One minute," I said.

I climbed down and moved the ladder, unlocking the door. The woman stared at me. "Are you Michael Found?"

I nodded.

"You look much younger than your brother."

"Yes," I told her. There was no way I could explain that to her. He'd chosen to experience old age. I hadn't. Just like he'd chosen to stay in Bradley and I'd chosen to stay on the road or at sea or uptrail or downstream. Any place that wasn't standing still.

She blushed and extended her hand. "I'm Sandra Matthews from Matthews and Donaldson's."

I shook her hand. "Yes. I knew your father."

"Actually, my *grandfather*."

Again, I'd found that explaining rarely helped. "Ah. Yes. My mistake."

"I saw the lights on and thought I'd stop by. I heard you were in town. I have some things to go over with you regarding your brother and the business at some point."

Mordecai Matthews had been one of Reverend McKay's strongest supporters. A deacon in the church and an expert marksman. He'd been with the Reverend on the day we were found. And when it became obvious that we weren't like our neighbors, his office became the keeper of our secret and the machine that made our lives possible.

"I'd be happy to meet and go over everything." I said. I paused and glanced from the statue to the ladder. "Is there any chance that my brother left a letter for me in your care?"

Sandra shook her head. "Not to my knowledge, but I can go through the file to be sure." I found myself wondering how big that file must be given how far it went back. The Found Brothers were easily their oldest clients. And Mordecai's granddaughter was processing that better than I expected. It was one thing to deal with a man my age by mail as I'd done with their offices since

leaving town so long ago. It was another to look me in the eye and
see what made me different from her and the rest of her kind.
Something quietly unsettling that Thomas had set about repair-
ing by learning to fit in. I'd never seen the point.

Of course, I'd not seen the point in staying here. Or in growing old. Or dying, for that matter. But Thomas had for whatever
reason. And whatever message he might've had for me was most
likely lost within the apocalypse of our bookstore.

Sandra's card materialized, cream against the lighter cream of
her hand. "Call me and we'll set up an appointment."

I took the card and slid it into my shirt pocket. "I will."

She smiled and let herself out. I went back to the statue and
the shelf I was hanging.

I stood beneath its stare when Victoria's keys jangled in the
back door. "It looks good," she said as she dropped her backpack
behind the counter.

"That's where he wanted it?" I'm not sure why it had become
so important to me but it had. More urgent in the moment than
even the letter. Still, that urgency was at least some kind of emotion. I glanced at Victoria.

"Yep," she said. "That's even the shelf he picked for it."

We were the Found brothers. We could finish one another's
sentences. And one another's projects. It was part of why not finding his last words to me was so perplexing. "I found it in the back
room," I said. "I found the screws in the drawer."

Victoria hung her coat. "Well, you're off to a good start.
What next?"

We spent the morning making more of a dent in the store,
getting books up on shelves and out of the way. She started a box
of free books to put on the sidewalk, weather permitting, and I
focused on going through the scattered apocalypse of loose paper.
Bills, receipts, notes, requests, doodles, forgotten napkins stained
with petrified bits of jelly. And after another full day, this time the
dent more noticeable, I still had nothing from him.

I felt the tickles of panic and wondered at it. I should feel sad.
Or lost. It's how I felt when the Reverend died. But all I'd felt so far
was urgency that was now balanced on a sharp edge of fear. And
yet it still didn't feel as if he were gone.

We closed up and Victoria waited by the door. "How are you

doing?" she asked.

The question surprised me and I didn't want to answer. "I'm fine," I said.

She nodded. "You're probably still in shock over it all."

I shrugged. "Probably."

She put her hand on the doorknob. "So . . . tomorrow then?"

"Yes. Tomorrow."

Victoria reached out and squeezed my shoulder. "We'll find the letter. I'm sure of it."

I offered a weak smile as she slipped into the dusk.

I stayed in that night and went to bed early. But sleep evaded me and at ten minutes to midnight, I turned on the shoplights and sat in the overstuffed reading chair we'd discovered earlier that day beneath a mountain of books.

I opened the copy of Poe and glanced at the statue.

The pallid bust of Pallas just above my chamber-door. I read the words and smiled. Then I settled into the chair and read until the dull chime of midnight made me jump. I chuckled at myself.

But I didn't jump when I heard tapping at the door. Between the book and the bust, I wasn't surprised. And it explained why I didn't feel as alone in the world as I should have.

I stood, put down the book, and went to let my brother in.

He hopped into the room with many a flirt and flutter and I locked the door behind him. Papers ruffled as he flapped his wings and launched himself toward the ceiling, finally settling onto the statue.

"Ta-da," quoth the raven.

I shook my head and chuckled again. "Hello, Thomas."

He cocked his head. "Pretty good, huh? I see you got my message."

"Eventually," I told him, pointing to the book. "I should've guessed sooner."

"Didn't Victoria tell you?"

"She thought it was a letter." Of course, now I realized there'd never been a letter. There'd been a carefully placed book and a carefully marked poem. A buried bust. A hidden chair.

"Ah," he said. "Semantics. It was more of a message dressed

up like a conjuring."

"Yes." I felt relief now and in it, I could feel the tension in my body easing. "And now I know why it didn't feel like you were gone."

"Exactly," he said. His eyes sparkled like pools of ink. "I'd never leave without saying goodbye."

I felt nothing at his funeral but those words—leave and goodbye—hit me like rocks. "But why leave at all?"

Thomas picked at his wing with his beak. "We've been here a long time. I'm ready for something else."

Now I was feeling even more of my emotions. Fear that tickled and anger that reared up without warning. I waved my hands at the room. "You've spent most of your time locked away here in this little town, this microcosm of reality. How can you be ready?"

He paused and looked away. "I just . . . am." Then his eyes met mine and were steady. "I supported your decision to leave and see the world. To stay young and steer clear of your roots." He didn't say the rest but he didn't need to. He had supported all my decisions because he was my brother and he respected my autonomy.

I nodded. "You're right, of course."

"And we know there was something before all of this. They found us on the mountain and time has proven that we're more than misplaced children or lost orphans. So I'm certain there's something after. Maybe a moving forward or maybe a coming home. I want to see that."

I thought the words and wanted desperately to not say them. I failed, because now I knew that the loss I'd not felt before was only delayed in its coming. "But what about me?"

"I don't know about you. We came here together, I know that. But I don't think we need to leave together." He hopped from the statue to the counter. "Maybe you'll catch up to me when you're ready." He paused. "I only know about me, Michael. I'm ready to see what's next. What about you?"

I sighed. "I don't think I'm done yet." I looked at my hands and the fine dark hair of my forearms. "I'm not even ready to let my body age."

Thomas's chuckle was more of a cackle. "That one took some getting used to. The weight and wear of time's passage on the body and the mind. Shuffling off the mortal coil at long last."

I shuddered at the thought of it. And yet, here he was.

"So the raven was *your* idea?"

He hopped back to the statue and held his wings out. "It felt right."

And it suited him. I still didn't understand exactly how he'd done it. Or why he was going. But his words rang true. It felt right. For him, at least. And my next question was more for *me* than him. "What's next, then?"

"I thought we'd catch up here and then take a trip." He chuckled and it was the caw of a hungry predator. "Obviously you'll have to drive."

"No," I said. "I mean for me."

"Ah." Thomas waited and watched me for a moment. "You'll know when you know. But I can tell you: I have no regrets about my life here in Bradley. None. I saw enough of the world. The best part of it were the ones we met the first time we set foot upon it. My tribe here in Bradley." He cocked his head. "And you, of course. But I've known you for all my lives."

More truth. I can't remember anything before the day that Reverend McKay found us naked and wandering in the snow. But I knew in my bones that there were other mountainsides, other findings, and that someday it would be time for my brother and me to leave this place and be found all over again. Maybe in that life, I would stay in one place and he would wander. Or perhaps do some of each together. Until now, I'd never questioned our choices but the sorrow of his departure weighed on my chest, heavy as a boulder.

"I wish I'd spent more time with you in this one. I wish I'd known you were planning to go." Bargaining come early as grief finally reared its head.

"I didn't want it to be a spectacle," Thomas answered. "I wanted a quick, simple goodbye the night before."

I nodded. "After it was too late to talk you out of it."

More laughter like fingernails on a slate. "Exactly."

We drove in moonlight and starshine until the forest swallowed us. I turned off the headlights and let my senses guide us, window-down, onto the gravel spider-web of roads leading up into the foothills.

My brother clutched the passenger seatbelt with his talons, beak pointed out the window. We were quiet as we went. We'd done all the catching up we needed to do.

As we went, the forest came to life around us. Bears and elk and coyotes and bobcats formed their ranks on each side of the road. They knew us for who we were, unlike the others, and we drank their adoration as we remembered where we came from and how we mattered in the Slow Moving Wheel. The mountain that was our mother on this plane loomed above us and I felt her call upon my brother. It was a gravity flooded with joy and I knew I could expect the same when it was my time to follow.

We parked and stepped out into the cold. The ground here was white and crunched beneath us. A light snow fell and I could hear each snowflake singing—a billion-voiced choir in the night—as they drifted down.

I walked as my brother flew ahead through the trees until we found the clearing. I went to the tree right away. It had grown in the decades and decades since I'd last seen it but I found the markings and ran my hand over the initials we'd carved there so long ago.

"So this is it," Thomas said. He hopped onto a fallen tree that rotted on the edge of the clearing. "I trust your judgment on the store but I hope you'll make sure Victoria is taken care of."

"I offered it to her the other day. She said no."

He chuckled. Then he was quiet and silence settled over us. "I'm going to miss you," he finally said. "But hopefully I'll see you soon."

"We're the Found brothers," I told him. "We'll find each other."

"Over and over again," he replied.

"Evermore," I told the raven. "Evermore."

There was that raucous laugh again. This time, I joined him. "Good one."

"Thanks, Thomas."

"You're welcome, Michael. I sure do love you."

"I sure do love you, too. See you soon, eh?"

With that, my brother lifted off into the air and beat his wings against a sky that refused to hold him down. He flung himself upward at the moon and stars and the veil of cloud and the mountain that awaited. He flung himself at all of that and flew free across the night's Plutonian shore.

I watched until I knew that he was gone and then I sat in the car and let grief begin its work in me.

I drove in the dark alone with my tears and paused at the cut-off to Bradley. I had an apartment—nearly empty—in Vancouver. And any number of ships to work. I could have my bag packed and be back on the road before Victoria arrived to open the shop. I could call the attorney—Sandra Matthews—and arrange for the store to be sold and for Victoria to be retained.

Or like my brother, I could decide it was time for a change. I could pack up my few belongings, move south, and take on the store. Maybe even write a book or two of my own about my life here. And then, when the time was right, follow him up the mountain for whatever world waited beyond.

"I don't need to know right now," I told the empty car.

For now, I had a store to finish cleaning. Days to spend in the smell of dust and paper while I made up my mind.

The bakery was open when I hit town. The coffee was hot and the donuts were fresh. I bought a dozen and realized as I climbed back into the car that the snow had followed me down the mountain. I watched it settling upon the shoulders of the statue of Reverend McKay. I listened carefully and far, far away I thought that I could still hear it singing.

I wondered if it meant my brother had been found again. If the cycle had started up again. I wondered where and how I would find him and myself be found again.

But I knew that I would learn this soon enough.

When it was my time to follow.

AFTERWORD AND ACKNOWLEDGEMENTS

A Fourth Pass Through
My Imagination Forest

WELL HOWDY. IT'S HARD TO BELIEVE THAT WE'RE BACK for a fourth pass through my Imagination Forest. I can remember quite clearly in my mind just the other day thinking how amazing it would be if I sold a single short story. Back in those days I imagined that with time, maybe I would have enough short stories out in the world to merit a single short story collection and then suddenly before I knew it I saw one then two and then three collections of my short fiction slip out into the world. As I sit and compose this Afterword I am nearly 25 years in print as an author and it leaves me shaking my head with Wonder.

This fourth volume captures mostly stories that came out in print between 2015 and 2024 including the tiny handful of stories I wrote during my hiatus from writing to focus on other things after finishing the decade-long logging trip into my Imagination Forest known as The Psalms of Isaak. Funny thing. Just as this book was coming together, I started thinking it was time to return to the universe of my series with some longer stories. I'm not sure where I'll be in the process by the time you're reading this, Dear Reader, but a new series, Pilgrims of the Dream, is slowly coming together. It picks up during the events at the end of The Psalms of Isaak and follows a group of people—some you met in earlier books—as they follow the Final Dream to the moon. Hopefully you'll be joining me there in those books as well.

Now here at the back of *this* book, it's time to talk about all of these stories and how they came to into existence. Then I'll take some time to thank all of the people who brought this book into your hands.

Ready? Here we go . . .

FIRST BAR AT THE END OF THE DAY

I suppose the only downside to having been at it for as long as I have is that now I've reached the point where I can't necessarily remember all of the origin details for my earlier tales. My document tells me it was created in November 2005, in the months after my Writers of the Future workshop. I have vague recollection of writing it in a Portland gay bar while I was waiting downtown for a ride home after work. That all makes sense because the original title was "That Gay Bar at the End of the Day." And then as happens with stories from time to time, it got lost in the hard drive and did not show up until more than a decade later. I started skimming the found document thinking maybe I had started a story that I hadn't finished, and imagine my delight when I reached the end and realized I had myself a tiny little space horror story. Not long after discovering this one, I learned from Sarah Chorn that the magazine she edited was looking for both reprints and new work. It was the beginning of a beautiful friendship with her and with *Grimdark Magazine*, that has now put a few of my older stories back into the world along with this previously unpublished piece.

This was the first of my sales to *Grimdark Magazine* and it's one of a handful of early stories that landed in this later collection of mine. It was also the front end of my friendship with Sarah Chorn and her work on that story started a snowball of friendship rolling that led ultimately to her editing and introducing this book.

MAKING MY ENTRANCE AGAIN WITH MY USUAL FLAIR

This is a story that I somehow missed for my third collection. As a matter of fact, I thought it *had* been collected and then was quite surprised to see I'd passed over it. And by the time a kindly fan pointed out the uncollected nature of the tale, I was in my hiatus and publishing far more slowly. So this one, written back in 2005 and originally published by *Tor.com* in 2011, is finally joining its story siblings.

"Making My Entrance Again With My Usual Flair" was my 24 hour story from the Writers of the Future Workshop. As a third place winner in 2005, I attended the workshop and award ceremony in Seattle and this story was homework for the class. Everyone had 24 hours to draft a story. We were given time in the library, a found object (mine was a little monkey made of beads that appeared to have three eyes), and time to wander the Seattle streets looking for people to interview (without them knowing we were writers on the prowl for stories.)

Initially, I started this much longer, much more serious story—it was the beginnings, I think, of a YA novel. I felt the call of the clown and the circus and his roadtrip friend but a comment by one of the teachers had me feeling oddly self-conscious and I was resisting Leroy my inner redneck muse and his pull toward the wacky and zany. Still, my interviews on the street had turned up a young man named Kamal and an unemployed circus clown. The signs were all there and pointing. I wrote 6k words of Something Not At All This, freaked out as my deadline loomed, then came back to it after a sandwich and a shower. This showed up and poured out of me. It was an early lesson in finding and following the right story and learning how to get unstuck.

The title was pretty easy once I had the tale underway. Send in the clowns. There ought to be clowns.

HARLEY TAKES A WIFE

The concept for this one goes back into the early 2000s. I found notes and even the start of a story called "Harley Finds a Wife" in my File of Forgotten Story Stubs. During my break between 2016 and 2024, I made a deal with myself that I'd say "Yes" to any short stories I was invited to write and sure enough, David Boop invited me to write a space western for his Baen anthology. I decided to dredge this old concept out of my hard-drive, set it in the universe of another older story, "A Good Hair Day in Anarchy," and sling it his way. It gave me an opportunity to explore the mail-order-bride concept in space along with some tongue in cheek humor about courtship and capers and talking cacti. Publisher's Weekly called it a campfire tale and I'll take that as a win.

I think at some point, I may go explore the Frontier System and Harlan Sussbauer and Dastardly Al's All Android Caper Gang a bit further. I think there may be more tales to tell. But this one works perfectly for the sweet little romance it is, dressed up as a space western caper story.

OF ANCHOR CHAINS AND SLOW REFRAINS AND LIGHT LONG LOST IN DARKNESS

While I was creating The Psalms of Isaak, I left a lot of bits laying around the workroom floor Very Much on Purpose. The new series, Pilgrims of the Dream, is one of those bits. There are several other future tales seeded in that soil. Including some story seeds about Rudolfo and Gregoric sailing with the pirate Rafe Merrique in their youth.

When Shawn Speakman asked me to write something for *Unfettered III*, I knew I wanted to return to the world of Lasthome and I also thought it might be a fine set up—a story using Gregoric as the POV character to pave the way for a few novellas (to come later) of Rudolfo at sea.

And since Gregoric was based loosely on my pal John Pitts, it became a bit of a love story about our friendship and brotherhood. Sadly, John passed before he had an opportunity to read this one. But I'm proud of the story and I think he would've given that knowing nod to it. It also features Drea Merrique, who ends up being a protagonist in the new project.

STUCK IN BUENOS AIRES WITH BOB DYLAN ON MY MIND

This is the story I was writing as my third collection came out into the world back in the summer of 2015 and was the second story earmarked for this current collection. I'd been approached by Bryan Thomas Schmidt to write something for a Baen anthology he was putting together.

This story gave me a chance to tap into my trip to France in 2013 along with the vast amount of music in my head and I was able to capture quite a lot of both in this story. When I went to France, Bragelonne's Leslie Palant met me at the airport and put a guitar into my hands. I played all over and it culminated in a big show at Dernier Bar Avant La Fin Du Monde, performed from an iron throne in a dungeon, amid piles of books that I signed for people. If you go looking on YouTube, you can also find about an hour of me playing at the Imaginale festival. And I did run into that Canadian with her somewhat snarky offer; and I did NOT correctly remember the capital of Canada.

I had a lot of fun with this story and I think it's a character and a universe I could come back to at some point.

GREATEST GUNS IN THE GALAXY

(*with Bryan Thomas Schmidt*)

For a guy who loves community, collaboration and connection, I really don't have many collaborations under my belt. Six total over 25 years. This one showed up just as I finished *Hymn* in 2016 while I was separated and charting my new course in life as a soon-to-be-divorced half-time father after being a stay home dad and full time writer for about three years.

Bryan and I had been going back and forth on my story for *Little Green Men—Attack!* and chatting about what my future held. I had a profound sense of peace regarding my body of work—that I had done enough between my five novels and my three collections—and that I was going to take a break. And that I was still going to do the part I loved most—short stories—but only when requested. At least for a bit. I had come back to writing in 1996 and was sitting at 20 years of treating it like a part time job that I had to show up for. I felt pretty done but I also knew those feelings would likely change. I also had other areas to focus on—a self-help book and coaching/consulting framework to research, music to perform and record, and a government job to go back to as I navigated it all.

Bryan had been invited to David Boop's weird western *Straight Outta Tombstone* and had the start of a story. I had told him my decision to say yes to short fiction and he very kindly invited me to collaborate with him to finish this up. I truly don't recall much of the process on this one; it was a foggy time for me. But I know he worked some tributes to John and Jay into the story and the story itself went out into the world without a hitch to do its part. I'm happy to present it here.

THE MONSTERS UNDERNEATH HIS BED

I wrote this story in the winter of 2002 and it's almost the oldest story in the collection. It was very much a therapy story captured from a raw and mighty time in my life. I had weathered my first parental loss—the death of my stepfather in 2001—and had left my first executive director position in Seattle to relocate to south-west Washington. I had no idea I was slowly moving to Oregon.

I know I wrote it quickly and without effort and that *The Monster at the End of This Book* was a loose inspiration, combined with a pretty and sweet librarian named Elizabeth that I was seeing. And it's a nod to a powerful movie, *The Sixth Sense*, that became part of the librarian's toolkit to inform Benjamin. I took my protagonist's name from a guy in the army I met who was originally from Portland.

Like most of my stories at the time, it went onto a list and went out to make its rounds of rejection. I kept that spreadsheet up until the book deal with Tor shifted my production to novels. By then, the requests for short stories were coming in fast and furious and I was no longer writing "on spec" but by invitation. No one had picked this one up by 2007 so it sat.

And then, one day, I found myself in a pandemic and Bryan Thomas Schmidt (a recurring theme in this collection) showed up asking for a story for *Surviving Tomorrow*, a charitable anthology he was editing to raise funds for medical supplies. I was delighted to give him this one. Later, I realized the story was also perfect for my spoken/sung show about C-PTSD which I've called *Making Friends with the Monsters Underneath My Bed*, featuring eight of my songs and a reading of this story.

LET ME HIDE MYSELF IN THEE

This is the longest piece in the collection and one I passed over for my third collection. Truth is, it was never intended to be all on its own and it's deeply tied to another foundational fixture in my life, Jay Lake.

Jay invited me to be part of the second MetaTropolis project with Audible, *MetaTropolis Cascadia*, and I incorporated his character, Bashar, into the end of my story "A Symmetry of Serpents and Doves," setting him and Charity Oxham onto a path of future (yet unwritten) adventures.

For *MetaTropolis: Green Space*, I was back but also in the co-editor seat with Jay. And this time, we tied our stories together. Of course, Jay and I didn't always see eye to eye on things. My vision was that the titles would sync up—"Rock of Ages, Cleft for Me" and "Let Me Hide Myself in Thee"—but he decided last minute to just go with "Rock of Ages" as his title, totally throwing my cleverness under the bus. Still, the stories were meant to hang out together and fulfill each other. If you want to experience the saga, you can pick up *MetaTropolis: The Wings We Dare Aspire* from Wordfire Press (capturing all of me and Jay's stories from the Audible series) or you can find the original Metatropolis series on Audible and give it a listen.

This is another one where I really don't recall most of the drafting but I know at the heart of it, there's a father and daughter going to breakfast. And that's one of my favorite father daughter experiences after nearly fifteen years of dadding.

BETTER DREAMS THAN THESE

I used to think (and say) that "Summer in Paris, Light from the Sky" was my most important story. But now, years after that one, I think maybe *this* is my most important story.

Bob Brown from B-Cubed Press approached me shortly after John (Pitts) passed and gave me an easy opportunity to say "Yes." He'd accepted a story from John and from our other good friend Manny Frishberg, and he thought it would be pretty neat to get all three of us into an anthology for the first time together.

I had met John and Manny on that rainy November day in Seattle in 1997 at Writer's Cramp and it had been a lightning strike of life-changing friendship. Now 22 years later, all three of us were established writers and one of us had slipped out of the party way too fucking early. When Bob asked me to write a Space Force story that could stand with John and Manny's in his new anthology, I gave a resounding "Yes."

The story found me on Valentine's Day 2020 on a hike in the forest. I remember the entire idea dropping at once and I even paused and recorded a quick talk about the power of nature to quiet our minds and uncover our creativity.

One of the inspirations for this was a picture of Patrick Stewart and Ian McKellan kissing. It captures my love of the 12 steps, nods a bit to Burroughs with my solar system emulating his work, points at the problems inherent with an unhinged Orange Prophet coloring our future, tips a hat toward *Star Trek*, and especially puts my growth and development as a human critter in the spotlight. You see, I'm a recovering bigot of the biggest kind, an ex-Southern Baptist preacher, programmed full of all kinds of nonsense about people not like me. The sifting and sorting of that heavy suitcase has been captured across my body of work for all to see. It's been a painful but beautiful process.

This is a story about finding love and hope and liberation from our worst beliefs. And about how we're never too old to change directions.

It's also the only story I've written where the world is ultimately saved by two old enemies making a gay space porno.

THAT WHEN I WAKED I CRIED TO DREAM AGAIN

This is the oldest story in the collection and has gone uncollected until now because it is such a difficult, early story of mine. But as Sarah said in her introduction, humanity is the backbone in my work and this story is a lot of raw humanity.

Like many of my early stories, it was very clearly me working things out in therapy. And like many of my stories, it was written for *Talebones* Live. I get a little uncomfortable, 21 years later, as I think about that first *Talebones* Live reading of mine, where I broke out this too-long, very uncomfortable story and inflicted it upon the room.

Don't get me wrong; I believe in what the story does. But I wouldn't choose it for that reading necessarily now at this point in my life. I have a trilogy of Hell stories and this is the second I wrote . . . and most raw. And it's a story about sexual abuse and how it warps the magic of childhood and creates a cycle of pain and potentially self-hatred. Something I learned from my dark childhood and the long road of recovery I've walked since. By the end of the story we discover that Archie's "hell" is one of his victims' "heaven" as our main character discovers he was the villain in this tale all along and is now earning his eternal reward.

OF HOMEWARD DREAMS AND FALLEN SEEDS AND MELODIES BY MOONLIGHT

This story was a happy accident of sorts also tied to Bryan. Originally, I'd been asked for the story that introduced Isaak and Rudolfo and formed the foundation for my novel *Lamentation* for an anthology he was editing with Robert Silverberg. *Robots*

Through the Ages was going to capture classic robot tales across SF history and I was very honored to see Isaak included in the project. Then the publisher suggested to them that a brand new Isaak story would be even better so once more, I said "Yes," and started pondering how I would tell a new Isaak story.

I knew going in that I couldn't give him a POV. So I would need a new character to experience him in the same way that Rudolfo and later Marta served. Tovin the Far-Seer showed up and a new story, set a few years after the end of *Hymn* showed up. In some ways, it helped pave the way for the new series in that it had me digging into the end of the series while pondering what comes next. Another story about finding home. A theme—the theme of my new series—emerged from saying "Yes" to this one.

And it is made mightier by the company it keeps. The anthology is a powerhouse of tales and mine looks really good there with all of the others. I highly recommend that you add it to your library.

BUSINESS IN GREAT WATERS

In 2015, I took a summer writing roadtrip with a writing friend. We drove a big loop out to the Oregon Coast and back with the express purpose of finding a story along the way. There were prompts (biplanes were one) and music (something by Dylan) to guide us along with the beautiful Oregon coastal region.

We spent our first night in Garibaldi and that got me started. I was up early that morning and found my way down to the little park with its locomotive.

By the time we were finished with our trip, I had the ingredients for this one bubbling in the slow cooker. I wrote this and then it sat for a bit until Shawn Speakman came looking for a story. I thought this quiet story about family and roadtrips might work for him and voila!

Naturally, I stole the title for this one from the Bible as a tip of the hat to my past life as Reverend Scholes.

EVERMORE I TOLD THE RAVEN

Closing out the collection with this one makes a lot of sense to me.

In 2014, Marshall Latham of *Journey Into . . .* podcast fame approached me and commissioned me to write a tribute to Edgar Allan Poe for the show. Poe was the first poet I fell in love with as a young fellow and I knew right away that I'd be paying tribute to "The Raven," my first favorite poem.

2014 was quite a year. It was the year Jay Lake died and his was the tail end of a long string of losses that included my parents, my father-in-law, a grandparent, some aunts, and a nephew. And this story was my first attempt at any words after Jay's death.

I'd been stuck and stumped and stalled many times before but never as much as this story. I made eight—EIGHT—attempts to land this one. Each start was slightly different but all were about loss. In the end, I went back to the very first attempt and it was the one that became this story about love and loss and brotherhood.

It captured my sense of brotherhood with Jay nicely and it pointed to other deeply rooted people in my life as well. Marshall produced an audio version of the story and then *Orson Scott Card's Intergalactic Medicine Show* ran the print publication along with an essay about the story's origins.

It's a great place to wrap up this trip through my Imagination Forest. This fourth visit was about a decade coming and I'm not sure when it will be time for a fifth. But I'm glad to wander it with you.

NOW I HAVE SOME PEOPLE TO THANK . . .

First, I want to thank all of the editors who requested stories from me. I love that you asked me. It was a pleasure creating these for you and my delight that you put them out into the world in such fine company.

Second, I want to thank Sarah Chorn for editing and introducing this collection. A great friendship has grown up out of you reaching out to me about *Grimdark Magazine* and I'm excited about the work ahead.

Third, I want to thank Fairwood Press. Patrick Swenson, the literary dad who discovered me and now keeps my short fiction out in the world, and his brother, Paul Swenson, who constantly amazes with the covers he creates for them. I'm deeply grateful. Not the first time an English teacher has changed my life.

Last but not least, I want to thank you, Dear Reader, for following me into the forest once again. I hope you've had a good time and I hope we'll all do this again real soon. And if you haven't wandered the other three volumes, I hope you'll spend more time in my Imagination Forest.

Ken Scholes
Cornelius, Oregon
2024

ABOUT THE AUTHOR

KEN SCHOLES is the award-winning, critically-acclaimed author of five novels and over fifty short stories. His work has appeared in print for nearly twenty years. His series, The Psalms of Isaak, was published by Tor Books and his short fiction has been collected in three previous volumes published by Fairwood Press.

PUBLICATION HISTORY

"First Bar at the End of the Day" originally appeared in *Grimdark Magazine*, July 2022 | "Making My Entrance Again With My Usual Flair" originally appeared at *Tor.com*, January 2011 | "Harley Takes a Wife" originally appeared in *High Noon on Proxima B*, Baen Books, 2023 | "Of Anchor Chains and Slow Refrains and Light Long Lost in Darkness" originally appeared in *Unfettered III: New Tales by Masters of Fantasy*, Grim Oak Press, 2019 | "Stuck in Buenos Aires with Bob Dylan on my Mind" originally appeared in *Little Green Men—Attack!*, Baen Books, 2017 | "Greatest Guns in the Galaxy" with Bryan Thomas Schmidt (© Bryan Thomas Schmidt and Ken Scholes) originally appeared in *Straight Outta Tombstone*, Baen Books, 2017 | "The Monsters Underneath His Bed" originally appeared in *Surviving Tomorrow*, Aeristic Press, 2020 | "Let Me Hide Myself in Thee" originally appeared in *METAtropolis: Green Space*, Audible Frontiers, 2013 | "Better Dreams than These" originally appeared in *Space Force … and Beyond*, B-Cubed Press, 2021 | "That When I Waked I Cried to Dream Again" originally appeared in *Insidious Reflections*, January 2006 | "Of Homeward Dreams and Fallen Seeds and Melodies by Moonlight" originally appeared in *Robots Through the Ages*, Blackstone Publishing, 2023 | "Business in Great Waters" originally appeared in *Unbound II*, Grim Oak Press, 2022 | "Evermore I Told the Raven" originally appeared in *Orson Scott Card's Intergalactic Medicine Show*, July 2015

OTHER TITLES FROM FAIRWOOD PRESS

*Obviously I Love You
But If I Were a Bird*
by Patrick O'Leary
small paperback $11.00
ISBN: 978-1-958880-37-1

Space Trucker Jess
by Matthew Kressel
trade paper $20.95
ISBN: 978-1-958880-27-2

Shifter and Shadow
by Sharon Shinn
trade paper $16.99
ISBN: 978-1-958880-36-4

When Mothers Dream: Stories
by Brenda Cooper
trade paper $18.99
ISBN: 978-1-958880-35-7

Changelog: Collected Fiction
by Rich Larson
trade paper $20.95
ISBN: 978-1-958880-33-3

*A Catalog of Storms:
Collected Short Fiction*
by Fran Wilde
trade paper $18.99
ISBN: 978-1-958880-31-9

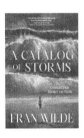

Black Hole Heart and Other Stories
by K.A. Teryna
trade paper $18.99
ISBN: 978-1-958880-29-6

One Last Game
by T.A. Chan
trade paper $15.99
ISBN: 978-1-958880-34-0

Find us at:
www.fairwoodpress.com
Bonney Lake, Washington

www.ingramcontent.com/pod-product-compliance
Lightning Source LLC
Jackson TN
JSHW022250290725
88477JS00007B/49